JANE PEART

ZondervanPublishingHouse

Grand Rapids, Michigan

A Division of HarperCollinsPublishers

The Pledge
Copyright © 1996 by Jane Peart

Requests for information should be addressed to:

ZondervanPublishingHouse
Grand Rapids, Michigan 49530

Library of Congress Cataloging-in-Publication Data

Peart, Jane.
    The Pledge / Jane Peart.
      p. cm.
    ISBN: 0-310-20167-5
    I. Title   II. Series: Peart, Jane. American quilt series ; bk. 2.
PS3566.E238P54 1996
813'.54—dc20   96-7450
                                              CIP

Edited by Robin Schmitt
Interior design by Sherri Hoffman
Frontispiece illustration by Michael Ingle
Part title illustrations by Adam Bloom

Printed in the United States of America

96 97 98 99 00 01 02 /❖ DH/ 10 9 8 7 6 5 4 3 2 1

Part One

Hillsboro, North Carolina
Spring 1861

Prologue

～～

Johanna Elizabeth Davison sat at the small maple desk in her bedroom, writing a letter to Wes, when she heard her aunt's voice calling, "JoBeth, come down here at once! Harvel's brigade is marching by. Do hurry!"

She tucked a stray dark curl behind her ear, then put her pen back in the inkwell. Before getting up, she slid the half-written to Wes letter under the blotter. Hurrying into the hallway, she met her mother, Johanna, just coming from her sewing room. They exchanged glances. Although full of understanding, her mother's eyes held a message that JoBeth dared not ignore. JoBeth nodded and together they went down the winding stairway to the hall, where Aunt Jo Cady stood at the open front door.

"Come along, you two!" she called over her shoulder as she went out onto the porch, down the steps, and along the flagstone walk to stand at the gate. JoBeth and her mother followed.

The May morning was warm, bright with sunshine. Residents from the houses on the street were rushing out to the strip of grass on either side of the road. In the distance, they could hear the drums beating, the brisk sound of marching feet, the clatter of horses' hooves. Then the line of gray-clad soldiers rounded the bend and came into sight. People began to shout hurrahs and wave small Confederate flags.

Where had they got them so soon? JoBeth wondered. North Carolina had only seceded a few days before. Although, of course, secession had been discussed for months, ever since South Carolina's secession and Fort Sumter. When President Lincoln called for troops from North Carolina to subdue the sister state's rebels, Governor Ellis's response had been immediate. "I can be no party to this violation of the laws of this country and to this war upon the liberties of a free people. You can get no troops from North Carolina." The state had enthusiastically rallied to the Confederate cause.

After that things had happened with lightning speed. JoBeth's uncle Harvel Cady had immediately formed a brigade, and there had been no lack of men ready to join up.

As the soldiers marched by, everyone began to clap. The officers were mounted on splendid horses and crisply uniformed with shiny braid and buttons, sash fringes streaming in the wind, sabers glinting. Harvel, leading astride his gleaming, roan-colored mount, did not look at his relatives nor show any sign of recognition. It would have been unsoldierly to do so. But as he went by his mother, he seemed to sit a little straighter, jutting out his chin with its bristle of mustache and well-trimmed beard.

Among the rows of erect soldiers were many JoBeth knew—boys she had played with, had gone to school with as children, later had danced with, flirted with, teased. Now they were almost unrecognizable with their military bearings and their new, serious expressions, eyes straight ahead, not looking to right or left.

As she looked at the passing parade of familiar faces, JoBeth felt an enormous sadness. Only one person was missing. For her, the most important one: Wesley Rutherford, who was at college in Philadelphia. And even if he were here, he would not have been in the group. Wes had already expressed his deep doubts about the division among the states, saying, "Both North and South fought to create the United States; we shouldn't break apart now."

Next month, when he graduated, Wes would come back to Hillsboro, where he had made his home with his relatives, the Spencers. JoBeth worried about what would happen then. Will and Blakely, twin cousins his own age, had already gone to Raleigh to enlist.

In spite of the warmth of the day, JoBeth shivered. She had a feeling of impending trouble, a kind of premonition. The bright day seemed to darken. Suddenly, even though surrounded by family, friends of a lifetime, she felt cut off from everyone else. All at once JoBeth realized that she was the only one in the crowd not happily cheering.

Chapter One

After supper, JoBeth helped Annie, the Cadys' elderly cook, in the kitchen, drying the dishes and putting away the silver, one of JoBeth's regular household chores. It wasn't until JoBeth went back upstairs to her bedroom that she had a chance to complete the letter she had started earlier.

She was more aware than ever, from the evening's dinner-table conversation, that war was now inevitable. Hillsboro was a hotbed of anti-Union sentiment. This was what Wes would be returning to in a few weeks. What would be his reaction? More to the point, how would they respond to his reaction? All his talk of brotherhood, settling differences peacefully, not taking up arms—all part of his Quaker grandmother's influence and his years at college in Philadelphia—was in direct opposition to what had been discussed among her relatives.

JoBeth pulled her half-finished letter out from under the blotter on her desk and began to write.

> *Everything here is talk of war. My uncles were here for supper, and the whole evening was spent in blaming President Lincoln for bringing about all this trouble. Uncle Madison kept pounding on the table and booming, "States' rights." Of course, Harvel and Munroe agree. They say,*

"If we're invaded, we'll defend ourselves." Would the president really send troops into North Carolina?

JoBeth paused, thinking about what had led up to all this. All the previous fall and winter, JoBeth had witnessed the growing resentment against the government in Washington. Every Thursday evening, friends and associates of her Uncle Madison gathered at the Cady house. Before the country's present crisis, it had been an evening of convivial fellowship, friendly conversation, congenial company, sometimes a game or two of cards. More recently it had become increasingly political. Often voices rose in not-so-gentlemanly confrontation. Most of the men present believed strongly not only in states' rights but also in the Union, and roundly put down the idea of secession as seditious and not to be considered.

The ladies of the house were never a part of the discussions, although they heard Madison's own opinions the next morning at breakfast. No one offered any comment. It would have been useless to do so, because naturally Uncle Madison never expected any difference to be voiced in his own household. However, JoBeth knew that Wes's views were almost directly opposed to her uncle's. This troubled her a great deal.

She dipped her pen in the inkwell and started writing again.

I wish you were here. All this would be so much easier if you were here to explain it to me. I miss you. I can't wait to see you.

JoBeth hesitated. Her pen hovered uncertainly. How should she sign this? Would "Love" be too bold? Although she *did* love Wesley and was pretty sure he loved her, too, they had not said those words to each other. Although they had nearly done so the day before he had left last Christmas.

JoBeth wished she had some small piece of poetry or something she could send with her letter, as Wes sometimes did with his. She reached into the pigeonhole in the desk, brought out his last letter to her, and read the poem he had enclosed.

Never seek to tell thy love,
Love that never told can be;
For the gentle wind doth move
Silently, invisibly.

Certainly that said *something*, she thought as she read it over. Through their correspondence this year, they had become much closer. It had been easier somehow to write about feelings than to speak about them. JoBeth tapped the end of the pen thoughtfully against her chin. Finally deciding that "discretion was the better part of—" she simply wrote

As ever,
JoBeth

She sealed the letter and again slipped it under the blotter. She would take it herself to the post office the next day and mail it.

As she got ready for bed, JoBeth thought of last summer. It had been a wonderful summer, a perfect one. At eighteen, JoBeth was an accepted part of the lively circle of young people in Hillsboro. Parties, picnics, dances, church socials, barbecues, and outings at the river. Wes spent half the year with his grandmother in Philadelphia while at college, but his summers were spent with his cousins in Hillsboro.

Of course, they had known each other long before that. In fact, Wes Rutherford was JoBeth's first friend in Hillsboro. JoBeth, her mother, and JoBeth's little brother, Shelby, had come back to live there after her doctor father, Ross Davison, had died. Her mother's family had lived there for several generations, and there were lots of aunts, uncles, cousins. Still, JoBeth had felt forlorn.

She missed her father, their mountain home, Granny Eliza, her cousins, and the life she had known. Life with her great-aunt Josie and great-uncle Madison was as different as could be from their life before. Here there was order, discipline, and nonnegotiable times to do everything from morning prayers before breakfast to wearing starched petticoats and high-button shoes that pinched little feet used to going bare six months of the year.

At first she was desperately homesick for the mountains, her freedom to roam, to wade in the streams, to pick berries and wildflowers. Gradually, with the natural resilience of children, she and her brother adapted to life in town, Shelby sooner than JoBeth. A quiet, handsome little boy with a naturally sweet disposition, he quickly became the household pet. Aunt Cady declared he reminded her of her own two boys, now both grown-up men.

JoBeth was entirely different. She was restless, imaginative, stubborn, often a trial to her mother and frequently the despair of Aunt Cady, who had envisioned bringing up a perfect, ladylike little girl.

In spite of their differences in personality, JoBeth and Shelby were very close. They played, read together, shared each other's secrets, and were each other's confidantes.

JoBeth blew out her lamp, climbed into the high, poster bed, recalling her first meeting with Wes.

That fall she had been enrolled in school. Shelby was too young, so JoBeth had to go alone. In a small town where everyone knew everyone else, she had felt lost and lonely. It was agony for her to sit quietly among a roomful of strange children.

One day soon after the beginning of school, JoBeth had been making her way slowly homeward, limping from a blister forming on her heel from the new shoes, when she met John Wesley Rutherford.

Wes, as he had told her he was called, was the Spencer twins' cousin. JoBeth had heard about him at the Cady dinner table, where all local news was discussed. His mother— Mr. Spencer's younger sister, who had "married North"—had recently died. Wes, her only child, had been sent to stay with his Hillsboro kin.

That day, Wes had offered to carry her books so she could slip off her shoes and walk the rest of the way on the soft grass. In that unusual gesture of compassion, JoBeth knew that Wes was different. Different from most boys their age, whose delight was teasing and tormenting girls. He was certainly different from his cousins, the boisterous Will and Blakely Spencer. Those two rode their ponies to school, then raced each other home with wild whoops, scattering dust and stones in their wake.

Wes had shown her a stream that ran under a stone bridge near the churchyard, where she could soak her burning foot in the cool water to ease its soreness. He had sat there with her on the bank, and they had talked easily. The fact that they had both lost a beloved parent gave them an immediate bond. From that day they had become friends.

Why was she so drawn to Wes? JoBeth wondered. Perhaps he reminded her in some ways of her adored father, had those same qualities she admired: loyalty, idealism, and personal honor.

Wesley was not particularly handsome, although JoBeth liked his looks—the sandy-brown hair that always seemed tousled, the strong, straight nose, the slow smile. He had a sensitive face with an intelligent expression and candid eyes. What JoBeth found most appealing about him was his generous nature, his honesty and openness. There was no shallowness at all in Wes Rutherford.

Was what she felt love? A kind of love, certainly. They had been friends for what seemed like forever. She felt more comfortable with Wes than with anyone else. She could share things with him, even the not-so-nice things, as when she was feeling upset or angry with someone or had had her feelings hurt. Wes always seemed to understand whatever her mood was, glad or down in the dumps. He could always make her laugh, too, jolly her out of the doldrums. Over the years, Wes and JoBeth's friendship had remained strong. Last summer it had reached another level. Both eighteen, they had discovered new things about each other. When Wes returned to college in Pennsylvania, they had written to each other. When he came for the Christmas holidays, they had spent a great deal of time with each other, and things had taken a decidedly romantic turn.

She had missed him terribly when he left, and through their letters that winter, they had become closer. Now JoBeth was counting the days until Wes came home.

Was this what love is? She would just have to wait and see.

June 1861

Chapter Two

❧

$\mathcal{M}$adison Cady, home for his midday dinner, was a solidly built man in his early fifties with graying blond hair, kind blue eyes, a pleasant expression. A successful merchant, he had the self-confident look of someone secure in his position in the community and in his role as head of the household. Seating himself at the head of the table in the dining room, he glanced around with satisfaction. Nodding to his wife at the other end, her widowed niece, Johanna, on his right, and her pretty daughter, JoBeth, on his left, he greeted them, then bowed his head and intoned the family grace.

Annie, in a crisp turban and white apron, came in from the kitchen and stopped beside his chair, holding a tray on which were two bowls. As he helped himself generously to a serving of rice and then some okra and tomatoes, he casually remarked to JoBeth, "By the way, missy, I ran into a friend of yours as I was coming out of my office. Young Wesley Rutherford."

JoBeth nearly dropped her fork. Her heart beat excitedly. She looked at her uncle expectantly as he went on.

"Just off the noon train, as a matter of fact. Told me he'd graduated college."

JoBeth held her breath, waiting for more information.

A smile tugged at the corners of his mouth. "Oh, yes, he sent his kind regards to you, madam"—he inclined his head to his wife—"to you, Johanna"—he nodded at JoBeth's mother, then paused, chuckling, and turned back to JoBeth—"and he said he hoped to come in person to give his regards personally to you as well, young lady! I told him I thought you'd be mighty happy to hear that, seeing as how you've just about worn out the rug on the staircase, and the path to the postbox, near every day lookin' for a letter from Phil-a-del-phi-a."

"Oh, Uncle Madison!" she exclaimed in amused indignation.

It was a family joke how the letters arriving from Philadelphia came at a rate that caused Aunt Cady to raise inquisitive eyebrows when the post was delivered and JoBeth came running down the hall.

"Did he say when he'd come by, Uncle Madison?" JoBeth tried to keep her tone light.

"Well, no, honey, now that you ask," Uncle Madison said solemnly. "I didn't inquire, either. I thought it might not be in keeping with how young ladies like to keep young gentlemen guessing. Maybe you might be entertaining some other young beau this afternoon. So I just told him he was always welcome to come visit." Uncle Madison's tone was level, but his eyes were twinkling with merriment.

"Oh, Uncle, you are a tease!"

JoBeth always tolerated Uncle Madison's teasing. He enjoyed doing it and she didn't mind. But if Wes *was* coming by this afternoon, she wanted to change into her new dress.

"What does Wes plan to do, Madison?" Aunt Josie asked him.

"Well, a few months ago his uncle told me he planned to ask Wesley to read law in his office with him. But I reckon that's all changed now. Wes'll probably join up with the same regiment as his cousins."

The conversation went on past the subject of Wes's return to Hillsboro. At least for the others. JoBeth, distracted by her own excitement at the prospect of seeing Wes again, was filled with nervous anticipation. *How would it be after all these months? Half a year with nothing but letters? Had she said too much? Or too little? Did he still care about her? Or had he changed?*

After the meal was over, Uncle Madison went back to his office, Aunt Josie for her nap, and JoBeth's mother to her quilting frame. JoBeth hurried upstairs to her bedroom. From the armoire, she took out the dress she had saved to wear for Wes's homecoming. It was a pale pink French lawn, sprigged with tiny blue flowers, its waist sashed in blue moiré, its flounced skirt made to billow out over the three starched petticoats she would wear underneath.

Dressed, she sat down in front of her mirror and tried a half dozen hairstyles. Not an easy task, for JoBeth's hair was naturally curly, thick, and inclined to be stubborn. Finally, flinging down her brush in exasperation, she impatiently tied her shoulder-length curls back and secured them with a blue satin ribbon at the nape of her neck.

Then she settled herself at the window, where she had a good view of the street, of the corner at its end, where, coming from the Spencers' house, Wes could be seen walking toward the Cadys'. As she waited, she was filled with uncertainty. What did Wes think about the secession of the states, including North Carolina? The firing on Fort Sumter and its aftermath had happened while he was at college in Pennsylvania.

JoBeth was more knowledgeable about current events than some of the other young women her age in Hillsboro. One of JoBeth's chores was to tidy and dust the parlor and

Uncle Madison's study. Although newspapers were not considered proper reading material for young ladies, JoBeth had a curious mind. As more and more reports of the raging debate between the states made bold headlines, JoBeth found herself picking up the daily papers her uncle discarded and reading the fiery editorials. It had all sounded ominous. Now the war was a reality.

Holly Grove, the spacious house at the end of a lane of holly trees, had once been her mother's childhood home. There the Cadys' son Harvel now lived, and there the latest events had been discussed at length for months. At first the sentiment was mainly for states' rights, although most present were opposed to secession.

Every time the family gathered, their lively dinner-table talk often became a heated discussion of the crisis hovering over the country. JoBeth had heard all the points her relatives argued, and knew they were not Wes's convictions. So when Uncle Madison suggested what Wes would probably do, JoBeth knew he was wrong. No matter what the Spencer twins did, Wes was still as different from his cousins as night and day.

JoBeth had been around the three enough to know that whenever the cousins had a difference of opinion, Wes was always able to diplomatically, logically, and sensibly settle it. However, *this* time she was not sure he would prevail. War fever was burning rampantly throughout the South, and the usually conservative state of North Carolina had caught it as well.

JoBeth remembered a conversation Wes and her uncle had had when Wes was here during the Christmas holidays. Wes had come to escort her to the McKennas' party, and since she had not been quite ready, Uncle Madison took him into the parlor to wait for her. She was just coming downstairs when she heard their voices. To her surprise, their tone of voice was not casual or jovial but tense. Halfway down, she stopped to hear what they were talking about.

She heard Wes say, "I'm sorry, sir, but I was taught that slavery is wrong. To go to war over something like that— well, I just can't agree that it's the right thing to do."

"It's not so much slavery that's the point here, Wes. How many people do we know personally who own any?"

Listening outside the door, JoBeth thought of Annie. Annie had already seemed old to her when JoBeth came to live here. Now the mahogany face was webbed with wrinkles, and her movements slow. But Annie still ruled the kitchen, and it seemed to JoBeth that both her mother and aunt were a little in awe of the venerable cook. A slave? She had never thought of Annie as a slave.

She strained to hear what else Uncle Madison was expounding upon.

"No, that's just the flag those Northerners are waving! They want to dominate us, because they outnumber us in the Congress! What it is, is a matter of principle. States' rights, my boy."

"But states' rights over the Union, sir? That doesn't seem right. Both my great-grandfathers fought the British to form the Union. I was brought up to believe that to be loyal to that is every citizen's duty. . . ."

"Well, Wesley, I reckon you got filled with a lot of Northern thinkin' up at that Pennsylvania college. Folks up north think and feel differently about things than we do. All I can say is, you're going to bring a heap of trouble down on yourself and your family if it comes to war." There followed a long silence that, to JoBeth, seemed to stretch endlessly.

"I hope it won't come to that, sir."

"You might rightly hope so, Wesley." Uncle Madison's voice had been solemn. Had it also been threatening?

"Yes, sir, I do." Wes's voice sounded strong.

Outside in the hall, JoBeth let out a long breath and hurried into the parlor. At her entrance, both men stood up.

"Well, now, lookahere!" Uncle Madison had exclaimed. "If this isn't the prettiest young lady I've seen in a month of Sundays. I'd say she was well worth the wait, wouldn't you, Wes?" He beamed at his niece, thinking what an attractive, graceful young lady JoBeth had become from the gypsyish tomboy she had been.

It was in that aura of pleasantness that they had gone happily off to a wonderful evening.

However, JoBeth hadn't forgotten that overheard conversation. So much had happened since. What they had all dreaded had happened. They *were* at war with the North. What was Wes thinking now?

She didn't have a chance to guess at the answer to her own question, because she saw Wes rounding the corner. JoBeth jumped up and ran down the steps to the front door before the doorbell might wake Aunt Josie or rouse Annie, who was probably nodding in her ladder-back rocker on the sunny back porch.

As he came up the steps, JoBeth caught her breath. He looked different somehow—taller, broader through the shoulders, handsomer. In spite of all the letters they'd exchanged, the things they'd written, she felt suddenly shy.

"Wes!"

"JoBeth!"

He stood there looking at her through the screen door. Then she opened it and stepped out onto the porch. "It's so good to see you," she said, holding out both hands.

He took them and held them tightly. "It's been so long. I can't believe I'm really here and seeing you," he blurted out, then blushed. JoBeth was pleased. His words seem to evaporate that first awkwardness.

One of the things she loved most about Wesley. He was so open, so without guile or pretense. He said what he thought, spoke what he felt.

"Would you like to sit down?" She gestured to the white wicker furniture on the porch. "I can have Annie bring us some iced tea or lemonade?"

"I'd really rather take a walk—to our favorite place, JoBeth. Past the churchyard, down by the creek that runs under the old stone bridge. I have so much to talk to you about, and"—he hesitated—"all the way down on the train, I kept remembering how we used to go there and talk."

"Then, wait till I get my bonnet and parasol and run upstairs to tell Mama I'm going," she said and went inside. Lifting her skirts and crinolines, she skimmed up the stairway and down the hall, then tapped on her mother's sewing room door.

Johanna Shelby Rutherford was known for her beautiful quilts, her original designs. Mountain Star and Carolina Lily were two of her most popular patterns. When she had returned as a widow to Hillsboro to live with the Cadys, Aunt Josie had fixed up a small room—once a dressing room adjoining one of the large bedrooms upstairs—for her. Here a permanent quilting frame was set up for Johanna's use. Soon she had a thriving business, which enabled her to send JoBeth to a good female academy, and Shelby to a fine boy's boarding school.

Some of JoBeth's earliest memories were of her mother bent over her quilting frame, her face rapt with concentration, her hand moving gracefully as she plied the needle in and out in a smooth, gliding motion.

JoBeth opened the door put her head inside. Her mother looked up questioningly.

Johanna Davison retained a youthful beauty—only tiny lines around her wide blue eyes and tender, vulnerable mouth traced the passage of years. She could have remarried. Upon her return to Hillsboro, several men had been eager to court the lovely young widow. But Ross Davison had been the love of Johanna's life. No one could ever replace him. Her life had centered on her two children. At the sight of her daughter, a smile softened her expression.

"What is it, dear?"

"Wes is here, Mama, and he wants to go for a walk."

"That's fine, dear. Go along then. Be sure to tell him hello for me and that Aunt Josie wants him to stay for supper."

"Yes, Mama, I shall." JoBeth turned and hurried back down to the porch, where Wes was waiting.

Opening her ruffled parasol, she took his arm and they went down the steps, out the gate. They both knew the way to the path that led past the church where both their families worshiped and up the hill to the arching stone bridge. Below flowed the broad stream where JoBeth had soaked her blistered foot the first day they had become friends.

The fact that Wes was here seemed like a dream to her. After all the months of writing to each other and waiting, to actually be together at last made JoBeth euphoric.

For the first few minutes, they talked about mutual friends. But the more news JoBeth told him about their acquaintances, the quieter Wes became. Gradually she sensed his thoughtful demeanor and stopped. She felt a little twinge of uneasiness. She and Wes had never had any trouble finding things to talk about before. In fact, one of the things she loved about their relationship was that they never ran out of things to say to each other. They delighted in each other's company, preferring it to the many social events they were invited to. That's why the sudden silence that fell between them frightened her. Was something wrong? Maybe Wes's feelings for her had changed and he didn't know how to tell her.

On the bridge, they paused for a few minutes, looking down to where the clear water rushed over the rocks. Then Wes turned gave her a long, searching look, smiled and said, "You're so much prettier than I remembered."

JoBeth felt her cheeks warm. She had hoped he would mention how becoming her dress was or how her blue bonnet ribbons matched her eyes, but this was much better. His words made *her* happy, but she wished *he* looked happier.

"You look troubled, Wes," she said rather uncertainly. "Is anything wrong? What did you want to talk about?"

"I'm sorry, JoBeth. I don't mean to worry you. I didn't mean to bring it up—at least, not right away. Not on my first day home."

"You look awfully serious."

"I guess I do. I guess—well, it *is* serious."

She pretended a pout. "Not about the war, I hope. That's all we seem to hear nowadays." She tilted her head and looked up at him quizzically. "What is it? You might as well tell me and get it over with. Then maybe we can enjoy the rest of the day!"

"I always could talk to you, JoBeth. The trouble is, I have to decide something. Uncle Wayne has asked me to come into his law firm to read law there—"

"Oh, Wes, how wonderful!" Impulsively she reached out, put her hand on his arm. "Then you'll be staying in Hillsboro. People said you might go back to Philadelphia, since your grandmother is there and you went to college there. Now everything you wanted, worked for, has come true, hasn't it?"

"Yes, everything has come true—except that everything else has changed."

"What do you mean?"

"The war, JoBeth," he said sadly. "Our country is at war."

"I know that. But people say—at least everyone here says—that it won't last . . . that it will all be over in a few skirmishes, maybe . . . then the politicians will settle things." She broke off impatiently. "Oh, Wes, do we have to talk about this now? You've just come back! And I'm so happy. Please don't spoil it with all this gloomy talk."

"I'm sorry. All right, I'll stop for now. But I can't avoid *really* thinking about what I am to do." He leaned toward her and took one of her hands. "Eventually you and I must talk about it. Because it affects us."

"The war? *Us?*"

"Yes, JoBeth. Sooner or later everyone's going to be affected. You, me." He hesitated, then said, "It's because I love you, JoBeth."

Wide-eyed, JoBeth gazed at him.

"I mean, *really* love you. I hoped you'd come to know that through my letters. I guess I've loved you for a long time. Last Christmas I *knew* it. I just felt I couldn't say anything until I had finished my education. I had to have a way to support a wife before I could ask you to marry me. Now all that's changed."

She took a deep breath and said, "I love you, too. So how has it changed, Wes?"

"Oh, JoBeth, don't you see?"

"No."

Wes shook his head, and his mouth tightened into a firm line. "This war, it's changed everything. I *know* how everybody in Hillsboro feels. Your relatives *and* mine. It's not that simple. In fact, it's very complicated."

She frowned, looking puzzled. "Why is it?"

"Because I guess you could say *I'm* not simple." He sighed. "Uncle Wayne wants an answer. Either I stay and go into law practice with him or I join up. Blakely and Will are all het up, ready to go."

"Well, you've never played 'follow the leader' with *them!*" she declared. "So what does what they do have to do with us? Oh, Wes, can't we just be happy?" JoBeth asked, knowing it was a silly thing to say, but she couldn't help it. Wes had just told her what she'd been longing to hear, and now he was ruining it by bringing up the war and all the things she'd rather forget.

"Because people have to choose. And it's splitting our country in two. Splitting families. That's what I'm facing. That's what I had to talk to you about. I don't think secession is right. To take up arms against our government. But I know what's probably going to happen if I make these kinds of statements here, to my uncle, to your folks."

JoBeth felt an awful tightness in her throat, the feeling that she was going to cry. She looked back down into the stream, wishing all her dread of what was going to happen would go away.

"Believe me, JoBeth, I wish we didn't have to talk about all this," Wes said earnestly. He leaned on the stone ledge, clasped his hands together, stared down into the water. After a long moment, he said quietly, "I felt I had to—*wanted* to—talk to you before I talked to Uncle Wayne. I had to know how you feel, whatever I decide."

JoBeth felt as if all the sunshine had gone out of the afternoon. "We may as well go back," she said plaintively.

Wes caught her hand, brought it up to his lips, kissed it.

JoBeth looked up at him, his face suddenly blurred because her eyes were full of tears. She couldn't speak.

"I love you, JoBeth."

"Love is supposed to make people happy, Wes," she said forlornly.

"I know. I'm sorry."

Slowly they retraced their steps back to the Cadys' house, not saying anything more. JoBeth's mother and aunt were sitting on the front porch as they came up the walk. They greeted Wes cordially, then Aunt Josie asked, "You will stay to supper, won't you, Wesley?"

"Thank you kindly, Mrs. Cady, but this being my first night home, Aunt Alzada's expecting me there."

"Well, certainly I can understand that. You've been away such a long time. But another night, surely. Tomorrow, then?"

"Yes, ma'am, that would be a pleasure. Thank you."

"Then, we'll look forward to seeing you tomorrow evening. Madison will be eager to talk to you about how things are up north."

Inwardly JoBeth shrank. She knew Wes was too respectful of his elders to argue with Uncle Madison. However, he was not a person to sit quietly and let his silence give consent if he disagreed with what was being said. Now, with his new determination to follow his conscience, JoBeth dreaded to think what might take place at the supper table the next evening.

She walked back to the gate with Wesley.

"Tomorrow I'll have my talk with Uncle Wayne," Wes said in a low voice.

"I'll be praying everything will go fine, Wesley," she said, not knowing what that meant exactly. Fine for whom?

He squeezed her hand. "However it turns out, JoBeth, I love you," he whispered.

"I know," she said over the lump in her throat. After he left, she stood for a minute at the gate before going back up to the porch. Preoccupied with her own heavy heart, JoBeth didn't notice that her mother and aunt exchanged puzzled glances.

Chapter Three

The next evening, Wes arrived almost at the same time that Uncle Madison arrived home from his office. Greeting Wes heartily, Uncle Madison invited him into the parlor. JoBeth hoped Wes wouldn't bring up anything controversial and upset Uncle Madison. At least not until after supper. She knew Wes had determined to make clear his feelings about the war, and there was nothing she could do about that. She just wanted them to have a pleasant meal.

With a lingering glance at the two men, JoBeth went into the kitchen. Annie had asked for the evening off to visit her sick sister, so her mother and aunt were going to serve the dinner Annie had fixed ahead of time.

Johanna was busily spooning spiced peaches into small, cut-glass condiment dishes. Sniffing appreciatively the savory smells of baking ham and candied sweet potatoes, JoBeth asked, "What can I do to help?"

Her mother smiled at her. "You can get the extra silver servers out and fill the cream pitcher."

Aunt Josie, her cheeks flushed from the heat, closed the oven door and turned from the stove. JoBeth looked at her aunt admiringly. Even in the kitchen, the woman managed to look elegant, not a hair out of place, sapphire drop earrings twinkling. Aunt Josie untied the strings of a blue cotton apron that covered her lace-trimmed flowered dress and asked, "Are Madison and Wes having a nice chat in the parlor?"

"Yes, ma'am," JoBeth answered, sincerely hoping so.

Aunt Josie's brow puckered slightly. "Hope they're not arguin'."

"No, ma'am." JoBeth looked at her aunt warily. "Why should they be arguing?"

"Well, I'm sure it's nothing to be fussed about. It's just that I saw Alzada Spencer's sister in town, and she told me she'd heard that Wesley was going back up north—that he'd refused his uncle's offer to come into the law firm. That they had some bad kind of falling out. It's probably nothing, just one of those rumors that fly around."

JoBeth felt a sinking sensation in her stomach. How quickly word spread in Hillsboro! She held her breath as Aunt Josie continued.

"But then, everybody knows that Wayne Spencer's got a hot temper, and"—she shrugged—"sometimes young men pick up ideas that don't really fit into the lives they're going to live after they graduate, but they like to test them out. Of course, some folks couldn't figure out just why the Ruther- fords let him go to *Philadelphia* to get his education. When there are several good colleges around here."

"Well, his grandmother lives there, for one thing," JoBeth began, but at her mother's almost imperceptible head- shake, she halted.

"Well, you know Madison—he always feels he has to set a young person's head straight," Aunt Josie said. Picking up a quilted hot pad, she opened the oven again and peered into it. As she lifted the lid of the roasting pan, delicious clove-scented steam filled the air. "The ham's done, and the sweet potatoes are just right," she said with satisfaction. "Go tell the gentle- men they can come to the table, honey," she directed JoBeth.

JoBeth left the kitchen and hurried down the hall. As she neared the parlor, she heard raised voices. In his best lawyerly tone, almost as though he were addressing a jury, Uncle Madison was saying, "But Wes, there're North Carolina brigades starting up. *Your* friends, some of your schoolmates, chaps you've known all your life—couldn't you see your way to joining up with these troops?"

JoBeth held her breath for Wes's reply. There was a pause. Then he said, "No, sir, I couldn't fight for slavery."

Her stomach in knots, she moved closer, placing her head in the crack of the door in order to hear her uncle's response. She knew her uncle and she was afraid. It was not long in coming.

"Well, Wesley, I'm sorry to hear this." A pause, and then, "I'm sure you know that my wife and I set a great store by our niece, and it hasn't escaped our notice that you and JoBeth have fond feelings for each other." Uncle Madison cleared his throat before continuing. "I wouldn't want to see her burdened by your decision and brought to divided loyalties and unhappiness."

"No, sir. I wouldn't want that, either," Wes replied. "I do love JoBeth. Under other circumstances—I mean, if things weren't so uncertain—I would ask you and her mother for the privilege, the honor, of asking her to marry me. I have no intention of bringing her any unhappiness."

JoBeth pressed her hands tightly together. She didn't know whether to tiptoe back to the kitchen and let Aunt Josie call them to dinner or to retrace her steps and then make some warning noise to let the men know she was approaching the parlor. As it turned out, Aunt Josie called from the dining room, "What's keeping those men? Madison! You and Wesley come along while everything's nice and hot."

JoBeth dreaded the meal. However, when both her uncle and Wes joined them at the table, the conversation seemed pleasant enough. Everyone seemed to be making an effort to avoid controversy. As sensitive as JoBeth was, both to Wes and her uncle, she felt decidedly tense throughout the meal. JoBeth had the distinct feeling that the truce between her uncle and Wes was simply for courtesy's sake. It seemed to her that when Wes said he must leave, Uncle Madison's goodnight was untypically cool.

She walked out to the porch with Wes when he left. They stood for a minute at the top of the steps. She felt instinctively that Wes was about to tell her something she didn't want to hear.

"Blakely and Will have already joined the Confederate Army. Uncle Wayne assumes I will, too."

Surprised, she turned to him. Had he possibly changed his mind? Hope flared up. "So will you? Is that what you've decided?"

Wes shook his head. "No, of course not. I can't. I couldn't fight for something I think is wrong." He clenched his hands in a double fist. "I don't know whether I can even fight for what I believe is right."

"Is that because—I mean, are your feelings, like everyone says, because you went to school up north?"

"Yes, that could be a part of it. It influenced my thinking. But it goes even deeper than that. Ever since I was young, even when I was a little boy, eight or nine, I had these feelings ... about slavery, about folks owning other human beings. I couldn't put it into words then. It was just an uneasiness that it was wrong—"

"I don't think of *Annie* as a slave," JoBeth protested. "She's always been with us, as long as I can remember, but ..." Her voice trailed off weakly.

"That's just it, JoBeth. It's a way of life we've all just accepted. Until now. Now people have to decide. Do what their conscience demands."

"I know what you've told me the Quakers think about war, what your grandmother taught you about taking up arms." She frowned, genuinely puzzled. "But in the summers, when you're here, you go to *our* church. And they never say anything about slavery or about fighting. Everyone here feels it's only honorable to defend yourself. I guess I just don't understand. If it's wrong to fight at all, why do you have to choose sides?"

"That's the dilemma, JoBeth. I can't answer for anyone else. It's my own conscience I must answer to. My own belief. I never became a Quaker, although I attended their meetings when I was with my grandmother. Probably unconsciously absorbed their teachings." He sighed. "That was when I was a child, JoBeth. Remember the Scripture 'When I was a child, I thought as a child'—First Corinthians, thirteen, eleven? 'I spoke as a child, I understood as a child, I thought as a child, but when I became a man, I put away childish things.'" He paused. "Now, however, as a man with my own convictions about what is right or wrong, I have to choose." He sighed again. "And I don't think that the Union should be broken apart. I think it should be protected. Much as I hate the thought of fighting people I know and love, I have to make a choice and go with my own conscience."

"You mean—"

"I'll have to leave Hillsboro, JoBeth. Go back to Pennsylvania. Then I'll—"

"Oh no, Wes!" Her voice sounded almost like a sob. "Please, isn't there some other way?"

"I don't see that there is, JoBeth." Wes's voice grew husky. "I can't stay, feeling as I do, knowing how others will view my decision."

"You've told your uncle, then?"

"Yes. Of course he's furious. We had a terrible row. Aunt Alzeda went to bed with a terrible headache. The whole

33

household is in an uproar. The sooner I can make arrangements to go, the better for everyone." He gave a harsh laugh. "I'd better be gone before the two conquering heroes arrive back from Raleigh."

"Blakely and Will?"

"Yes." Wesley turned and drew JoBeth into his arms. "Oh, JoBeth, forgive me for what I'm doing to you." His words were muffled against her hair as he drew her even closer.

She clung to him, her cheek pressed against the starched, ruffled shirt. *This should be one of the happiest moments in my life*, she thought. *So why do I feel as if my heart is breaking?*

Just then Aunt Josie came to the door, holding an oil lamp.

"Oh, is Wesley still here, JoBeth?" she asked, of course knowing he was. They broke apart guiltily. "My, what a lovely night. Looks as if a new moon is coming up," Aunt Josie said. "Do give my regards to Alzeda, won't you, Wes, dear?" Then to JoBeth she said, "It's getting rather cool, isn't it, JoBeth? Either get a shawl, dear, or come inside."

There was no mistaking the subtle reprimand in her aunt's voice.

"Yes, Auntie," she replied, then whispered to Wes, "I guess I'd better go in."

"I'll come by tomorrow and let you know my plans," Wes said.

"No, maybe it had better not be here. Let's meet at the bridge instead. We can talk more freely there."

"Yes, that's a good idea. Tomorrow, then. Say, three o'clock," he replied. Raising his voice slightly, he said, "Good night, Mrs. Cady. Thanks again for supper." He started down the porch steps. JoBeth watched his tall figure walk through the gate and disappear into the shadowy night.

What tomorrow or the day after would bring, she had no idea. She had only a feeling of dread that her life was going to change drastically.

She'd had that same feeling once before, long ago.

Even at age seven, JoBeth had been old enough to remember the day of her father's funeral clearly. As they lowered the simple pine coffin into the ground her father had loved all his life, Reverend Tomlin, his voice breaking as he spoke the words, read from Matthew 25:34.

"'Come ye blessed of my Father, inherit the kingdom prepared for you from the foundation of the world. For I was sick and ye visited me. Inasmuch as ye did it unto one of the least of these, my brethren, ye did it unto me.'"

JoBeth had understood how much Ross Davison had been beloved by the members of the mountain community that he had served so faithfully for so many years. With no thought to his own comfort, he had traveled the hills in any kind of weather to bring aid to the sick, treating injuries and all sorts of illnesses.

His dedication had been unquestioned. At great risk to his own health and safety, he had given generously of his skill, his knowledge, his determination, and it was in treating a dangerous and deadly disease that he had at last succumbed himself.

But what JoBeth hadn't fully understood was why they had to leave Millscreek Gap.

She and her five-year-old brother, Shelby, had listened while Johanna explained that they were going down to live in Hillsboro with their mother's relatives. All JoBeth really heard was "leaving the mountains." But *why* must they leave? she had asked stubbornly. Why couldn't she stay with Granny Eliza?

"Johanna Elizabeth," her mother had said sternly. "You must not complain and whine and carry on like this. Your daddy is gone—we can't stay alone up in the mountains. You and Shelby have to go to school. That's what your father would have wanted. I must make a living there for us. Aunt Josie and Uncle Madison have been kind enough to offer us a home, and we should be grateful. I will work, making quilts to sell, in order to give us money enough to be independent— but Shelby must have his chance. A *man*, nowadays, needs to be educated. Maybe he'll become a doctor like your daddy, or a lawyer like Uncle Madison ... but he's got to have his opportunity. This is the only way I could make sure that he does."

JoBeth hadn't said any more. But it was with a sense of hopeless loss that she helped pack up their belongings, said good-bye to her beloved grandmother and to her mountain cousins, climbed up on the wagon seat alongside her mother— with Shelby wedged in between them—and started the torturous trip down the narrow, winding road to Hillsboro.

"Will we stay at Holly Grove?" she had asked once they came into town.

"No, honey. Grandmother Shelby lives in Charleston with Aunt Cissy now. Our cousins Harvel and Marilee live at Holly Grove these days. We'll be going to the Willows, to the Cadys' house."

JoBeth had nodded, not really sure if she knew just who the Cadys were. Her mother had so many "town kin," so many aunts and cousins, that JoBeth had found it hard to keep them straight when they came down to visit. That hadn't been often. In winter the mountain roads were impassable, and in the summers—well, there was always so much to do on the long summer days.

As they finally came to a stop in front of a large, white, pillared house just at dusk, JoBeth's memory had been stirred. She had suddenly remembered that Aunt Johanna Cady was the "fussy" one of her mother's aunties. Just then she had felt a sharp sense of loss over her father's death. She had recalled his deep, kind voice, the way he would swing her up in front of him onto his saddle, cuddling her in his strong arms, leaning down and asking affectionately, "Well now, Miss Johanna

Elizabeth, what kind of a day did you have?" Tears came stinging into her eyes. It was at that moment, in some indescribable way, that she knew in her child's heart that her life was forever changed.

Now, remembering that, JoBeth felt again the sensation of being on a road whose end she could not see.

Wes had warned her, *It's not that simple.* But she was yet to discover the full price of their love, their commitment to each other.

Chapter Four

Wes had been right when he said that things were complicated, JoBeth thought on her way to meet him the next afternoon. Everyone had his own opinion about the war. First the argument had been whether or not North Carolina should have seceded, then they debated what kind of president of the Confederacy Jefferson Davis would make, now it was a disagreement about what the generals were doing. Even within JoBeth's family, there were sharp differences.

In the mountain community, there were few hotheads for war, she found when she visited. Granny Eliza Davison had spoken for many when she said, "'Tain't our fight. Why should I send my grandsons to die for someone I don't even know to keep their slaves?"

Shelby, now in his first year of seminary, seemed to be having some private inner struggle. He had been unusually quiet since coming home this summer.

JoBeth saw Wes waiting for her and quickened her step. The very sight of him made her heart turn over. Everything she had imagined feeling about him as she wrote to him and received his letters was real. It set her pulse pounding and made her lightheaded. This was the love she had always dreamed of knowing.

The sad part of it was that the kind of idyllic, romantic time she had imagined for them when Wesley came home had not come true. When she reached Wes, it was evident from the look on his face that things were not any better at the Spencers'. In fact, Wes's expression, the sadness in his eyes, told the story, without JoBeth's asking for details.

"If it hadn't been for Aunt Alzada, I think my uncle would have ordered me out of the house right then and there," Wes said dejectedly. "There's no going back. All affectionate exchange between us is gone. He said he was bitterly disappointed in me. *Ashamed*, actually, that I was willing to go against my own people, my state." He shuddered. "He doesn't realize just how painful it is for me. Everything would be fine if I'd recant"—he snapped his fingers—"if I'd say I was wrong, he was right. But I don't believe that."

"What is he most angry about? Is it your view of slavery?" JoBeth frowned. "The Spencers only have house servants, just as my aunt and uncle do—"

"It's not just over slavery, whether a man has a right to own slaves or not. More importantly, it's whether a state can leave the Union at will. It's about how important the union of *all* the states is."

She had heard this argued among her relatives for months. So much so that she had begun to deliberately stop listening and instead to think about other things while the discussions went on. She had not really believed it would affect her life. Now she realized she had been mistaken. Still, she wanted—*needed*—to be convinced.

She gestured impatiently. "Yes, yes, I know all that. But what does this really have to do with *us*?"

"Everything. People are taking sides. No one can remain on the fence, JoBeth. We're all going to have to stand up for what we believe or what we're against. It's going to get people angry and bitter, and it's going to go on for a long time."

JoBeth felt as if a cold wind had blown over her, chilling her to the bone.

"There's no point now in asking permission to marry you. Now that your uncle knows where I stand, he as much as told me it was impossible."

"Oh, Wesley, did you have to be so *honest?*" she demanded with mock despair.

"Would you love me if I weren't?"

She threw out her hands helplessly. "I suppose not."

"Then you *do?* You do love me?"

"Yes, of course!"

He frowned deeply. "You have to be prepared. Now that they *do* know, they may forbid us to ever see each other again—"

"Oh, Wes, don't say that. Don't even *think* that."

"You still don't truly understand, do you? How deeply emotions about this war run? I wish to God you didn't have to, JoBeth." There was a desperate edge to Wes's tone.

"I'm trying to understand," she hastened to assure him. "I guess I just didn't want to understand. It hurts too much. To think your aunt and uncle would let something come between their love for you and what you believe. I mean, you've been like another son to them both."

Wes looked so sad. She knew how much Wes loved the Spencers, respected them, had always wanted to please them. She understood how much their approval meant to him. Impulsively JoBeth reached up on tiptoe and put her arms around his neck, kissed him on the lips. He drew her close, and the kiss deepened into a long, tender one, full of sweetness, tenderness, and tentative hope.

"I love you, Wes. Nothing else should matter."

"I love you, too, JoBeth. But I'm afraid other things *do* matter. At least at this time, in this place." He kissed her again, then gently released her, saying, "I'm also aware that what I'm going to have to ask you to do will take more than love. It will take everything either of us has within us. And we can't do it by ourselves. We're going to need God's help, JoBeth. It won't be easy. In fact, it might be the hardest thing we've ever been called on to do."

That evening, JoBeth found out just how hard it was going to be, when she timidly approached her uncle. "Uncle Madison, I know Wesley has told you how he feels, and though I know you don't agree with him, I hope—"

Before she could finish, he cast aside his newspaper and declared vehemently, "It's not the government's place to tell us what we can do with our own property—"

"Uncle Madison, can't you try to see it from Wes's viewpoint? He's an idealist, and—"

"How many idealists do you find in history books? Not many, I'll tell you. It's the doers like Andrew Jackson we remember, the kind of men that stand up for what they believe."

"But that's exactly what Wesley is doing! Don't you see that?"

"I see that you're a foolish young woman who doesn't know dreams from reality," he said coldly. "Reality never measures up to anticipation, and expectation is usually the precursor of disillusionment. You're heading for a cruel disappointment, my girl."

JoBeth felt a rush of antagonism that he should dismiss Wes's beliefs so harshly. But she would not allow anyone to snatch away her dreams so ruthlessly. Even though she had to remain under this roof and accept that she and her mother were living here mainly at the largesse of their relatives, she was determined not to be defeated by her uncle's attitude nor to doubt Wes's staunch convictions.

JoBeth glanced away as if examining the silver epergne in the center of the table. She knew it was useless to argue further, to plead Wes's case. Uncle Madison's mind was closed. In his way of thinking, Wes had become a traitor.

That night, JoBeth thought long and hard about everything that had transpired in these past three days.

From being a romantic figure of fantasy and imagination, Wesley had become the central person in her life. Someone on whom so much revolved. In the matter of a few hours, everything had changed. There would be no long summer in which their romance would progress at a leisurely pace. All the things she had dreamed of doing when Wes came home—strolls by the river, long talks, reading poetry together—had been eclipsed by the need to make life-changing decisions. Suddenly they were living out a real drama. One for which there had been no rehearsal, she herself in a role she had never sought to play.

Wes had said everyone had to take a stand. He was right. She was being forced to choose sides: Wes or her family.

For her mother's sake, for the peace of the household, she had to keep her thoughts, her feelings, to herself—and yet she would not betray her loyalty and her love.

Because she knew now, without doubt, that she loved Wes. Something in him drew her irrevocably. A few days ago, even a few hours, she would never have had this certainty.

Remembering Wes's words "We're going to need God's help," she threw herself on her knees beside her bed. JoBeth prayed. But no peace came. Her soul was still in turmoil.

The serene, safe world she had known, the circle of love and acceptance, of affection and hospitality and shelter, had cracked. Hostility, resentment, anger, had been thrust into its quiet warmth. All the things she had taken for granted seemed to be slipping away.

Burying her face in her hands, she saw a mental picture of Wes standing alone outside the circle. In that moment, she knew she could not let him stand there alone or turn and walk away from her. *I'm mad about him*, she thought. *I'm half sick with it*. She was quivering. Life was so scary and unpredictable.

It's not that simple, Wes's words came back to her. No, it certainly wasn't. It wasn't like deciding to accept an invitation to a party, choosing a dress pattern, selecting the color of bonnet ribbons, the simple kind of choices she had made easily most of her life. This choice was different and not simple at all. One choice meant she might never see Wes again. If his conscience demanded he sacrifice everything, his hometown, cousins, family, friends, his love, then she had to decide if she would support that conviction. It was not, after all, debatable.

She knew she could not let Wes leave without telling him she was willing to stand by him. She got up from her knees, strengthened but trembling.

JoBeth did not realize she had entered a battle of her own making: the battle between loyalty and love. She had no intention, no matter what the opposition or provocation, of giving Wes up.

> *I never spoke that word "farewell" but with an utter-*
> *ance faint and broken;*
> *A heart yearning for the time when it should never more*
> *be spoken.*
>
> Caroline Bowles

Chapter Five

⊶≈⊷

Three more days passed. Days of anguish and silent misery such as JoBeth had never spent before in her entire life. JoBeth was well aware that the whole Cady household seemed to be walking on eggshells as they tried to avoid mentioning the subject of Wesley Rutherford around her.

Finally a note from Wes came, asking her to meet him. Heart racing, she slipped out of the house at a time when no one would miss her and hurried to their favorite place.

Although she had prayed, hers had been rather undirected prayers: for courage, for strength. She had not dared pray for Wes to change his mind. In her heart of hearts, she knew that the parting she dreaded was about to come. Even knowing that this was inevitable, she had no way to prepare herself for it.

When she reached him, they clasped hands silently. Was it her imagination, or had Wes aged overnight? He looked pale and there were dark circles under his eyes, as though he had not slept. JoBeth's heart winced in sympathy, as if his pain were her own. Only she fully understood how heart-wrenching it was for him to leave the home that had been his own since childhood, to say good-bye to the aunt and uncle he cherished. Worse still was the way of the leave-taking. In disgrace. As a turncoat. A traitor.

For a minute, they simply looked at each other wordlessly. Then Wes said brokenly, "I'm so sorry, JoBeth. The last thing I ever wanted to do was hurt you."

"I know."

"I thought it would all be so different—our future, I mean. I even dreamed we might be married this summer. Now that's out of the question. Your relatives would never let you marry me now."

Impulsively JoBeth burst out, "Oh, Wes, I'd marry you tomorrow, with or without permission."

He looked at her with a slight smile. "I wager you would, JoBeth. That's your sweet, generous nature. But I wouldn't ask that of you. It was wrong of me to even—"

"No, it wasn't. I love you, Wes. I say yes, now or whenever," JoBeth rushed on, knowing it was unseemly, unladylike, unheard of, but she didn't care. What did all that matter now? There was so much more at stake here than that.

"Bless you for saying that. If it weren't for you"—he paused—"I would feel totally alone, abandoned. I hope to God I'm doing the right thing, that it's worth all the people that are being hurt by my decision."

His sorrow was too deep for tears. Anything she might have said to ease his suffering would have seemed shallow, banal.

They walked along in silence, holding hands. There was so much they wanted to say to each other, but it was difficult to speak. Each was locked into a private sense of desolation. Memories still fresh of the past, dreams of the future they had hoped to share. They were both conscious of the heavy shadow hovering over them, the good-bye that must be said.

They climbed to the top of the hill, where they could look over the town. A soft summer dusk began to fall, and as it deepened, here and there a light winked on. People were setting their oil lamps at the window to welcome others or on a table ready for a family dinner. A kind of timelessness stretched over the scene. From where they watched, it all looked so safe, secure, almost like a toy village. It seemed impossible that such a picturesque scene could harbor hostility, anger, and flaming antagonism.

Reluctantly JoBeth said, "I'd better be getting home, Wes. There'll be questions...."

"Yes, I know, we have to go. But first ..." He drew her close, pressed his cheek against hers. Gently stroking her hair, he said, "Before we do, I have something to show you." He drew a small chamois bag from his pocket. "I guess I was too optimistic—took too much for granted. Here, look for yourself." He pressed the bag into JoBeth's hand. She untied the string that closed it, and shook out the contents. Two rings fell out into her palm. Each was a narrow band with two sculpted clasped hands. "Press it gently on the back," Wes instructed in a low voice. JoBeth did and the tiny hands sprang apart, revealing a heart.

"Oh, Wes!" she breathed softly. "How lovely!"

"I had them especially made from a twenty-dollar gold piece, by a Philadelphia goldsmith. One for you and one for me. The smaller one is yours. I intended to give it to you at the end of the summer, when I planned to ask you to marry me. Like a betrothal ring."

"They still can be, Wes. Betrothal rings."

"You mean that? You still would marry me, in spite of—"

"Of course, and not in spite of, Wes—*because of*. I admire you so much. I respect your courage." She hesitated. Then, with a catch in her throat, she said, "I love you."

He drew her into his arms, held her hard against his pounding heart. "JoBeth, it's *you* who is brave. How did I ever deserve you?"

She clung to him, feeling her heart throb wildly, feeling dizzy with the enormity of what was happening. After a minute, he released her and took one of her small hands in his. "Here, I'll put yours on, then you can put mine on."

She tugged her hand away. "But Wes, I can't wear mine on my finger, where everyone will notice—" Her voice faltered. "I wish it could be for all the world to see."

"Of course. I should have thought of that myself."

"I'm sorry—"

"No, I understand. It's better, safer that way," he said quietly.

"I'll wear it around my neck on a chain. That way it will be closer to my heart."

"What a girl you are, JoBeth," Wes said softly, taking her tenderly into his arms again. They kissed and in the kiss was tenderness, sweetness, commitment, and promise. Finally they drew apart and, arms around each other's waist, started back down the hillside.

As they passed the churchyard, Wes paused, looked at the old brick building heavily hung with ivy. He glanced at JoBeth as if for consent. She nodded, understanding what he meant. He agilely hurdled the stone wall and then, putting his hands around her waist, lifted her over it. Winding their way through the cemetery with its monuments, crosses, and stone lambs, they moved into the arch of the entrance to the church.

Wes took out his ring and handed it to JoBeth, and she gave him hers. Then he took her left hand and said solemnly, "JoBeth, if anything should happen, or if I shouldn't come back, I don't want you to feel that this is binding—"

"Don't!" With her right hand, she placed her fingers on his mouth, stopping whatever else he was going to say. "Never! Don't even think it!"

"All I meant was, if—if that did happen, I would want you to feel free to find someone else—"

She slipped her hand down from his lips and placed her palm against his heart.

"Wesley, let's pledge ourselves to each other for now. No one knows what's ahead. What we feel at this moment is what counts."

"You're right." Wes's voice was husky as he slipped the ring on her third finger.

"I, John Wesley Rutherford, pledge my life, my faithfulness, my enduring love, to you now and forever. Now you," he coached gently.

"I, Johanna Elizabeth Davison, pledge myself to keep this promise to love and wait for you. However long the separation, however long the war lasts, I will be true."

Wes leaned down to kiss her and discovered that her cheeks were wet with tears. He wiped them away gently with both thumbs. "Oh, darling, don't cry." Then they were in each other's arms again. She heard the drumbeat of his heart where her ear was pressed against his chest. At length Wes said gently, "It's getting dark. I'd better get you home."

"When will I see you again?"

His mouth tightened. "I didn't want to tell you, but I'm packed, ready to go. I could see that things were not going to get better. Too much has been said that can't be unsaid. The sooner I leave, the better, the less unhappiness and resentment I'll cause." He hesitated. "I've decided to leave tomorrow. On the morning train."

"So *soon*? Oh, Wes!" she exclaimed, then said, "I'll come to see you off."

He pressed her hands, shook his head. "No, I don't think that's a very good idea," he said slowly. "To be seen with me might—well, it would get back to your family. They would be angry. It would just make things harder—"

"Oh, it's so unfair. So cruel!" she cried. They stood there in the darkness, heart to heart, both fighting to hold back tears. After a moment, hand in hand, they walked on, not talking.

On the porch post of the Cadys' house, a lantern had been lit and shone out, illuminating the way from the gate. They walked up the path with lagging steps. Just before they reached the porch, Wes pulled her gently back. Turning so the light shone on her face, he took it in both his hands, lifted it, and looked down into it. "I want to remember how you look, so after I'm gone, I can close my eyes and see you."

"I'll send you my picture," she whispered.

"Yes, do that," he said huskily. Then he took one of her shiny dark curls, wound it gently around his finger. "Goodbye, darling JoBeth. I do love you so." He drew a deep breath. "Maybe it won't be long, and after the war, when I come back, we can marry"—he halted, adding in a voice that shook a little—"and live happily ever after."

Before she went in the house, JoBeth took off the ring Wes had placed on her finger and put it back inside the small chamois bag, then into her pocket. All evening long, every once in a while, she would put her hand down and touch it as if to see if it was there and if what had taken place between her and Wes that afternoon had really happened. She amazed herself that even while her thoughts were on Wes, she was able to carry on a conversation at supper, help Annie clear the table and assist her in the kitchen, then hold her aunt's skein of yarn while she rolled it into a ball. Was he packing, making his sad farewells, meeting coldness and disapproval as he prepared to leave? Not once did she give way to her feelings. Perhaps this was preparation for what lay ahead of her in the time she and Wes would be separated by this cruel war.

It wasn't until later, when she was alone in the privacy of her own bedroom, that she took out the ring. Inside the little bag, she found a piece of paper folded in tiny squares. Unfolding it, she saw that Wes had written something on it. Taking it closer to the oil lamp by her bed, she read it.

My Darling JoBeth,

In medieval times, the exchange of rings in betrothal was made in church. I found this and thought it appropriate for us. It's from Hosea 2:19–20: "I will betroth you to me forever, I will betroth you in loving kindness and understanding, I will betroth you with faithfulness."

Ever your loving,
Wesley

JoBeth reread the Scripture several times. She wasn't familiar with it. However, Wesley was right. They were pledged to each other. Whether anyone else knew it or not, she intended to keep the promise she had made that day *forever*.

Chapter Six

❧❧❧

*W*es was gone. And there was a void in JoBeth's life that she could not freely share with anyone. Any voicing of how much she missed Wes would bring cold stares, even some remark—perhaps unintentional but pointed—expressing the speaker's personal viewpoint. That would cut her to the quick. Was there no one in all of Hillsboro who shared Wes's abhorrence at the thought of war, of the dissolution of the Union?

Neither of them could possibly have imagined that a shot fired at Fort Sumter would resound throughout the land and like a cannonball shatter all their lovely plans.

Less than a week after Wes declared himself and left town, Alzada Spencer came to pay a call. Her intention for doing so was soon made clear, as was her opinion about her nephew.

She was seated in the parlor with Aunt Josie and Johanna. When JoBeth joined them, bringing in the tea tray and setting it down for her aunt to pour, she realized that Wes was the subject of the conversation. She quietly sat down and listened intently.

Mrs. Spencer gave a dramatic sigh and declared, "None of us can understand it, I declare—we simply cannot. It's all because of Grandmother Blakely, who, bless her soul, cannot help that she was raised by the Philadelphia branch of Lewis's family and adopted the Quaker religion. Wesley has absorbed it all, ever since his own folks died and he was sent up there to live. Then, of course, he went to that Quaker college— and the damage was done. It's hard to blame him, but he *is* a grown man *and* also a North Carolinian by birth. Wayne has tried to explain it to me"—she shook her head until all her clustered blond curls danced—"and I do try to take a Christian attitude about it, but my dears, if he goes into the Union Army, he will be, the Lord forbid, perhaps someday aiming his gun . . . at one of his cousins. . . ." She took a dainty handkerchief out of her velvet purse and brushed the tip of her small nose and sighed again.

"But Mrs. Spencer, I don't think Wes intends to fight, to carry a gun. That in itself is against Quaker beliefs. . . .," Johanna tried to gently suggest.

JoBeth, her hands locked in her lap, said nothing.

But she didn't escape Mrs. Spencer's lugubrious glance and direct comment, "I do feel sorry for *you*, darlin'. You know, Wes confided in me last Christmastime his hopes about you." She whisked the handkerchief again, sighing. "It's such a shame. I know what you and Wes were plannin', and we couldn't have been more pleased, and I'm sure you, Josie and Johanna, felt the same." She paused with a sniff and shook her head again. "But of course, now it is all just ruined—"

JoBeth sat up straight and her mouth opened to protest, but just then she caught her mother's warning glance and stopped. It would have been unthinkable to contradict Wes's aunt, rude to argue with a guest. JoBeth pressed her lips tightly and clenched her hands but thought, *Oh, no! No! Everything's not ruined. We're not giving each other up, no matter what. I love Wes and he loves me, and it will, please God, work out.*

"I can only be thankful that my own boys knew their duty and did it without question," Alzada continued.

Of course! Her sons, Blakely and Will Spencer, were reckless and wild, JoBeth thought indignantly. They'd do anything to avoid books, classes, or lessons. They had been among the first to join up. A few days after the April attack on Fort Sumter, they and some of their classmates from the university had gone up to Raleigh to enlist. They had come home saying they couldn't see sitting in classrooms while the threat of invasion from the "Northern aggressors" was a possibility. Only days later they had come over to the Cadys' house to show off their officers' uniforms. JoBeth had to admit they looked dashing, all spit and polish, complete with sashes and high boots.

JoBeth had to bite her tongue as she listened to Alzada's bragging about them. As far as JoBeth could remember, neither them had ever had a serious thought in their lives! Much less had they developed a philosophy or conviction about anything. Having known them since they were boys, JoBeth knew they weren't fighting for some cause they believed in. For them, riding off to war was an adventure, like so many of their other escapades.

Politeness kept JoBeth quiet, but she was relieved when Aunt Josie asked her to freshen the teapot and she was able to leave the parlor. In the kitchen, while waiting for the kettle to boil, she had a chance to get control of her feelings.

Where was Wes? Back at his grandmother's home? She hadn't heard from him. He had promised to write as soon as he knew his plans. Already the days he had been here were beginning to grow vague, faded. The conversations they'd had were becoming mixed up. What had they talked about and when? Had he actually asked her to marry him? Or was it she who had spoken first of love and commitment? Oh, she had been shamelessly bold, she knew. JoBeth felt her cheeks warm at the things she had said, the kisses exchanged. It had seemed so real then. Why was she losing hold of it? *Please, Wes, write.*

She measured the tea, poured the boiling water into the teapot, and carried it back into the parlor. However, Alzada was putting her bonnet back on, saying she had to be going. As she moved to the front door, she patted JoBeth's cheek, saying, "Now, don't you worry, darlin'. There are plenty of fine young men ready to serve North Carolina who will find you a mighty sweet girl to court. I know it's a great disappointment, and my heart is truly heavy, but we must all go on—somehow."

JoBeth knew that Alzada meant well and that she was doing the best she could to bolster her own sadness over Wes. However, her words fell on deaf ears. At this moment, JoBeth could not imagine being interested in any other young man—especially not one in the gray uniform of the Confederacy, who might consider Wes the enemy.

Her mother gave her a sympathetic glance, and Aunt Josie raised her eyebrows, but neither added anything else to Mrs. Spencer's words. While the two of them saw their guest out, JoBeth carried the tea things back to the kitchen. She left them there on the table for Annie to deal with and went out the back door, through the garden, and out the back gate.

She needed to be alone, to think her own thoughts and avoid any discussion with her aunt or mother about Wes.

～❧～

There are few secrets in any small town. Hillsboro was no exception. The Spencers' dismay at Wes's defection to the North was common knowledge.

In the weeks that followed, for the first time JoBeth felt the full brunt of being associated with Wes. She had not realized how her name had been linked to the name Wesley Rutherford, which was now anathema to many. After he left, JoBeth began to feel that people were watching her, looking at her with curiosity. In the social circle to which they belonged, everyone had assumed that once Wes graduated from college and returned to Hillsboro, their wedding would soon follow.

She was the target of curious glances. At first, comments were made behind her back. Then, as time went on, they were said to her face as well. JoBeth knew that people expected her to denounce Wes's decision openly. She refused to do that. Not even to make things easier for her relatives. She was sure that both the Cadys had received their share of questions and criticism. Was their niece actually engaged to that Yankee sympathizer? Gossip fed by rumor was confirmed by fact. Alzada made no secret of her own distress over Wes's reason for leaving.

Even at home, JoBeth felt constricted. She went silently about her household tasks, avoiding any confrontation. Discussions about the war took place unabated at the Cady dinner table, where Harvel and Munroe were frequent guests. At family gatherings at Holly Grove, events of that summer were usually the topic of general conversation.

The war permeated the town in every way. Local men in small militia units drilled daily in the town park. War fever was everywhere. No one could avoid it! It was epidemic, infectious, and contagious.

The women had their own kinds of activities. There were fund-raisers of all sorts, bazaars, fetes, with booths selling palmetto pins in support of South Carolina's "gallant defense" of states' rights, and other Confederate symbols. Sales of the new red-white-and-blue Stars and Bars flag to display on porches or in yards were high. News of more states' seceding every day bolstered the patriotic fervor. Most of the girls JoBeth had grown up with boasted of sweethearts rallying to the call for volunteers to the cause.

JoBeth avoided her friends as much as possible. Why should she try to explain Wes to anyone? Let people think what they would. JoBeth kept a proud silence and walked with her head high in spite of it all.

It was only to her brother, Shelby, that JoBeth confided her own feelings. "Oh, Shelby, it's so hard. I am trying to understand why Wes did what he did. Why he felt he *had* to. But people are so cruel. They say such horrible things about him. And how can they? They've known him all his life. They know how honorable he is, how much things matter to him. He's following his conscience. . . ." Eyes bright with tears, JoBeth flung out her hands in a helpless gesture. "Uncle Madison makes it sound like—I don't know. He calls him an idealist, as if it were something contemptible."

Shelby was serious beyond his sixteen years. His deep-set eyes regarded his sister with sympathy. "I've always liked Wes. He's an idealist, sure, but he has convictions. People should admire him for that."

"But they don't! All people around here want is for everyone to feel and think and be the same way they are."

Shelby's expression showed his concern. His light-brown eyebrows drew together over gray eyes filled with compassion. "It's the same way at school," he said. "Everyone there thinks we had the right to secede. Freedom of dissent, they call it."

"Isn't that exactly what Wes is doing?" she asked in despair.

"I'm sorry, Sis. I really am."

"I know you are, Shelby. You're the only one I can talk to about this. Mama feels so obligated to Aunt Josie and Uncle Madison—well, you know how it goes." She sighed. "Oh, I wish this horrible war was over and everything was back to the way it used to be."

"I don't think it ever will be," Shelby said sadly. "Oh, eventually the war will be over—I didn't mean that. But I don't think things will ever be the same again."

JoBeth looked sorrowfully at her brother. How tall he'd grown since Christmas, how lanky. His face had lost its round boyishness and was becoming that of a young man. Would he too, before long, have to go into the army? Boys as young as sixteen and seventeen were joining up. Her heart lurched in loving fear. Ever since he'd been born, JoBeth had adored her little brother.

They had always been close. Especially since they came to live in town. They shared the same childhood and recalled a world no one else in Hillsboro knew, a world of tall pines, shadowy glens, mountain streams.

JoBeth longed to hear from Wes. To learn what he had done. Had he joined one of the Pennsylvania regiments that were forming as fast as the ones in the South, in defense of the flag, the country, the Union? It seemed so long since he had left, and she'd had no word. JoBeth wondered if her letters from him might be being withheld. She quickly dismissed that as a possibility. This family prided itself on its honor and would never stoop to anything like that, no matter how they felt. Wes must just be busy with all his plans and with all the decisions that he faced.

She tried to be the first to get the mail, and at last one day she was rewarded. Her first letter from Wes arrived one morning early in July. She ran upstairs with it to her bedroom and there eagerly tore it open.

My Dearest JoBeth,

I apologize for not writing sooner. It is not because you haven't been in my thoughts constantly since I took sad leave of Hillsboro and all that was dear and familiar to me. But ever since my return here to my grandmother's home, my time has been occupied with making my plans. I have found that here reactions to the declaration of war differ greatly from those in Hillsboro. Here there seems to be a profound sadness at the thought of the dissolution of the Union. There are no firebrands, no fiery statements. At least none I've heard. My grandmother wept when I told her why I had returned and about Blakely and Will already joining up. She said, "Oh, my poor Southern kin! God forbid that it should have come to this, brother against brother. It will bring so much suffering to all of us. That I should have lived so long as to see this happen."

There is here, however, a determination to prevent a long war, and after much consideration and prayer, I have decided to join a local unit headed up by a longtime friend of our family. He is as fine a character as one would want for a leader and will make a good captain of our mostly unmilitary group—most of the men have never handled a rifle or firearm of any kind. My summers in the South— riding, hunting with my cousins—have made me at least able to do this. We will be deployed to muster into Federal service in a matter of weeks. Just now we are drilling daily. When we wear our uniforms and march, people come out to cheer us as we pass. Sentiment here seems to be supporting our intention. Rumor has it we will be heading south into the Shenandoah Valley.

I know you are anxious about the future. I cannot promise anything, as we both knew before I left. However, remember I love you and hold you in my heart, whatever happens. I will write as often as I can.

Ever your devoted,
Wes

He enclosed a poem by one of his favorites, Robert Burns, the Scottish poet.

Ae fond kiss, "One fond kiss" and then we sever,
A farewell and then forever.
Deep in heart-wrung tears I'll pledge thee,
Banish Fate's power to grieve thee
Hold high the star of hope shining
While cheerful and ever glowing light
No dark despair can him benight.

Hungrily JoBeth read and reread the letter. There was no one with whom she could share her feelings, a mixture of relief, pride, love, and anxiety.

⚜

JoBeth had to keep the letter, its contents, and her feelings to herself. However, it was with a sense of doom that she learned that Harvel and Munroe's regiments were heading out to go north. There they would join a regiment under General Thomas J. Jackson, who was massing reinforcements for a threatened Union invasion into Virginia.

Upon hearing this news, JoBeth felt a sinking sensation in the pit of her stomach. Her hands turned clammy with dread. Was it only a premonition, or was it possible that in Virginia her uncles and their men would meet and engage in terrible conflict the Union troop of which Wes was a member?

Sick with secret dread, JoBeth stood nearby the day her uncles came to bid their parents good-bye. Uncle Madison struggled valiantly to control his emotions as he embraced his oldest son and said with a choked voice, "I only wish I were young and able enough to go with you, Son." He clasped Harvel's hand tightly, then turned to Munroe. "You two are brave, and we are more than proud of you both."

JoBeth felt like an intruder at this farewell scene. Her own heart felt as if it were split in two, divided in love and loyalty. She watched in a kind of frozen agony as Johanna embraced both cousins and gave them each the gift she had made for them. How much Harvel and Munroe knew of her own relationship to Wesley, JoBeth was not sure. However, both were too gentlemanly to betray anything, by word or gesture, that would indicate any resentment. They kissed her good-bye as tenderly as they had the others.

Then both men gave a last hug to their mother, saluted their father, and left the house. Everyone followed them out to the porch. In front of the house, their horses, held by their aides, waited. Before mounting, Harvel turned for one last look, brandishing his wide-brimmed hat in a kind of flourish. As they moved forward down the road and out of sight, Aunt Josie broke into sobs, and Uncle Madison put his arm around her, saying, "Now there, my dear." Together they returned into the house, heads bowed in mutual sadness.

Left together on the porch, JoBeth exchanged a glance with her mother, who was wiping away her own tears. Seeing that, JoBeth had another image, that of Wes's grandmother weeping as she kissed him good-bye. All the women, North and South, were going through this same heart-wrenching experience. Sending their men off to fight in a war that would last who knew how long, not knowing if they would ever see their beloved ones again.

❧

It was a silent meal that evening. Under the circum-stances, it could have been expected. Everyone seated around the table had his or her own personal sadness, and yet there were no mutual words of comfort to exchange. The Cadys were openly grieving the absence of their two sons. Unable to share her own sorrow at Wes's departure, JoBeth sat quietly, yet she understood more than anyone what pain they were experiencing. She had told her mother of Wes's decision to join the Union Army, and she was conscious of Johanna's frequent anxious looks during the meal. JoBeth understood her reluctance to express sympathy for her daughter, because she knew it would offend her aunt and uncle. But she was not surprised when later her mother came into her bedroom. JoBeth didn't try to hide the tears she had been shedding. Johanna sat down beside her on the bed, cradling JoBeth's head against her shoulder.

"It's so hard, Mama," JoBeth sobbed. "To love someone as I do Wes and to have nobody care. He's in as much danger as Harvel and Munroe will be, and he believes in what he's doing as much as they do."

"I know, and I wish there were something I could say or do to make it easier for you, my darling."

"You can give us your blessing!" challenged JoBeth.

"That I do. All is in God's hands, anyway, JoBeth. Whether it happens or not, whatever the outcome of this war is, nothing comes to us but what is ordained. If you and Wesley are to be together, then it will come about."

Johanna knew what it was like to love so completely and have others oppose that love. She understood the ache of loneliness, the pain of being separated—perhaps forever.

Chapter Seven

❧❦❧

When the news of the battle of Manassas arrived, Uncle Madison came rushing home from the telegraph office at the train station that hot July day, red-faced and excited. It was the first major battle of the war, and the Confederates claimed victory. There was wild, triumphant reporting that the Yankees had turned tail and run. And there was pride that the Confederates had held their position unwaveringly, bringing acclaim to their commander, General Jackson, now nicknamed "Stonewall."

A wave of dizziness swept over JoBeth. Had Wes been among the routed Union troops? How would she know? JoBeth prayed for news yet dreaded hearing it. If he had been killed or wounded, would the Spencers be notified as next of kin? Or was his grandmother considered a closer relative, so that she would be the first to know? JoBeth could not enter into the victory celebration. It was all too awful. She concealed her anxiety as best she could and rejoiced with the others that neither Harvel nor Munroe had been injured or worse.

A letter finally reached JoBeth, informing her that Wes had not been in the battle of Manassas—in fact, he had not seen any action yet. She was relieved for a time. However, as summer turned into fall, letters were few and far between, and JoBeth spent much time wondering where Wes was or what he was doing.

Before the end of the summer, JoBeth and Shelby rode up to Millscreek Gap to visit their grandmother Davison and their father's relatives. In the first few years after they had moved to Hillsboro, their mother used to take them for a week's visit every year. As children, they had looked forward to a degree of freedom they had in the mountains, freedom they didn't enjoy in Hillsboro. They played, swam, and fished with their cousins Jesse and Reid, who were Uncle Merriman and Aunt Jenny's boys and just a few years older. Granny Eliza delighted in how they'd grown and in how much they'd learned, and she spoiled them with her special dishes. Her daughters—Aunt Sue, now the postmistress, and Aunt Katie, a schoolteacher—who were home for the summer, also took great pleasure in their adored older brother's children. It was always a time of special pleasantness for all of them.

This year, war talk had reached even this remote mountain community. Jesse and Reid, now grown men, helped Uncle Merriman on his large tobacco farm. They seemed eager to hear what news their town cousins brought but were reluctant to leave home to join up. Granny Eliza held to her staunch belief that it wasn't mountain folks' fight. "Let them as has sumpin' to protect, go. We'd have more to lose than gain. 'Sides, I don't hold with killin' for somebody else's purpose."

JoBeth spent many hours with her grandmother on this trip. Eliza seemed to have aged a great deal since the summer before—she was a little more bent, a little slower in her movement, though still sharp, with a dry, ironic wit. She still was at her quilting frame a good part of every day, and JoBeth was more interested in the skill than she had ever been before. She marveled that Eliza's gnarled, rheumatic fingers could yet ply a needle so deftly, making tiny stitches.

"What do you call this pattern, Granny?" JoBeth asked one day as she sat beside her at the frame.

"This here's called Jacob's Ladder. But there's other names for it. Most quilters change things in a pattern to make it their own. Your Mama's real good at that! She's done fine with her quilts, she has. Earned enough to send Shelby off to that fine school to get his education."

JoBeth nodded. "She's doing more than ever. Besides the quilts people order, she's making quilts for the soldiers too. She and Aunt Josie and the other aunties meet once a week to quilt."

"And what about you, missy?" Eliza turned a sharp glance at her granddaughter.

"I help, cutting out patches. I'm not really that good at quilting." She didn't add that she'd never been much interested. JoBeth was too active, too impatient, to spend hours perfecting the skill needed to produce the beautiful quilts her mother did.

Turning back to her work, Eliza said, "My next quilt will be for you. What kind would you like? What shall it be? The Double Wedding Ring pattern or"—she chuckled—"the Old Maid's Puzzle?"

JoBeth laughed ruefully. "Maybe it had better be the Old Maid's Puzzle!"

"What? No young man beatin' a path to your door?"

Before JoBeth had to answer, Aunt Katie came in from the garden with a basketful of ripe corn and enlisted JoBeth's help in shucking it so they could have it for supper.

❧

When Shelby returned to school early in September, JoBeth felt lonelier than ever.

That autumn seemed particularly beautiful. But its beauty made her even more melancholy, reminding her of how she and Wes had walked the hills, glorying in the winey, crisp weather, the smells of burning leaves, and the scent of ripening fruit in the orchards. Those weeks and months she walked a lonely path. Not a day went by that JoBeth did not think of him, long for him. She would close her eyes and try to remember his face, those clear, blue, truthful eyes, the hair that never seemed to stay put, the kind, gentle mouth.

In addition to JoBeth's anxiety about Wes and his safety, she also began to worry about Shelby. His letters to her were very different from the ones he wrote to their mother, the ones Johanna so proudly read aloud to the rest of the family. Those were filled with descriptions of his classes, his instructors, his fellow seminarians. But to JoBeth he told of his feelings that he was a "slacker."

> *While other fellows my age are out on the firing line, putting themselves at risk every day, I am poring over translations of Greek gospels. It seems wrong that I am safe behind these "ivy walls," tucked away in an "ivory tower" for that faraway day when I may be of some possible use to someone. And don't write and tell me that I've been called. I know that—I felt that (unless I've been deluded and self-deceived). However, might not the question be asked, Would I not be even better able to serve my fellow man if I'd been tried in the crucible so many of my peers are facing now? If I'd had my "dross burned away into silver"? You and I have always been able to tell each other our real feelings—I long for those heart-to-heart talks we used to have. I hope that when I come home, we can find a way to go to one of our old haunts. I need to confide in one I know will not only listen sympathetically but also help me find some answers. Don't think I don't know and understand that you, too, are going through your own troubled time. As we struggle together, may we both find the right path.*

JoBeth thought long and hard about what should she write back. It was all too much to put into words in a single letter. As he had suggested, their real confidential talk would have to wait until he was home. But she wanted to send him some reply, even if it was inadequate. She wrote, reminding him how hard their mother had worked, making and selling her quilts to pay his school tuition and fees, how disappointed she would be if he gave it up and joined the army.

All of us have our own purpose in life, Shelby. Yours may be of greater value than taking up a gun and going out and fighting. No one should doubt your purity of intent, and no one could ever call you a coward.

Before she signed and sealed the letter, JoBeth had an inspiration. She wanted to add something that would speak to Shelby's heart in a special way. She got out her little concordance and, whispering a prayer for guidance, thumbed through it to look up the reference she wanted. When she found it, she quickly copied it onto the bottom of the page.

Jeremiah 29:11: "'For I know the plans I have for you,' declares the Lord, 'plans to prosper you and not to harm you, plans to give you hope and a future.'"

I can't wait till Christmas, when you'll be home and we'll have a chance to talk.

Always your loving sister,
JoBeth

❦

December 1861
The family Christmas was to be held at Holly Grove. Both Harvel and Munroe had secured leave. The war that

was supposed to be over by Christmas cast its dreadful shadow still. In spite of that, Marilee, Harvel's wife, declared they would have a party just like in the old days.

JoBeth tried to enter into the preparations with the same anticipation the others had, doing her best to hide her own downheartedness. She wrapped presents with her mother, welcomed Shelby home for his school holidays, went with Aunt Josie to help decorate the church for Christmas services.

Her mother had made her a new outfit—a bright-red merino wool skirt and short Spanish jacket trimmed with black braid, and a popular Garibaldi blouse of black satin to wear under it. It was enormously becoming, but JoBeth's first thought was that she wished Wes could see her in it.

Two days before Christmas, she received a letter from Wes. It was on the hall table when she came in from shopping one afternoon. No one mentioned that it had arrived, nor asked her about it afterward. Wes was a subject never brought up, never referred to, in the Cady household.

JoBeth took the letter upstairs to read it in private. The battered envelope looked as though it had passed through many hands, had endured a hard journey before reaching her.

Dearest JoBeth,

I have started several letters to you, then stopped. There is so much to say, and I don't know where to begin or how to say it.

Being in the army is not at all what I thought. I imagined that everyone fighting for the Union would have the same high resolve as I did coming in, that the spirit among my fellow soldiers would be high, the ideals and conversation lofty. I'm afraid it is not at all that way, at least among us common soldiers. To say I have been sadly disillusioned is to put it mildly. Not that there aren't good-hearted men among us, but most seem not to know what it is we're supposed to be fighting for, and there is a great deal of coarse talk that, without my taking a superior attitude would be resented, I have to hear.

If I didn't have you to think about, this life would be unbearable. At least after a day's march (no encounters with the "enemy" as yet), I can carry my bedroll apart from the others, lie down on my blanket by my fire, and concentrate all my thoughts on you. What we had together, how lovely you are, how sweet and pure, and how much I love you.

I hope we have made the right decision, the right choice. Others who oppose this war, I've heard, simply took themselves and their families away, to Europe or England or out west. But I don't think you can run away, escape from your responsibility. This is my country, and I have to believe it is worth fighting for. That you have to suffer is a great sorrow to me. At least I am among those who have chosen to fight on this side—you are daily among people who despise your allegiance to a man whom they consider a traitor. God willing, we will soon have peace and both sides will be reconciled.

That, I fear, may be a long time coming. Longer than either you or I thought. It all seems such a waste— of time, men, and of the beautiful country our Creator gave us to live in and enjoy. As yet I haven't been in any battle, not even a minor skirmish, but I have seen troops returning, seen men with wounds that defy description, and listened to horror tales from veterans. I do not relish when my time comes to face—I cannot even call them the "enemy." My nightmare is that as we rush at each other from either side—and there is much hand-to-hand combat, I'm told—I will see the faces of men I know!

Reading this, JoBeth felt her heart wrench. Not only was Wes suffering the hardships of army life but his sensitive soul was in agony. There was a second page, more hastily written, and she realized from its date that it had been added later.

> This may be my last opportunity to write for a while, so I want to have a chance to say this, for I know not what may befall. I love you, JoBeth. I pray God it will not be long until we are together again. But I fear the worst. No one talks anymore of an early victory or a peaceful settlement.

She couldn't hold back the tears that streamed down her cheeks. She read it over and over, the tears falling on the pages so that they became blotted.

The thought of going to the party at Holly Grove the day after next and pretending things she didn't feel seemed impossible. But she knew she had to. There was no alternative. No one would understand if she stayed away. She would have to go.

Determinedly she buried her heartache and joined the family for supper, keeping up her end of the conversation by sheer willpower. Only Shelby seemed aware that all was not well with her. He did his bit by turning the attention from her so that her unusually subdued manner was not noticed or commented upon by their uncle, aunt, or mother. He rendered stories of schoolboy pranks and other events, lightening the hour for everyone. JoBeth was grateful. When Shelby suggested a chess game with Uncle Madison afterward, she was able to slip away without any trouble.

On Christmas morning, after attending early church service, they came home to breakfast and to open their presents, then drove over to Holly Grove. Marilee had carried out her promise to have the kind of Christmas party that Holly

Grove was famous for. Evergreens tied with gilded ribbons were arranged on mantels and windowsills, candles glowed, and the long table in the dining room, spread with a Battenberg lace cloth, was beautifully set with gleaming silver, sparkling glassware, and a pyramid of cloved oranges and pine cones as a centerpiece.

The house was festive, as was the company. The Cady grandchildren were a lively bunch and had the run of the place. Their father, home for such a brief time, had suspended all discipline, so no one tried to stop the shouting, the tooting of tin horns, or the beating of toy drums, all of which were presents they'd been given. The mood among the military men was buoyant. Harvel and Munroe and the friends they had invited as guests were all in some branch of the Confederate service. As JoBeth listened to them talk, she heard a far less sober perspective of the war than she had read in Wes's letter. They were sure of victory, sure of their superiority in spirit and fighting skills.

Quite suddenly JoBeth could bear it no longer. Listening to all the bravado, knowing it was all directed against the man she loved and what he represented, she felt the blood rush up into her head. The room seemed to become stifling, the fire burned red-hot, the walls tilted dangerously. She thought she might faint. She had never before fainted in her life, but she now felt very much as if she were about to. *I must get out of here, get some fresh air,* she thought. She stood up, edged toward the parlor door, murmuring some excuse, and slipped out of the room. She rushed down the long hall, knowing that at the end there was a door leading out to the back porch. She pushed it open, went out into the darkening evening, and leaned on the railing, gulping the cold air. The pounding in her heart, the throbbing in her temples, mercifully slowed. Then the chill air penetrated her clothing and she shivered. She knew she had to go back, get through the rest of the evening, not let on that anything was wrong.

But it *was* wrong, horribly wrong. And she didn't know how long it would be going on. Wes didn't know, either. It was so hard to live in a house where Uncle Madison did nothing but talk about the war and what they were going to do to those Yankees. She shivered again. *I feel torn to pieces,* she thought, closing her eyes and hugging her arms around her shoulders. *I love Wes. I want to believe that what he is doing is right. But what about the others? Uncle Harvel and Uncle Munroe are both good men. Even the Spencer twins. And maybe Shelby will have to go if the war lasts any longer. Wes thinks it will—Oh, dear Lord, help me! I don't know what I think or feel or even who I am anymore. What will become of me?* Tears rose into her eyes, and she wiped them away. She couldn't go back if her eyes were all red. They would all wonder why she was crying when everyone else was celebrating. *Dear God, help me be brave like Wes. Bless and keep us both, please.*

In a few minutes, JoBeth felt calmer. Resolutely she went back inside. There she rounded up the children and got them into a rollicking game of blindman's bluff, much to the relief of their mother and aunties. The gentlemen had removed themselves to the study for brandy and cigars, so the ladies settled down for a nice chat. Shelby joined JoBeth and later gathered the little cousins around him in a storytelling that quieted them down enough so that eventually they could be put to bed.

Driving back to the Willows in the winter dark, JoBeth realized with a twinge of sadness that this was the first time in her life that she was glad that Christmas was over.

Part Two

*A quilt, woven of love, dreams, and threaded with
grief, joys and laughter sewn into its patches, tells of life
beyond the shadows of hidden love, secret messages.*
Carrie A. Hall

Chapter Eight

❦

Against all predictions, the war edged into a second year. No one had dreamed it would last this long. Both armies had been camped through the winter months, with little action on either part. However, with the coming of spring, everyone on both sides braced for the battles that inevitably would happen.

JoBeth wasn't sure just when or how the idea of the quilt came to her. *Of course!* she thought. It would be so simple, so subtle, so innocuous, that no one would guess, no one would suspect. Every young woman made quilts for her hope chest. No one would think anything of one she would design for herself. The secret would be her own. The hidden truth. She would keep working on the quilt all the time Wes was gone, as a kind of talisman to their promise, their pledge to each other.

She took out a sheet of paper and, with a pencil, began sketching her idea. Each square would have a dove in the corner, an olive branch in its mouth, and in the center would be clasped hands holding a heart!

Her mother seemed mildly surprised at JoBeth's sudden interest in quilting and readily told her to rummage in her scrap bag or among her many various lengths of cloth to select material for her design.

Her choice for the center of the square was a blue-gray calico with a tiny pattern. The dove shapes were white, the clasped hands she cut from pale-pink cotton, and the heart was red, as was the binding of each square. The olive branches she would embroider in brown and green thread after the patch was completed. Satisfied with her selection, she began work with high hopes. Perhaps it wouldn't be too large a quilt—perhaps the war would be over soon.

JoBeth's optimism, however, was short-lived. There was too much evidence to the contrary. Harvel's letters were full of the hardships the Confederate forces were suffering, camped as they were in winter weather that most of the Southern men were unused to. There were difficulties in reaching the troops with supplies and food as well as medical necessities. All this was discussed and worried over at length in the Cady household. JoBeth, who knew that Wes was suffering the same kind of discomfort, distress, and deprivation, had no one with whom to vent her own anxieties. When Aunt Josie enlisted Johanna's help in packing boxes with warm quilts, homemade jellies, knitted scarves, and gloves to send to her sons, JoBeth's desire to do the same for Wes had to be suppressed.

It was so unfair, yet she could do nothing about it.

The days were long and the work on the quilt went slowly. JoBeth started diligently enough, but then her thoughts would wander, bringing Wes dreamily to mind. Was he cold, hungry, weary? The long marches, the battles he might be fighting, the danger, all played on her vivid imagination. If only she would hear from him! Mail was slow and irregular, especially that coming through the lines from the North. All such mail was probably considered suspicious, she thought, and was more than likely opened and read to see if it contained any information that could be used or could be damaging to the enemy.

JoBeth had also started keeping a journal into which she poured her thoughts, her feelings, her fears, her hopes, her dreams. It was a place where all their secrets could be safe. JoBeth hid both the growing stack of letters from Wes and her journal under a loose floorboard under the rug in her bedroom.

She often echoed the plaintive question that Wes had written in one of his letters that spring.

> *Why are we killing each other? We are all the same, descended from the same band of brave men who founded this country in the first place. If we have such differences, why can't we settle them peacefully? What if men on both sides simply refused to fight, demanded that the politicians settle this some other way?*
>
> *Forgive me, my darling, for burdening you with all this. But I have no one else to talk to who would understand, who knows my heart, mind, and soul as you do. I miss you more than I can say. Pray that this wretched war comes to a speedy end with victory for the Union, saving our wonderful country. I long for the day I can come back to you, kiss your sweet mouth. I love you, JoBeth. Pray for me.*
>
> > *Ever your devoted,*
> > *Wesley*

If only Uncle Madison could read what Wes was feeling, maybe he would understand and forgive him. That was impossible, of course. JoBeth could not show this letter to anyone. As she read his letters, she realized that Wes was thinking deeper, becoming more mature, more spiritual. She had never heard any of the men in her family—for that matter, any of the men she knew—express such feelings. Her one comfort was the pledge quilt she was making. Hiding all in her heart, she stitched on her quilt, counting the finished squares as milestones until she could be with Wes again. Strengthening herself, she would think over and over, *No matter what anyone says or thinks, I love him and he will come back! We will be together.*

One day Aunt Josie asked, "Aren't you ever going to finish that quilt, JoBeth? Seems to me you've been working on it quite a spell."

"Yes, ma'am, I know," JoBeth answered noncommittally. No one knew her secret pledge not to complete it until the war was over and Wesley returned safely.

Spring arrived and the war picked up momentum—battles fought, battles won. First the Confederates seemed to be winning, then the Union forces. Elation or depression came and went like the tide. Letters from Wes were rare. Sometimes JoBeth would get two or three at once, and other times weeks would pass before she heard from him. The letters she received did nothing to lift her spirits.

She herself was surrounded on every side by those who are all "hurrah for the South." Of course, she understood. *Their* dear ones were in danger, fighting for what they believed was right. Sometimes it was hard to take so much talk edged with mean-spirited comments about "Yankees" as though they were an alien people. Did not people on both sides of the conflict bear a similar appearance, pray to the same God?

❦

November 1862

With the bleak November weather, JoBeth experienced an eerie sense of doom. The war was never going to end. It would go on and on, just as her pile of patches grew. How many would she have to make before the war was over, before Wes was home? She began to feel like some kind of prisoner condemned to piecework, turning out a required number of units day after day. Each new one she cut out and started sewing added to her sentence. A self-imposed sentence. She would go on making them—she didn't care how long or how big the final quilt became. Sometimes she almost lost heart, but something—fear as much as anything else—doggedly compelled her on. *It isn't superstition*, she told herself. Wasn't she praying constantly all the time she worked on it—for Wes's safety, for the war to end? As the patches accumulated, so did the days and months drag by. She continued writing to Wes. Even if she wasn't always sure he got the letters, it helped her to write them. It relieved some of her tension to express the feelings she had to suppress in her daily life. The fall dragged into winter, and JoBeth dreaded facing another Christmas without Wes.

Chapter Nine

❦

*I*n an unspoken agreement, everyone seemed determined to follow Dickens' suggestion to celebrate Christmas. In spite of the war, in spite of shortages, in spite of worry and deprivation, all bent every effort to appear cheerful and optimistic.

Harvel was due home for a leave, so Holly Grove was again going to host the holiday dinner. It was the largest home in the family circle and thus could easily accommodate everyone in the family, as well as the few extras who were always welcome. Besides, it would be the right place for Harvel to spend his homecoming—among his young children. Each family group could bring some special dish, cake, or pie. Nowadays no single larder had the abundance of the past, so every contribution would add to the feast.

A few days before Christmas, JoBeth went over to help Marilee decorate the house. She was on a stepladder, arranging festoons of evergreen boughs on the mantelpiece, when Alzada Spencer stopped by. Not noticing JoBeth at first, she announced that the twins also had obtained leave and were coming home, bringing one of their fellow officers with them.

"It will be just like the old days—all of us together!" she declared happily. Marilee cast a quick glance at JoBeth, and Alzada, suddenly aware of her, gave a little gasp and flushed. Still she did not mention Wes, and she soon left.

Even as JoBeth continued at her task as casually as she could manage, her thoughts were bitter. She bit her lip to hold back the quick tears at the dismal thought of where Wes might be spending Christmas. Would he even receive a Christmas box, other than the small one she had been able to smuggle out of the house and post to him? It seemed such a heartless thing for the Spencers to ignore the boy who had spent every Christmas of his growing-up years in their house as part of their family. She had heard of families disowning their sons. How could Wayne Spencer—or especially, tenderhearted Alzada—so coldly cut Wes out of their lives?

JoBeth knew there were many others in Hillsboro who held deep feelings about a North Carolinian who would desert the Southern cause, join the ranks of the "enemy." Only a few weeks before, she had been over at her great-aunt Honey's, helping her put together a quilt. JoBeth's job was simple, consisting of basting the top onto the cotton batting, then whipstitching the flannel-back top to its underside. While she was there, a longtime family friend, Patsy Faye Wrightman, dropped by for an impromptu visit. JoBeth had gone on stitching while Aunt Honey, always the gracious hostess, urged Mrs. Wrightman to stay for a cup of tea.

JoBeth, concentrating on keeping her stitches straight, had paid little attention to the murmur of conversation behind her in the room. That is, until she heard Mrs. Wrightman say furiously, "I simply can't abide him. A hometown Yankee sympathizer." Aunt Honey gave a small warning cough, which was followed by a moment's silence. Without turning around, JoBeth felt sure her auntie was sending some kind of signal to her guest. Evidently it didn't matter to the lady, nor did it diminish the "righteous indignation" she was expressing. Instead, Mrs. Wrightman wiggled her plump body like a ruffled hen puffing up her feathers, shot JoBeth a scathing glance, and said sharply, "Oh, I pretty near forgot. *Wesley Rutherford* is one of them Unionists! I'm sorry, Honey, but maybe if *you* had three nephews and goodness knows how many dear friends' sons fighting for *our* safety and well-being, you'd feel the same way I do! I can't abide *any* of them turncoats." Without an apology to JoBeth, Mrs. Wrightman picked up her shawl, gloves, and purse and stood up, saying haughtily, "Well, I'd best be on my way. I'm rolling bandages this afternoon for *our* poor wounded boys. . . ."

The echo of the remark hung in the air in the hollow quiet after the front door closed behind Mrs. Wrightman. There was no sound other than the ticking of the mantel clock, the rustle of Aunt Honey's skirts as she came back into the parlor, the clicking of the cups as she began gathering up the tea tray. At last she cleared her throat and said, "Don't pay her any mind, JoBeth. Patsy Wrightman never thinks before she speaks. I'm sorry if she hurt you, dear—"

"It's not your fault, Auntie. I know that plenty of people feel the same way. It *does* hurt. Especially when I know how hard it was for Wes to make the decision he did, knowing no one would understand." She added sadly, "But that's the way it is. It happens even at home."

She heard Aunt Honey sigh, then the rattle of teacups as she carried the tray back to the kitchen.

She continued working on the quilt, wishing she could share with Aunt Honey the letter she had received from Wes just a few days before.

Received your letter of the 25th. It arrived somewhat the worse for wear, having passed through who knows how many hands to reach me. I read it hungrily. Seeing your handwriting brought tears to my eyes. I had taken it aside to read it so that none would be witness to whatever unconcealable emotion it might evoke within me. Not that my fellow soldiers are so hard of heart that they would not understand—all here long for loved ones as deeply as I—but there are some things a man wants to keep private and precious, as I do my feelings for you.

Until recently we had not had a regular chaplain and consequently no religious services. About three weeks ago one was assigned to this regiment, at least on a temporary basis, and conducted a meeting. The Scripture from which he drew his sermon was very much on the same order as you described.

Second Chronicles 20:15–17: "Thus saith the Lord to you: 'Do not be afraid nor dismayed of this great multitude, because the battle is not yours but God's. Position yourselves, stand still and see the salvation of the Lord, who is with you.'"

The men seemed to take great heart from that. Although I cannot say there is great religious fervor among soldiers, without this kind of preaching we would all grow lax and weary with the dreary routine of daily life in the army. I must not, however. Since we have had the chaplain, there is a stirring within the troops, and small groups are meeting for prayer. We all need the Almighty so as not to lose sight of the real purpose of this fight, to free men from bodily bondage, as we have been freed from spiritual bondage.

Our unit got its orders to pack and be ready to move out in the morning. It has been raining for days, and we all live in mud, sleep in mud, and almost eat in mud. I have no idea where we are headed or to what battlefield *we may be called upon to do what we have come to do. I don't think they want to kill me anymore than I want to kill them! More and more, I understand my grandmother's abhorrence of war. It is madness.*

The very next Sunday, JoBeth was seated in church. She was not being too attentive to the sermon. That summer, their old minister retired, one who had been an inspiration to and was so fond of Shelby. In fact, he had encouraged Shelby to go to seminary. His replacement was as fiery a Confederate as the most militant general would ask for. Suddenly his forceful words brought JoBeth to quivering attention.

"Listen, church, to what the Scripture is saying to all of you. Recently we have heard with awe the number of men and weapons the enemy is gathering to come against us. So I say to you, search for your answer, your strength in our cause, in the book of Nehemiah, chapter four, verse fourteen. It is as true today as it was then: 'So I arose and said to the noble, to the leaders, to the rest of the people, "Do not be afraid of them. Remember the Lord great and awesome, and fight for your bretheren, your sons, your daughters, your wives and your homes."' Amen?"

There was an enthusiastic round of "Amens" from the congregation, which was usually known for its quiet and decorum. In fact, some of the gentlemen rose out of their seats and applauded. If they had not been restrained, JoBeth would not have been surprised if the famous "rebel yell" had been shouted to the rafters. Instead of feeling enthusiastic and aroused by this, JoBeth's heart sank. As Wes had said, "We all pray to the same God, the Creator of us all." So whom was God listening to?

~∙~

Christmas afternoon, JoBeth dressed to go to the family party at Holly Grove, wishing Wes could see her in the new dress her mother had made for her. It was red poplin, and it had a molded bodice with a froth of white lace at the throat, and wrists banded with black velvet ribbon. She gathered her hair into a crocheted black silk snood tied at the top of her head in a wide black velvet bow. As she slipped in her small freshwater pearl earrings, she tried not to think about where Wes might be spending this Christmas. She just prayed it wasn't somewhere cold, miserable, and that he wasn't in any danger. He had sent her a small picture of himself in uniform. He looked wonderful, manly and brave. She had spent hours studying it, but of course she could not show it to anyone. The blue uniform was hated by everyone she knew.

The Cadys left for Holly Grove earlier than the three Davisons. Their carriage had been so crowded with goodies and gifts for Harvel and his large family that there had hardly been room for Aunt Josie's skirt, let alone Johanna, JoBeth, and Shelby. The Cadys then sent their driver, Jonas, and carriage back for the trio.

It was always a nostalgic trip for Johanna to visit her childhood home. As the carriage rounded the bend of the road and started up the holly-tree-lined driveway, dusk was just falling. They could see the candlelight from the windows of the house, glinting on the snow.

"Oh, look, children! My, it looks lovely! Just like old times!" Johanna exclaimed, clutching JoBeth's arm.

JoBeth tried to put aside any melancholy thoughts and strived to join into the spirit of the day when she entered Holly Grove. The sound of laughter, children's voices, and general merriment almost drowned out the greetings of Marilee, Harvel's pretty wife, as she met them at the door. She looked like a happy bride instead of a wife of sixteen years with a half dozen children. Her radiance was due, JoBeth was sure, to the happiness she felt at her soldier husband's homecoming. All her anxiety for his safety was put aside for one glorious evening. Harvel, looking fit and ruddy in his tailored gray uniform and sporting newly acquired gold captain's bars, came out to welcome his cousins.

"Happy Christmas!" he said heartily, kissing the cheek Johanna turned to him and pumping Shelby's hand vigorously. Turning to JoBeth, he winked. "Just what we needed— a pretty girl to liven up the party for some of my bachelor officers. Come in, have some eggnog, and meet our guests."

The parlor was gaily decorated, the windows festooned with red bows and swags of evergreens. Red candles shone from candlesticks on the mantelpiece, between garlands of galax leaves and gilded pine cones. The Cady children and assorted cousins were running in and out, dodging and playing among the booted legs of the men and the billowing skirts of the ladies as people clustered in congenial chatting groups.

The merry scene before her dismayed JoBeth instead of pleasing her. The parlor seemed to be filled with gray uniforms!

She took a deep breath, willing herself to smile just as Blakely Spencer, hardly recognizable with a just-grown, curly beard, came up to her, gave her a hug and kiss, then grinned mischievously, "Rank has its privileges, and I'm doing the honors for our—dear *departed one*."

Startled by his words, JoBeth stared at him in confusion. Then, realizing what Blakely meant, she smiled. Blakely was always a cutup, never took anything seriously. Remembering this, she felt both relief and a new warmth for him. At least *he* did not harbor any animosity for Wes, no matter how the rest of the family felt. She knew Wes considered his twin cousins "almost brothers."

Blakely leaned closer and whispered, "How is the old scalawag?"

She made a small grimace. "It's a long time between letters," she told him in a low voice. "I hope and pray he is all right."

"Probably having a jolly old Christmas for himself in Yankee land." Blakely gave her a wink and squeezed her hand. "Now come along, JoBeth, I want you to meet someone." Taking her by the arm, he led her toward the piano, where Dorinda, Munroe's wife, was playing familiar carols that could hardly be heard above the din in the room. A gray-uniformed man, his back to them, was leaning on the piano. Blakely tapped him on the shoulder and announced, "Here she is!"

The soldier turned around. A direct gaze from intensely blue eyes momentarily stunned her. Blakely introduced them.

"JoBeth, may I present my brother-in-arms, Lieutenant Curtis Channing. Miss Johanna Elizabeth Davison."

The man introduced bowed slightly. "A pleasure, Miss Davison." She acknowledged his greeting and murmured something she hoped was appropriate, thinking that surely this was the most handsome man she had ever seen.

He might have stepped out of the pages of the romantic novels she used to ridicule. Tall and slim in his superbly tailored gray, he had coal black hair that fell in a wave across a high forehead. His features might have been considered too perfectly molded face too handsome, if it had not been for a tiny scar on his cheekbone. When he smiled, he revealed teeth that were very straight and white.

"What did I tell you?" Blakely demanded, gleefully nudging Curtis Channing with his elbow. Then he said to JoBeth, "I kept telling Curtis that Hillsboro has the prettiest girls in North Carolina—for that matter, in the entire Confederate states."

Never taking his gaze off JoBeth, Curtis replied gallantly, "Indeed you did, sir, you most certainly did. But you *under*-stated the matter."

"Curtis is from Georgia, JoBeth, and had too short a leave to make it home, so I brought him along so he could see for himself. Now I guess you believe me!"

"I certainly do," Curtis smiled.

Almost immediately the evening she had dreaded JoBeth began to enjoy. It had been such a long time since she had been with people her own age, exchanging light conversation, being flirted with, and even flirting a little herself. She almost felt guilty that she was having such a good time. Every once in a while during the evening, that thought would flash into her mind. In those fleeting moments, JoBeth hoped desperately that Wes had been fortunate enough to get leave and had perhaps gone to his grandmother's home in Philadelphia.

Actually, JoBeth hardly had time but to be in the present. Curtis Channing scarcely left her side for the rest of the evening. He was so attractive and charming, was such an amusing raconteur, that she was completely dazzled and entertained.

He seemed eager to tell her about himself, as if to make up for their short acquaintance and the brevity of his time in Hillsboro. When she attempted asking about his army life, he dismissed it as unimportant.

"It will all be over by summer," he said loftily. "The Yankees are no contest. Not for men like us, born in the saddle and knowing how to hunt! Most of them are clerks, farmers, shopkeepers, schoolteachers," he scoffed. "Most never held a gun or rode a horse."

He was much more eager to tell her about his family, his home, the life he loved and was anxious to get back to, a life of riding, hunting, socializing. He told her he had two younger sisters, Melissa and Anadell, whom he adored, a mother and father he loved and respected, two sets of grandparents, and an assortment of cousins, aunts, and uncles.

"Sounds like *us*!" JoBeth laughed, gesturing to the room full of Shelbys, Cadys, Hayeses, and Breckenridges.

"That's what makes Southerners strong," Curtis nodded, not arrogantly but with complete assurance. "We have unbreakable bonds of loyalty. We stick together, have pride in our land."

He talked about his horses, two fine thoroughbreds he'd brought with him into the brigade that he'd volunteered to join, and he added in a nonchalant aside, "I also brought Jericho, my groom."

His casual reference to his manservant after his horses jarred her. Later when she recalled her reaction, she wasn't sure why that had bothered her so much. Then she decided it was because she could imagine Wes's reaction. Putting a human being *behind* a pair of prized animals. At the time, she didn't have a chance to analyze it or question Curtis about the reference, because there was a general stir around them. Harvel called for everyone's attention. They were going to play "the farmer in the dell" for the sake of the smaller children, who would soon have to be put to bed.

The ensuing chaos chased away any serious talk for the rest of the evening. When the children were shepherded off to their rooms upstairs, the grown-ups went into the magnificent dining room, where a bountiful buffet was spread out. After that, the evening quieted down. People sipped coffee and ate fruitcake while Dorinda played softer melodies on the piano for all to listen and enjoy.

Gradually some of the guests began to depart, among them Uncle Madison and Aunt Josie. At this, Blakely and Will, with Curtis adding his pleas, begged Johanna to let JoBeth stay longer. They were going to roll up the rugs, declared another cousin, Ted Hamlett, and dance. They all promised her mother that they would escort JoBeth safely home later. Smiling, Johanna gave in to the chorus. Shelby decided to accompany his mother home and went to get her cape. JoBeth helped her mother on with it, and Johanna patted her daughter's cheek, saying, "I'm glad to see you having a good time, darling."

One by one the Munroe Cady children got droopy-eyed and cross, and reluctantly Dorinda and Munroe declared they had better take their children home, as they were dropping like flies and getting into little squabbles. Dorinda stood up regretfully to close the piano lid. Surprisingly, Curtis offered to replace her. At that the dancing gradually turned into a songfest, with the lingering guests gathered around the piano. JoBeth discovered that Curtis had a rich, true tenor voice and knew all the words to most of the popular songs.

Finally, at a little after midnight, everyone agreed it was time to depart and leave the household in peace and quiet. The last remaining quintet of Will, Blakely, Ted, Curtis, and JoBeth bade their hosts thanks and good night and went out into the starry December night. Outside, they linked arms as they walked, singing merrily some of the marching songs the young men had learned since enlisting. It was a short distance back to the Willows, and the crisp air and lively company made the trek seem short.

In the Cadys' wide front yard, Blakely, Will, and Ted succumbed to the temptation of an impromptu snowball fight, and Curtis walked with JoBeth up onto the porch.

"I can't tell you, Miss Davison, how glad I am that I accepted Blakely and Will's invitation to spend my leave here in Hillsboro. I cannot remember a recent evening when I have enjoyed myself so much."

The light from the porch lantern that was left burning for her return illuminated his expression as he spoke, and it was flatteringly sincere. Instinctively JoBeth stepped back from it so that he couldn't see the sudden blush that warmed her cheeks. She felt inordinately pleased and then immediately guilty. Why should she care that any other man besides Wes enjoyed her company?

"May I see you again? My leave only lasts three more days, and they will go very fast. I find myself not wanting to miss any possible time with you."

JoBeth hesitated. This evening had been enormous fun. Was it wrong to feel lighthearted and happy for a change? Was it a disloyalty to Wes? But then, she was sure *he* would be the last one to mind if she had a good time.

Curtis asked, "Is there something wrong?"

"No, it's just that I don't know whether it's such a good idea."

"Why not? Blakely tells me there are several other events planned for our time here—a ball tomorrow night, I understand, and if the temperature continues to drop, he says, the ice on Bedlow Pond may be solid enough for a skating party. Surely you're not going to miss those? Come now, Miss Davison, isn't it your duty to provide a brave soldier some respite from the war?" There was a teasing challenge in his question. "Besides, *I* want it very much, so please don't refuse."

How could she hold out against such persuasion? And what harm could it do to spend a few hours in such delightful company? Surely it would all be innocent enough. Besides, it would be hard to explain to Blakely and Will why she wouldn't accommodate their house guest. It would also be difficult to explain to her aunt and uncle, who, she could tell, had taken quite a liking to Curtis Channing.

"Yes? You will, won't you?"

She laughed. "Well, yes then. If it freezes tomorrow, I'd be happy to go skating."

"And even if it *doesn't*, may I call?" Curtis persisted.

She laughed again. "Yes, you may. And now I must go in, or else those fellows will wake the whole house!" She pointed to the other three, who were still scuffling and throwing snowballs at each other on the lawn.

She turned to open the front door, but Curtis caught her hand.

They both now stood shadowed by the porch columns, hidden from the frolickers in the front yard.

"Good night, Curtis," she said softly and gently tugged her hand, which he pressed and then very slowly released. Her heart gave a little warning flutter, as if alert to some unexpected danger. Quickly she went inside. After closing it, she peered through the glass panels on either side and saw Curtis leap buoyantly down the porch steps, join his comrades. Then the three of them, arms around each other's shoulders, went down the path, out the gate, whistling "Dixie" and singing at the top of their voices.

⚜

To her surprise, a light was shining out from the small parlor. Who might still be awake and up? Tiptoeing toward the stairway, she glanced in through the half-open door and saw her brother sitting by the fireplace, his sandy head bent over a book.

"Shelby? What on earth? Do you know what time it is?"

"Couldn't sleep," he explained with a smile as she came over to join him.

JoBeth tucked her skirt under and sat down on the low hassock opposite Shelby, asking, "Problems?"

"I suppose you might say that. Mostly what I've already written you about."

"Enlisting?"

"I'm torn between what's my duty and my calling," he sighed.

JoBeth put out her hand and covered his to convey her understanding. "I know. It's the same here. Bugles blowing, flags flying. Anyone who isn't in uniform gets a scorching glare or a questioning look or even worse! It's almost as if those people who don't go, no matter if they have good reason or whatever, are supposed to walk around with a placard tied around their neck telling why in bold letters."

Her mockery brought a slight smile to Shelby's lips.

"There're only ten left in our class of thirty-five. Of the ones who all started out together."

"But you're so close to being finished," JoBeth reminded him.

"I know, but it all seems so pointless with fellows my age out there on the battlefield. Wouldn't it make more sense for me to be out there, ministering in some way—not carrying a gun, necessarily, but taking God's message?" He halted, then gave an ironic shake of his head. "That is, *if* God goes out on the battlefield—*any* battlefield."

"You sound like Wes," JoBeth told him.

"I thought Wes was convinced *he* had chosen the right thing to do."

"Oh, yes, I'm sure he believes he has. But he doesn't think war is right, no matter what. The longer he's in it, the more bitter, the more disillusioned, he sounds."

"You've seen him? He's been here?"

"Oh, no! He couldn't come." She gave a harsh laugh. "He'd be shot as a spy! Uncle Madison would probably meet him with a shotgun himself!"

It was Shelby's turn to comfort. "I'm sorry, JoBeth. It must be doubly hard for you. A divided heart."

She nodded. "Oh, Shelby, you always put it so right. Yes, that's what I have, a divided heart, and sometimes I feel as if I'm bleeding to death."

The two siblings turned to the fire and were lost momentarily in their own dark thoughts. Then Shelby said firmly, "Don't worry about me anymore, JoBeth. I'll go back. I'll finish out this term, at least. Then we'll see what next summer brings. Maybe the war will be over by then—"

"Please, God!" she said fervently. "I think you've made the right decision. At least for now. Mama would be so disappointed if you left. She's so proud of you, Shelby."

"I know. And I realize how hard she's worked, making quilts, selling them to pay for my tuition, room, board, books. I know that. Above all, I do want to do the right thing."

"You will, Shelby. I trust your judgment." She got to her feet, leaned down, and tousled his hair softly, "You're a wise old owl for seventeen!"

"Sometimes I feel more like Methuselah!"

"Well, I'd better get to bed, get some sleep," JoBeth said.

"Good night, then. Thanks for listening." Her brother raised his hand in a saluting gesture. "See you in the morning."

"Yes, I'll be up bright and early. I've promised to go skating if the pond is still frozen. Will and Blakely's house guest has unlimited energy!"

"Good! You deserve to have some fun."

"Want to go with us?"

Shelby shook his head. "As Proverbs says, 'Do not boast about tomorrow, for you do not know what a day may bring forth.'"

"Spoken like a true seminary student!"

"Or 'Out of the mouths of babes . . .,' right?" Shelby said, laughing.

"I'd better get out of here before you shame me any more with your Scripture quotes," she said. "Good night, Shelby." She waved her hand as she went out the door.

"Good night, Sis."

Chapter Ten

❦

The next day, instead of dropping, the temperature rose. An unseasonable warmth melted the light layer of snow that had fallen before Christmas, so there was no skating party on Bedlow Pond. However, the Spencer twins and their guest arrived at the Cadys' house to call upon JoBeth the following afternoon. Warmly received by Aunt Josie, they stayed, enjoying Uncle Madison's special holiday punch and the congenial company. The Spencers, always known for their exuberant personalities, were true to form and in high spirits. The visit ended after a round of singing, with Curtis again doing the honors at the piano.

When it was at last time to go, Curtis lingered a little behind as the others stood at the door, thanking the Cadys for their hospitality. He asked JoBeth, "May I call again tomorrow? On my own?"

"Tomorrow is the bazaar, a fund-raiser the Ladies Auxiliary is holding, and I've promised to help my aunt at her booth."

Disappointment clouded Curtis's handsome face momentarily, then quickly disappeared as he asked, "An event, I presume, that is open to the public?"

"Of course! Provided you bring lots of money to spend," she teased.

"Done." He saluted her. "And if I empty my pockets, may I have the honor of escorting you to the ball tomorrow evening?"

She laughed. "That sounds very mercenary."

"Anything for our cause, right?" He raised an eyebrow and smiled.

When Curtis departed with the others, JoBeth realized, with a guilty start, that she had not thought about Wes all afternoon.

⁓ℰℊ⁓

The bazaar to raise money to send needed supplies for "our boys in gray" had been planned for a long time. All the proceeds would go to various relief services. Hospitals, soldiers' widows and orphans, people who had left their homes in fear of Yankee invaders, and other charitable groups were listed as recipients of the money to be earned. For the past several months, all the Hillsboro ladies had been busy making handiwork of all sorts to sell. JoBeth's mother, aunt, and other relatives in the family had been involved from the beginning. Aunt Josie, known for her organizational ability, headed up the committee, assigning the different booths, each with specialized items for sale. Homemade delicacies, preserves, jams, jellies, baked goods. Embroidered pillowcases, tea towels, spectacle cases, slippers, floral potpourri and sachets, scented bath salts. Several booths were planned that would offer practical knitted garments, such as mittens, scarves, gloves, wrist warmers, socks, havelocks for foraging caps. There would also be booths tapping the varied creative talents of Hillsboro "artistes," exhibiting and selling such works as hand-painted china, watercolor greeting cards, and sentimental quotations in small frames. There would be a booth devoted to displaying dainty baby accessories, which were much in demand and would prove to be a popular item. (As would infant apparel—at one of the first organizing meetings, Patsy Faye Wrightman had commented, "With all the many military marriages that have taken place since Fort Sumter, there should soon be a market for baby booties, bonnets, buntings, blankets, and the like.")

The Logan ladies, as JoBeth's great-aunties were sometimes called by those who knew them before they were married, combined their quilting skills to contribute a beautiful quilt for which raffle tickets would be sold. In order to finish it in time for the bazaar's grand opening party, they increased their "quilting bee" from one to five days a week. The pattern they had chosen to make was Star of Bethlehem in bright yellow, blue, and red, with pointed patches making the star, and the quilt bound all around with a band of orange.

Johanna made several crib-sized quilts. JoBeth put aside her own work on her pledge quilt to help her mother. On these days when mother and daughter spent time together on the project, a new closeness seemed to grow between them. There was something about the quiet task that initiated confidences and sharing. Often the sound of November wind or rain beating upon window or roof created an intimacy, shutting them off from the outside world. Sometimes JoBeth would ask her mother about the years in the mountains when she had first married Ross Davison.

"Oh, it was a wonderful time, such happy years." Johanna's voice grew soft. "Hard work, which you know I wasn't used to at first. But so rewarding, so worthwhile. Your father was so kind, so loving—such a fine man, beloved by all the people in Millscreek."

JoBeth had her own memories of the tall, rugged man who was her father. She remembered his coming home and swinging her up into his arms, times he had held her on his knee, read to her. She could still recall how his beard felt against her forehead when she leaned back on his shoulder, the smell of him, the scent of leather, balsam pine, the slightly medicinal aroma that clung to his clothes. She remembered the gentleness of his hands, and the sound of his deep voice.

Thinking back on those long-ago childhood days, JoBeth felt the sharp twinge of loss. Only when she closed her eyes and really concentrated could she bring back the smell of the pine woods that had puckered her nostrils, the feel of the brown-needled carpet on her bare feet when she would run down the path between their home on the hill and Granny Eliza's.

"Do you remember the gritted cornbread Granny used to make?" Johanna's question broke in on JoBeth's thoughts.

"Oh, my, yes!" JoBeth looked at her mother, eyes shining. "That was the sweetest, tastiest cornbread I ever had! Was it a secret recipe or something?"

"I'm sure not. She told me how to make it and I tried, but mine never turned out as delicious as hers." Johanna laughed and shook her head.

"As soon as the weather gets better, I must go visit Granny," JoBeth murmured. "Maybe when Shelby comes home in the spring, when the snow melts, we can ride up there together." She thought of the weathered cabin nestled under the cedars with a tender longing. It was a part of her life, a part of herself that somehow had got lost in the years since she was a little girl. She felt an urgency to recapture it, treasure it somehow. Everything about the past had taken on a special significance, because everything else was changing so fast. Holding on to happy memories was important.

<hr>

The morning of the bazaar, soon after breakfast, Aunt Josie supervised packing Johanna's crib quilts into large boxes, then directed Jonas to carry them out to the carriage. Then she said, "JoBeth, you come along with me now. I need you to help arrange the booth, help me to decide which ones to display first." Buttoning her fur tippet, she nodded approvingly to JoBeth's mother, declaring, "Your quilts are just the sweetest, Johanna. Doting grandmothers will certainly snap them up in a hurry. I'm sure they will all go like hotcakes."

JoBeth glanced at her mother, who seemed a trifle wistful at seeing some of her favorite baby quilts disappear. It was as though she hated to part with them. JoBeth knew that each one her mother made was special to her. She gave her a sympathetic smile as she kissed her cheek, saying, "You'll come over later, won't you, Mama?"

"Yes, indeed. Aunt Honey's picking me up in her carriage. We don't want to miss the raffling off of the aunties' quilt."

"Good! You've worked so hard, you certainly deserve a bit of pleasure," Aunt Josie said decisively, putting on her bonnet.

JoBeth was amused that sometimes Aunt Josie spoke to her mother as if Johanna were still a young girl. Maybe that was the price her mother paid for coming back to live in Hillsboro with a member of her family.

Not for the first time, JoBeth wondered what would have happened to them all if instead, Johanna had decided to stay in Millscreek Gap among her husband's people. What would their lives have been like, hers and Shelby's? Shelby might have become a farmer like Uncle Merriman, their father's younger brother. *She* certainly would never have met Wesley! But she could hardly imagine that.

"Come along, JoBeth. Don't stand there dawdling and daydreaming. We must be on our way. So much to do—," Aunt Josie said over her shoulder as she swept out the front door.

JoBeth glanced at her mother, who rolled her eyes in affectionate understanding, then JoBeth followed her aunt out to the waiting carriage.

When they reached the town hall, where the bazaar was being held, the place was abuzz with women's voices and the swish of their skirts as they bustled about. A cacophony of sound echoed in the vast building. People were issuing directions for the setting up of booths, the draping of bunting all around. Hammers banged as signs went up, and a large muslin banner hung from the rafters, declaring in gilt-edged lettering such heart-quickening words as "For Our Glorious Cause" and "For Our Gallant Men in Gray."

Aunt Josie was greeted by everyone. Mrs. Herndon, a portly lady in pink and mauve taffeta, the grand chairwoman of the event, rustled up importantly to lead her through the of maze of cardboard boxes, unfurled crepe-paper streamers, stepladders, and clusters of women busily erecting and decorating their individual booths. JoBeth tagged behind.

"We always look forward to you Logan girls outdoing the rest of us!" Mrs. Herndon simpered. JoBeth stifled a giggle at the referral to her elderly great-aunts by their maiden name and as "girls."

"As my own dear mama used to say, the Logan sisters do the finest needlework in town!" Mrs. Herndon said effusively. Then, gesturing with a flourish to a flimsy wood frame, she said, "Now here we are, Josie. I hope this position suits you? It is just to the right of the entrance door and will be the first thing anyone sees! I'm sure you will be sold out long before any of the other booths." She smiled at Aunt Josie, but her smile did not include JoBeth. Startled by this obvious snub, JoBeth wondered why not. Mrs. Herndon had known her most of her life. JoBeth had gone to school with the Herndon children, Billy and Maryclare. Slowly she understood. Mrs. Herndon was a neighbor of the Spencers. So of course she knew about Wes! *Her* son had joined Lee's army of northern Virginia. By ignoring her, Mrs. Herndon was expressing her disapproval of JoBeth's allegiance to Wes.

Realizing that this might be the general feeling of many of the ladies working at the bazaar, JoBeth, her face flaming, immediately went behind the booth. There she busied herself unpacking one of the boxes. Maybe she should have been prepared for that kind of treatment. JoBeth bit her lower lip as she bent over the boxes, wishing she could develop a hard shell. As it was, she couldn't help feeling hurt. More for Wes than herself. She laid some quilts neatly on one of the shelves, thinking, *I hope some Yankee women are doing for their soldiers what we're doing for*—She'd started to say *ours* to herself, then stopped. A bleak, hopeless feeling washed over her. She remembered what she and Shelby had talked about. *A divided heart! That's what I have! No wonder it hurts so much.*

JoBeth was sure that her aunt had been too preoccupied to notice Mrs. Herndon's deliberate coldness to her. Determined not to let her wounded feelings show, she began winding crepe-paper streamers around the spindly poles of the booth. Soon their booth was transformed into a bower of ribbons and clusters of flowers.

"Oh, that looks lovely, JoBeth!" Aunt Josie praised her, adding, "You certainly have your mother's artistic touch!"

For the next hour, they worked steadily, arranging, rearranging, setting out the lovely handmade items. Several of the other women working in various booths came by to admire and compliment them. Having been alerted by Mrs. Herndon's behavior toward her, JoBeth tried to act busy so as not to embarrass her aunt if any of the ladies refused to acknowledge her. She kept reminding herself that most of them were probably mothers who had sons off fighting and were sick with worry about their safety, so she tried to understand and forgive their resentment.

By the time they had placed the last patchwork pillow and agreed on the best angle to show off their favorite quilt, the bazaar had opened and people started streaming through the hall. From the size of the crowd, it appeared sales would be brisk. Most people seemed to first make the rounds—circling through the giant hall, admiring all the booths, browsing, getting an idea of all that was available—and then turn around and proceed to buy.

After two busy hours, Aunt Josie collapsed on one of the stools provided for the sales force. "Mercy me, JoBeth! I'm about done in! Do me a favor, darlin'. Like a good child, run along over to the food booth and get us each a bit of lunch. I heard tell they've got all manner of good things to eat, and I'm simply famished. I think we could both use a restoring cup of tea and a sandwich or two."

"Of course, Auntie," JoBeth agreed. "You just sit and rest. Now, don't do another thing till I get back, hear?"

"I couldn't if I wanted to!" her aunt laughed as she waved a pleated newspaper as an improvised fan.

JoBeth made her way through the crowded building to the refreshment booth. A long line of people was stretched out in front. It looked like a long wait to be served. Resignedly she took a place at the end. Others joined the line behind her, among them four chattering young women. Seemingly oblivious to anyone else, they were making no effort to keep their voices down. It was impossible not to overhear their conversation, and suddenly JoBeth began to catch some of it.

"The nerve of her—"

"She must think nobody knows—"

"Most likely doesn't care—"

"It's absolutely brazen, I think."

"With almost everyone here having *somebody*—brother, father, husband, sweetheart—serving!"

"It's outrageous, if you want *my* opinion."

"I should think Mrs. Herndon would have asked her to leave—"

"Or to not even come in the first place!"

"She could hardly do *that*! After all, the Cadys and the Breckenridges and Judge Hayes are all her relatives—"

"Even so—it's the principle of the thing!"

JoBeth's ears tingled, her cheeks burned. They were talking about *her*! *She* was the subject of this spiteful conversation. For the second time that day, the gossip about her and Wes that must be circulating hit her. Her heart hammered so loud, she wondered that people standing next to her didn't hear it! It even alarmed her with its banging. What if she fainted?

Should she turn around and confront them? Or just never let on that she had overheard? Her impulse was to whirl around, face them. But what could she say? How could she honestly defend being here at a fund-raising for the Confederacy when the man she loved was considered the *enemy*? All this raced through her mind. Her fists clenched. Part of her wanted to escape, even if it meant going back to her starving aunt empty-handed. Undecided, she debated. Then JoBeth heard her name spoken by several male voices.

"Miss Davison!"

"JoBeth!"

Dazed, she turned to see Will, Blakely, Ted Hamlett, and Curtis Channing! Within a few seconds, she was surrounded by four attractive, gray-uniformed officers. As she looked on in amazement, Curtis made a sweeping bow to the nonplused girls, the very ones who had been talking about her, and said in his most ingratiating manner, "I am sure you lovely ladies will give way to us"—he gestured grandly to his companions—"being that we're all heroic soldiers honorably defending your lives, homes, and country. Will you allow us to slip in line here? Yes, I was sure you would, seeing as we must soon be away again to the battlefields."

JoBeth glanced at him in astonishment. There was laughter in his eyes, a bold sureness of his own powers to persuade. Like magic, the disconcerted quartet stepped back and made way for the four officers. There was an amused ripple of laughter from others in the line, and looks of approval at the men. Someone was heard to say, "That's our rebels for you."

Escorted by the four, JoBeth moved up the line. Beside her, each handling two plates apiece, they quickly had them piled with sandwiches, frosted cupcakes, slices of pie. Blakely wheedled a tray from one of the booth ladies and loaded it with steaming mugs of fragrant tea to take back to the quilt booth.

Out of the corner of her eye, JoBeth saw the four indignant deposed gossipers staring at her with open envy. However, knowing that her companions' food purchases had totaled up a nice sum for the benefit's coffers, she walked off with her head high. Certainly, she thought, by the end of the afternoon other booths would find their cash boxes filled with the young officers' money as well.

Back at the booth, after consuming the delicious delicacies they'd brought back, the four men persuaded Aunt Josie to allow JoBeth to be their guide among the myriad booths. That way, they said, they could spend more money for "the glorious cause."

If unfriendly eyes followed her progress as she guided the good-looking cavalry officers from booth to booth, JoBeth knew they could not argue with the fact that the four were clearing out great quantities of the merchandise displayed.

JoBeth was ironically amused by all this. Underneath, however, the overheard comments still stung. But she thought it a small sacrifice on her part—Wes had made the much harder one.

In spite of the constant chaperonage of his three fellow officers, Curtis had a chance to whisper in JoBeth's ear, "Do I qualify for the honor of taking you to the ball tonight?"

Looking at his armload of pot holders, doilies, china bud vases, knitted scarves, and other miscellaneous purchases, JoBeth widened her eyes and exclaimed dramatically, "I should hope so."

Chapter Eleven

◆━◆

That evening, JoBeth got ready for the ball, with both her mother and Aunt Josie hovering like bees around a favorite flower. Each had suggestions to complement her appearance. Johanna got out her point lace scarf and insisted JoBeth wear it, draping it over the shoulders of her hyacinth blue velvet gown. JoBeth was just securing a high-backed comb into her swept-up hair when her aunt left the bedroom and returned, carrying a jewel case.

"Here's something that will set off your gown," she said, opening it and taking out amethyst-and-pearl earrings and a matching pendant on a gold chain.

"Oh, Auntie, they're beautiful!" JoBeth exclaimed. "But I couldn't!"

"Of course you must. I'll hear no argument. They'll be perfect," her aunt said firmly. "Here, let me fasten this around your neck."

Persuaded, JoBeth then slipped the earrings in while her aunt clasped the pendant's chain. Both Johanna and Aunt Josie murmured approvingly at the result of the added jewels.

"Thank you both!" JoBeth smiled, touching the lace then the earrings with her hand. "I feel like Cinderella in her borrowed finery and jewels."

"Except it won't all disappear at midnight!" Johanna laughed.

"Let's hope not!" declared Aunt Josie in mock alarm. "That set was Madison's wedding gift to me!"

Downstairs, Curtis, splendid in a dress uniform and polished black boots, waited for her. The gilt epaulets and the golden swirls on his sleeve cuffs gleamed against the fine gray broadcloth coat, the tasseled yellow silk sash a bright slash of color at his waist.

Curtis had brought a wrist corsage of hothouse violets for JoBeth to wear. As she held out her wrist for him to tie the purple and lavender satin ribbons, the admiration in his eyes was open and unabashed. It made her a little breathless.

Uncle Madison handed Curtis JoBeth's dark-blue velvet cape, and Aunt Josie said with satisfaction, "My, what a handsome couple you make!"

Catching a glimpse of herself and Curtis in the hall mirror, JoBeth felt elated and excited. It was a heady moment, and she needed to defuse it. She whirled around, shook her fan playfully at her aunt. "Oh, Auntie, you're prejudiced. But thank you." She slipped her kid-gloved hand through Curtis's offered arm. Then, kissing her mother, she said, "Thank you all, and good night."

"Have a lovely time!" her mother's voice followed them out into the crisp December night.

As they entered the ballroom, which was adorned with a random mix of Christmas decorations and patriotic symbols of the Confederacy and brightly illuminated by candles in brass wall sconces tied with gilt ribbons, the band was playing.

JoBeth felt her heart lift at the sound of the music, the slide of feet upon a floor sanded and waxed for dancing, the sight of whirling colors—cerise, orange, green, gold, pink— and the ballooning skirts of dancers circling. The gaiety of the atmosphere was irresistible. Suddenly all JoBeth's underlying sadness melted magically away. She was caught up and into it all. Curtis held out his hand to her and swept her out among the dancers.

Curtis knew every type of dance and executed each with finesse. His skill spoke of much practice and social experience. JoBeth had never felt so light on her feet as he guided her expertly in several intricate maneuvers so that she never missed a step. During the first part of the evening, she danced with many partners—with Blakely, Will, Ted, and a half dozen others. Many were hometown boys she knew and had grown up with but hadn't seen much of in the past several months. Most were in uniform, on leave, or coming or going to some military post or service. Although this was a military ball and had been given to honor and aid the cause, strangely enough nothing was mentioned about the reason for it all. For once in what seemed forever, the war was not the main topic of talk. Gaiety seemed the order of the evening, and JoBeth gratefully entered into it. She found it almost easy to forget what had been constantly on her mind for months. She slipped back into what had once been natural—carrying on banter of a light, silly kind. In fact, she had almost forgotten she was very good at it.

When intermission was called, Curtis led her to a table at which Blakely and Will and the girls they were escorting were already seated. When Curtis and JoBeth joined them, it made six crowded around it. JoBeth knew the two other girls, Trudie Hartman and Flavia Bates. Of late they had pointedly excluded her from the social occasions that previously she would have been invited to attend. Tonight they were conscious that she was accepted as part of the group they were with, and they were superficially polite. However, most of their attention was turned to their escorts as the two girls flirted with fluttering eyelashes and fans, giggling at the twins' outlandish jokes and flattery. Since Curtis was devoting *his* full attention to *her*, JoBeth hardly minded being ignored by her former friends.

When the music began again, a childhood friend, Kenan Matthews, came over from another table to ask JoBeth to dance. She excused herself from the others. Kenan had also been a friend of Wes, and for the first time all evening, she was asked about him.

"I realize how hard that must have been for Wes—and for you, too, JoBeth," Kenan said when she told him Wes was now in the Union Army. "Wesley Rutherford was the most idealistic, most honest, person I ever knew. Although I disagree with his decision, I admire him for his integrity."

"Thank you," JoBeth murmured, feeling her heart swell with pride at hearing these rare words of praise for Wes.

When Kenan returned her to her table with a courteous bow, she found that the other girls had left for the ladies' "refreshing room." The three men had been joined by cousin Ted, and although they had all risen and politely acknowledged her return, they resumed what appeared to be a heated discussion.

Curtis was saying, "I can't see what all the fuss about slavery is about. My father has a lumber mill down home and has about twenty men working for him there, and out at my granddaddy's farm there are people who have been on the land as long as I can remember and before. They all seem happy as can be. You should hear them singin' out in the fields—"

JoBeth experienced a sick sensation, a rush of blood to her head. The drastic contrast between Wes's long, agonizing soul-searching and Curtis's casual offhandedness about the same subject struck her like a blow. Her fingers clutched her little fan so tightly that she could feel the edges of its spokes.

Just then Curtis, as if aware of JoBeth beside him, seemed to lose interest in the conversation. He leaned toward her, smiling, and said, "I missed you." Then, lowering his voice and with his appealing little-boy grin, he said, "Let me have your dance card. I'm putting my name on all the rest." Disarmed, she handed it to him.

Watching him scrawl his name through the line of dances still left on her card, JoBeth knew she shouldn't blame Curtis for his attitude. Wes had even understood that. Like so many Southerners, he was only speaking from what he knew, what he had grown up with, never having learned any other opinion. Why should she expect any more from this charming man than an evening of flattering attention? With his graceful manners, his wit and good humor, it was impossible not to like Curtis Channing—and it would be easy to fall in love with him.

Back on the dance floor, Curtis said, "You know I go back day after tomorrow. This has been too—" He checked himself, as though he would have used a stronger way of expressing his frustration. "This has been *way* too short. At any other time that you and I might have met, we would have had a chance to get to know each other better—spend long, leisurely afternoons strolling, swinging in a hammock under the trees, playing croquet on the lawn, going riding. There are so many things I can think of I'd like to do with you." There was amusement, affection, in his eyes as he looked down at her. Then quite suddenly his eyes darkened. "I hate that we're missin' all that, Miss Johanna Elizabeth Davison." He spoke her full name as though he delighted in each syllable. "This has been one wonderful two and a half days." His hand on her waist tightened as he circled and then reversed in the final strains of the waltz. "Days I shall never forget."

The music ended, but he didn't take her right back to the table. Instead he stood, still holding her hand so tightly that she finally wiggled her fingers to free them.

The orchestra began playing the final piece of the evening—"Goodnight, Ladies"—and Curtis led her into the slow steps of the song, making a slow circle of the dance floor.

As was customary these days, the evening ended with a rousing chorus of "Dixie," which was finished with a flourish of trumpets, followed by some spontaneous renditions of the famous rebel yell inaugurated at the Yankee defeat at the battle of Manassas.

The Spencers' large carriage had been commandeered for their party. When they came out, they found the horses stamping their feet and blowing frosty breaths in the cold night air. They had to rouse the sleepy driver, Felix, who was bundled in front. The two girls were taken to the door of the Hartman's house, since Flavia was staying overnight with Trudie. JoBeth and Curtis remained together in the carriage. They could hear the high-pitched laughter and low voices saying whatever frivolous and foolish things were being said besides proper good nights on the doorstep.

Curtis made no move to give JoBeth more room on the seat on which the six of them had all been squeezed so tightly on their way from the ball. JoBeth did not move either, because she was cold and also did not want to call attention to the fact that they were sitting so close together.

At last the twins came running back and hopped into the carriage, and they went on toward the Cadys' house. When they reached it, Curtis helped JoBeth down. He then surprised her by leaning back into the carriage and saying, "I can walk home from here. You fellows go along." Before she could utter a protest, Will shouted up to the driver to go, and the carriage moved forward, leaving her and Curtis standing at the gate. For a minute there was silence. JoBeth hardly knew what to say about his bold dismissal of his hosts and their carriage.

"Did you mind?" Curtis asked in a low voice, taking JoBeth's hand and drawing it through his arm. "I hate for this evening to end. For our time together to end."

"You're to come to dinner tomorrow," she reminded him. Uncle Madison had issued the invitation before they left for the ball.

"Yes, I know, but he invited Will and Blakely as well, and from what he said, there'll be a bunch of people. We won't be by ourselves at all. Funny thing, but I've always enjoyed being around people until—well, to tell you the truth, all at once I find I want to be alone with you, JoBeth."

"It's late, Curtis. I'd better be going in," JoBeth demurred, thinking the conversation might be getting dangerous. She pulled her hand from his arm and placed it on the gate latch.

Curtis put out his hand and kept the gate from opening. He lifted his head, looking up. The night sky was studded with stars. "What a beautiful night. I can't remember seeing one so beautiful."

JoBeth felt she had to take charge of the situation.

"Yes, Curtis, it *is* very beautiful, but it is *also* very late," she chided gently.

Curtis laughed softly. "I know. My delaying tactics are pretty obvious, aren't they?" He didn't seem offended and pushed open the gate. They started up the walk, but Curtis's step was slow.

When they reached the porch steps, Curtis took her arm, keeping her from going up. "At the risk of repeating myself, JoBeth, I wish I could make this evening last. . . ." He paused, then almost in a whisper said, "I would like very much to kiss you."

Startled, JoBeth halted, staring up at Curtis. He hurried to say, "I know it's highly improper, as you may rightly say, since we have just met. Hardly know each other. But JoBeth, don't you get the feeling that these days, time is telescoped? Each day, each hour, each minute, counts." He paused, reached out with his other hand, turned her face toward him. "You have quite the most beautiful mouth I have seen in a very long time and—simply put, I want to kiss it."

She was stunned. She had not been kissed in months, and then by Wes. All other kisses before his had disappeared from memory, like figments of a dream. Now this handsome soldier's request stirred her.

"Since you haven't answered, I'll take the offensive as a good soldier should—" And Curtis bent and kissed her very slowly, sweetly. When it ended, both sighed.

"You are very lovely, Miss Davison, and I couldn't resist the temptation. Say you forgive me?"

He didn't sound at all remorseful, and JoBeth realized she wasn't sorry either. The kiss had been gentle, warm, and very satisfactory. It would be silly to *act* offended. Indeed, to *be* offended. Curtis was right—the days they were all living through were moving too fast, taking with them the time for leisurely courtships, old-fashioned restrictions of all kinds.

They went slowly up the porch steps. At the front door, he put both arms around her waist, interlocking his fingers so that he held her in a tight clasp from which she could not easily escape.

"Do you have a charm chain, JoBeth? One of those strings of buttons that girls collect?"

"How do you know about those?" she asked, surprised. She didn't know any man who was aware of the current fad that single girls had of collecting buttons. The legend was that the button last collected, if given by a male and placed on the chain, was from the one you would marry.

Curtis chided her gently. "Remember, I told you I have two younger sisters. I'm on to all sorts of feminine pastimes. They each have one of those chains, and they're always lengthening them, afraid the wrong fella will give them the last one. Girls!" Curtis chuckled, shaking his head in amusement. "They're somethin' else. You just never know what they'll do next." He paused, then asked, "So then, do *you*? Have a chain?"

JoBeth used to have one, as most schoolgirls did. But after she and Wes had made their pledge, she hadn't even thought about the silly tradition. However, not wanting to explain all that, she just nodded. "I confess I used to have a button collection."

Slowly Curtis released her. His hand went to the front of his tunic, grasped at the double row of shiny brass buttons, gave a hard tug, and a button came off. He held his hand out to her, then opened it to show the button resting in his palm.

"Here, JoBeth, will you take it? Let it be the last one on your charm chain?"

JoBeth was taken aback. She drew in her breath.

"But—but I'm not superstitious."

"No? Well, *I* am! I believe in fate, destiny, and predestination. That nothing happens by chance. My coming home with Blakely and Will on this leave. Meeting you. It's all in the cards." He paused, took her hand, and pressed the button into her palm. "Please take it. I want to go back to camp believing it means something."

Chapter Twelve

✧⟨❧⟩✧

The December morning was cold. Under a gray sky, a chill mist drifted. At the Hillsboro train station, the families gathered to see the "boys" off again. A kind of false gaiety prevailed—everyone chatted about unimportant things, marking time until the train came. Underneath the forced optimism ran an undercurrent of apprehension. They were sending them back to their regiment, back to the war—and no one really knew what these young men were going back to, what they might be facing in the next weeks or months.

As the group huddled together, making innocuous small talk, JoBeth shivered. Inside her small beaver muff, her hands were nervously clenched. Uneasily she met Curtis's fixed gaze. For the first time since she met him, Curtis's smile was not visible, and his eyes had lost their mischievous sparkle.

The evening before, which was spent in the company of the Cadys, the Spencers, and the Hamletts, had not been a success as far as Curtis was concerned. Impatient to be alone with JoBeth, he had endured an evening with company. Dinner had been festive, with all the ladies contributing their tastiest dishes, their finest cakes and pies, as a grand sendoff to the boys, who were used to army rations. Afterward there had been games, songs, and general conversation. As the evening progressed, Uncle Madison drew the young soldiers into a military discussion. Sitting across the room from him, only JoBeth had been aware of Curtis's growing frustration. Eventually the evening had come to a close. Good manners required the hosts to see their guests to the door, so at the end they had still been surrounded by other people.

All this JoBeth read in Curtis's eyes as he gazed at her this morning in the midst of the awkward group of family and friends.

Finally Curtis reached the end of his patience. He came over to where she stood. "I *must* speak to you," he said in a low voice. Then, ignoring the exchanged glances of the others, he took JoBeth by the arm and walked her to the end of the platform.

There, apart from the rest, he no longer felt obliged to present a bravado. Curtis's expression turned grave. "I didn't mean to be rude. But time is slipping fast, and I had to talk to you privately," he said. "I couldn't keep standing there pretending it didn't matter, when it does." His tone was intense. "I hate to leave with so much unsaid. I don't want to go back. It's not just going back. It's leaving *you*."

"Please, Curtis, don't—," JoBeth protested, but he didn't let her finish.

"No, JoBeth. You may not want to hear this, but I want to say it—*have* to say it. So please listen." He rubbed his hands together as if from the cold. "I attended church with the Spencers this morning. But the sermon was so long and tiresome, I got bored and started thumbing through the Bible. I came upon some pretty interesting stuff." He halted, then asked with mock severity, "Are you familiar with Scripture, Miss Davison?"

Surprised by his question, she replied, "Not as much as I should be."

"Well, neither am I ordinarily, I'm ashamed to admit. But this morning I had a revelation of sorts—I think you might call it."

"What do you mean?"

"Simply this. It was in Deuteronomy. I chanced upon something I heartily recommend—I scribbled down chapter and verse so I wouldn't forget it. Deuteronomy 24:5—this is what's written down right there in the Good Book, as a law to the Israelites—'When a man has taken a new wife, he shall not go out to war, but he shall be free at home for one year and bring happiness to his wife.'" Curtis's voice took on excitement as he quoted the passage. Looking directly at JoBeth, he said, "Now, *that* is a law I believe we should adopt in the Confederacy." A faint smile lifted the corners of his mouth. "And therefore I fully intend to bring this to the attention of my commanding officer. What do you say to that, Miss Davison? A good idea?"

"I suppose so. . . ." JoBeth smiled tentatively, as if waiting for the joke she expected would follow.

Yet Curtis seemed totally serious. "Should we not press for the enactment of such a law?" he demanded.

JoBeth looked at him in bewildered amusement. "I don't think I understand, Curtis."

"Miss Davison, would you consider marrying me? And let me spend one full year bringing you happiness?"

Suddenly JoBeth realized this wasn't one of Curtis's pranks or comical attempts to make her laugh. He meant it. He was proposing.

"Curtis, I—"

"Don't look so shocked, please. I've been very proper about it. I've spoken to your uncle who, I understand, is your guardian, and asked for your hand in marriage. And also received permission from your mother to address you. It took a good deal of maneuvering to do that last evening. I had to follow your mother into the kitchen, and I was forced to waylay your uncle early this morning. I was waiting at the gate when he went out for his walk. They were a bit taken aback, I admit, but they said it was up to you, so—" He rushed on. "I realize we haven't known each other long. Just met, in fact. But we've spent nearly three entire days together. I know I could make you happy! You'd love my hometown, my family—and they would love you. They're much like your family. We have so much in common, JoBeth. The same background, the same values, the same—"

"Stop, Curtis! I can't. Please, don't say any more. Let us part as friends. It's been a wonderful three days, but that's all it can be."

"*Why?* I don't understand."

In the distance, the thin sound of a train whistle pierced the winter air, startling both of them. A frown brought Curtis's eyebrows together over eyes full of dismay.

"JoBeth, there isn't any time. I love you. I know I can make you love me."

In his face, disappointment and possibility mingled. JoBeth had the feeling that Curtis Channing had been refused very little in his life. And nothing that he really wanted. She shook her head.

"No, Curtis, I'm sorry. There is someone else—I'm pledged to someone else."

He looked shocked, then angry.

"But you never said—you never gave any hint that— neither did your aunt and uncle nor your mother!"

"They don't know. It's a secret."

His frown deepened. "I don't understand."

"I'm sorry—truly I am," she said, and she meant it. She had not meant to mislead or hurt him.

The train rounded the bend and was clanking down the track, a spiral of smoke billowing out of its stack. With a hissing of steam, a screech of brakes, it pulled to a grinding stop. The small group at the other end of the platform started calling, beckoning, gesturing to them.

"I can't believe there's no chance," Curtis said forlornly.

"I'm sorry, Curtis. Perhaps if we had met some other time—"

Blakely was shouting to Curtis, motioning with wild, flaying arms. Hillsboro was what was called a "whistle stop." Even in wartime it had a schedule to keep.

Curtis grabbed JoBeth's hands, held them tightly.

"Isn't there anything I can say to change your mind? Can't you give me some reason to hope?"

"No, that would be wrong—it wouldn't be true." JoBeth's voice broke. "I'm sorry," she said again.

He pressed her hands so hard, they felt crushed.

"I respect loyalty, JoBeth. If you are promised to someone else . . ." His mouth tightened. "Another soldier? I can accept that."

Something inside JoBeth shrank from telling him. If he knew *who* the soldier was and *what* he was fighting for— would Curtis be so noble, so understanding?

"I'm sorry, "she said weakly, knowing it was inadequate.

The shouts grew frantic. "Curtis, come on! You're going to miss the train. Hurry up!"

"I will never forget you—nor these three days—for the rest of my life." Curtis's voice was hoarse, ragged, above the warning shrill of the train's whistle.

Impulsively JoBeth raised herself on tiptoe to kiss him lightly on the cheek. But before she could, his arms went around her, drawing her tight against him so that her feet were lifted off the ground. He kissed her with passion and desperation. When he set her back down, she was breathless, deeply stirred by his kiss. "Good-bye, darling JoBeth," Curtis said huskily, then he took one or two steps, backing away from her. "Good-bye." He started down the platform, then turned, took one last, lingering look at her before he began to run toward the train. The locomotive was sending up great clouds of steam and the whistle shrieked again.

JoBeth watched him swing up into the car even as the train started moving down the track. He leaned out, waving his arm. She raised hers feebly and waved back.

As the train disappeared around the bend, she shuddered. A rising wind tore at her bonnet strings, tugged at her skirts. Still she stared down the empty tracks, standing away from the rest of the people at the other end—standing apart, standing alone.

❦

JoBeth got back into the carriage. On the way home, Aunt Josie leaned over and patted her knee. "What a lovely young man, honey. And so taken with you. I don't know when I've seen such an example of love at first sight. Why, I could tell the minute he laid eyes on you the other evening at Harvel's—he never looked at anyone else. It was clear as a bell to see."

"As fine a young man as the Confederacy could ever have to defend us," was Uncle Madison's comment. "Good stock, good breeding. You can't miss it."

"And beautiful manners!" chimed in Aunt Josie. "He was so easy and gracious, you can tell he was brought up well."

JoBeth did not know how to reply. She knew her family assumed that her downcast mood was because of Curtis Channing's leaving and were treating her with considerate deference. She *was* sorry—not so much that he was gone but that she had hurt him. She hadn't meant to, but it couldn't be helped. Should she let their assumption go on? How could they possibly think she had so quickly forgotten Wes? They seemed to. People often saw what they wanted to see. They had been upset about Wes, so no wonder they hoped she would be attracted to the charming Curtis. In their minds, who could be more acceptable as a suitor for their niece than a well-born, well-mannered, handsome Confederate cavalry officer?

Arriving back at the house, JoBeth immediately went upstairs to her room, shut the door. She needed to be alone with her guilty conscience. Ever since Wes left, she seemed to be living a lie, hiding her correspondence, never speaking his name. Mostly to please her aunt and uncle, she had outwardly participated in Hillsboro's social life. All the time, she had been hiding her secret. Now her family happily believed she was interested in Curtis Channing.

She knelt down on the carpet in front of the fireplace and poked the sputtering fire to life. The look in Curtis's eyes haunted her. If she had misled him, there was no way to undo the damage, to avoid the consequences.

She regretted that she might have inadvertently led Curtis to imagine romantic possibilities for them. Worse still was her remorse that in enjoying his delightful company, basking in his flattering attention, she had betrayed Wes. How could she have—even for a few days—forgotten what *he* had given up, what he was going through? She put her face in her hands and wept bitterly.

That evening she got out her neglected pledge quilt squares and sewed diligently. Tears fell on the cloth as she sewed, and at times blurred her eyes so that she couldn't stitch properly. Finally, exhausted, she prepared for bed. Hopefully, after a good night's sleep everything would seem clearer. But sleep refused to come. Obsessively her thoughts kept returning to the scene on the train station platform, and Curtis's good-bye.

Chapter Thirteen

All the following week, the hints, the innuendoes, and the inferences from both Aunt Josie and Uncle Madison began to mount. JoBeth assumed that Curtis's supposed proposal had been circulated among the close-knit family. She was sure the consensus was that she had best not summarily dismiss the courting of such a gallant young man. It was as if the combined family were holding its breath and waiting for her to make the announcement.

JoBeth simmered under the covert glances sent her way. She could just imagine the discussions about her that were going on within the family circle. While they held an idealized image of Curtis, they seemed to have forgotten all Wes's fine, brave qualities—his integrity, his courage. What hurt her the most was the fact that Wes had grown up in this town. They had known him since he was a little boy. They knew his parents as friends. Wes had often been a guest in all their homes, and now they had all turned against him in favor of someone they had just met. And only because Curtis wore the right uniform! Finally JoBeth reached the end of her tether. She went to her mother and told her about Curtis's proposal.

"Of course, I told him I was pledged to another. I don't see why Aunt Josie and Uncle Madison presume I could forget

Wes like that." JoBeth snapped her fingers. "They *want* me to be engaged to someone like Curtis, for their own sakes. So they won't be embarrassed any longer by a niece promised to a Yankee sympathizer. I don't think they even realize that Wes has joined the Union Army!" She got up from the chair on which she had been perched near her mother's quilting frame and began to pace. "No matter what they want, I am in love with Wes, *pledged to him*! Nothing or no one, no matter how charming or attractive or eligible in their opinion, will change that. I wish they'd stop insinuating otherwise."

"Do you want me to speak to them, darling?" Johanna asked sympathetically.

"Would you, Mama? Please? I'm afraid I'd just get defensive and get into an argument." JoBeth sighed. "I love Aunt Josie and Uncle Madison. I don't want this to cause any more misunderstanding."

Since Wes's departure, there had been an unspoken rule in the Cady household never to mention him. It was a rule that no one had yet disobeyed.

That evening at dinner, JoBeth guessed that her mother had broken the rule. Her aunt and uncle's attitude spoke volumes. There was an unnatural stiffness in their very postures. JoBeth could not only feel the disapproval but see it in her uncle's face. Aunt Cady regarded her with hardly concealed impatience, her mouth pressed as though she were trying to keep from speaking her mind about JoBeth's stubborn and distressing stand.

Uncle Madison never could keep from expressing himself on any subject for long, and before the meal was half over, he addressed himself directly to JoBeth.

"I understand you turned Curtis Channing down, young lady." Uncle Madison's tone was bitter, implying that he was a man who felt he had been greatly wronged. "In my opinion, that was a very rash and unwise decision. You would do well to reconsider that refusal. A finer specimen of an upstanding Southern gentleman it has not been my pleasure to meet. And from what Blakely tells me, a fine officer as well, admired by his comrades and well-thought-of by his superiors. I understand he will probably make captain before long—you should be proud that such a man has asked you to be his wife."

It was too much. After all, Wes had been welcome here since he was a little boy. He had sat at this very dinner table, had brought flowers and his gracious manners to her aunt and mother. Yet now he had become anathema, as though he had never even existed.

"Yes, indeed." Uncle Madison was waxing eloquent as to Curtis's qualities. "That young man is certainly an outstanding example of what is best in a Confederate officer—"

But this time he got no further. JoBeth could stand no more, and she turned furiously toward her uncle and interrupted, "Curtis Channing doesn't have the remotest idea what the war is all about—or even what he's fighting for."

At first, Uncle Madison looked stunned at this startling outburst.

Then his face reddened and he banged his fist on the table. "Well, he damn well knows what's the *right* side to be fighting for!"

At this, tears threatening, JoBeth flung down her napkin and jumped up from the table and ran from the room.

❧

JoBeth's outburst at the dinner table that night ushered in a dreadful period of strained relations with her aunt and uncle. Uncle Madison maintained a dignified silence as he came and went, and he kept his contact with his niece to a minimum. Aunt Josie fluttered between her husband and niece, begging them both to relent and resume their former affectionate relationship.

Both were stubborn. At last Johanna intervened with her daughter, saying it was *she* who should apologize. Uncle Madison had been like a father to her all these years, she reminded JoBeth, and she should honor and respect him, no matter their differences. JoBeth, knowing she had been wrong to react as she did, finally yielded. She went to her uncle one evening, upon his return from his office, and asked his forgiveness. Wes was not mentioned.

"We'll say no more about it, my dear," was Uncle Madison's stiff rejoinder. After that the household seemed to regain its balance. However, under the surface, all knew that things might never be the same again.

Part Three

Chapter Fourteen

～❧～

*T*hree letters from Wes, all looking "battle scarred," arrived for JoBeth at the same time. One touched her deeply but filled her with a feeling of apprehension. There was something about it that sounded so final, as though it might be the last time she would ever hear from Wes.

> *Lying here on my cot in the tent on this dark night, my dreams are filled with visions of your dear face. Even though now it seems endless, I know our separation must someday end. And we will find our love and happiness again. I take your letters out and press them to my lips—it seems your perfume still clings to the pages, and I am most aware of the sweetness of your memory, the scent of your skin, your hair. How I long to hold you once more. Pray God it will not be too long until that happy day comes.*
>
> > *Ever yours,*
> > Wes

The letters had no dates, so JoBeth could not be sure when Wes had written them or where he might possibly have been at the time.

> *Long march today, feet aching, legs weary, shoulder burdened with heavy pack. All made light, easy, because*

I let my mind wander to thoughts of you—the bright days of summers we knew . . .

I had a terrible dream. I woke feeling suddenly desolate. I dreamed I could not remember your lovely face. How could this be? At night when I lie awake waiting for sleep to come, your beautiful eyes appear, smiling, and gradually your image comes to comfort me. I think sometimes I can even hear your voice.

I do think of you as my bride. Then I consider the price I've asked you to pay. My love for a life of sorrow? Alienation from your family, from those you hold near and dear? This cruel war that has parted us, that has sent me away from you. For what? For home and country? I have left the only home I've known, my land, my people. I am an orphan, in truth. Except for your love, my dearest—that is all that holds me staunch. And I believe our cause to be a just one.

～≈§≈～

Spring brought the war even closer. With the battle at Chancellorsville in May, the Confederates won a remarkable but costly victory against the Union Army. The losses were heavy, something that the Southern forces, with less manpower, could not easily bear. Worse still was the tragic death of General Lee's right-hand man, accidentally shot by his own pickets.

At the news of Stonewall Jackson's death, flags were flown at half-mast in Hillsboro. Some even wore black armbands, like Wayne Spencer, whose sons had fought under the brilliant general. Still, the success of Lee's army lifted spirits and gave a renewed hope that the Confederacy would eventually be victorious.

A letter from Wes came, and JoBeth sensed a difference in tone from the previous ones. There was a sense of fatalism about it that frightened her.

June 1863

My Dearest,

In the silence around this encampment, the tension is almost alive. We expect attack or some action anytime. . . . We know the Confeds are somewhere camped in the hills just beyond the ridge. We speak of the enemy, but all I can think is that these are my former playmates, my classmates, my fellow college students, my brothers. . . . Are we not all God's children? This horrible conflict must soon be resolved. Oh, JoBeth, I can close my eyes and see your dear face, see your sweet smile, the dark, silky curls falling on your shoulders, hear your tender voice. I remember the words we spoke, and they echo in my despairing heart. Will they ever be said again? When I finally drift off to sleep, when I wake, your name is on my lips.

No more letters came for three more weeks. Anxiety about Wes was JoBeth's constant companion. Yet she could share it with no one.

It was in July, however, that the tide of the war was about to turn dramatically. Ironically, it would happen on the national anniversary celebration of American independence.

Hillsboro on the first day of July was blistering, not a breath of air stirring. The ladies were out on the Cadys' front porch, waiting for Uncle Madison to come home for noon dinner. JoBeth was sitting on the steps, and her mother and aunt were in rocking chairs, fluttering palmetto fans and discussing a new quilt pattern. All of a sudden Aunt Josie sat up straight, exclaiming in alarm, "Will you look at that! Walking so fast in this heat, he's liable to get a stroke. Madison ought to know better."

JoBeth turned to see her uncle striding briskly down the sidewalk toward the house.

Aunt Josie got to her feet and went to the porch railing, ready to rebuke her husband the minute he came through the gate. But something in his expression stopped her. He came puffing up the steps, mopping his red face with his handkerchief as he said breathlessly, "News has just come over the telegraph wires. A great battle is underway near a small Pennsylvania town called Gettysburg. And we're winning! Surely now Lee will bring about a glorious victory—whip those Yankees once and for all."

A worried Aunt Josie urged him to sit down and rest a bit while she brought him a glass of iced tea. He did, under protest, and eventually he caught his breath, and they all went into the house for a delayed meal. However, Uncle Madison could hardly eat a bite and left without taking his usual short nap. He wanted to return to his office downtown to be close to the telegraph office, where further bulletins would be posted as soon as received.

Soon after he departed, Aunt Josie put on her bonnet, saying she thought she'd go over to Dorinda's. Munroe's wife was expecting a new baby, she said, and it might be well for someone to be with her, in case ... She left the sentence dangling, but Johanna and JoBeth knew the fearful thought she had left unspoken. Both Harvel and Munroe were with Lee's army and probably in the midst of the battle now raging. *And was Wes too?* JoBeth wondered. She had to keep her dread question to herself.

That night at the supper table, Uncle Madison was still in an excited, optimistic frame of mind.

"Lee's invincible! Everyone says so. Harvel told me at Christmas that even the Union generals agree he is a military genius. This could be the turning point!" He slapped his hands together in obvious anticipation of victory.

Suddenly the tension that had been building inside her over the past weeks and months came to the surface, and JoBeth turned to him tearfully. "Men and boys are *dying*, uncle! Being killed! On *both* sides in this awful war, don't you know? There's nothing to feel good about!"

She shook off her mother's restraining hand and continued to face her uncle, tears streaming down her cheeks.

Uncle Madison visibly paled. He stared at her.

"You forget yourself, young lady," he said in a trembling voice. "I have two sons most probably in the thick of it. But they are fighting for a cause that affects us all—you, your safety, our life here even this far from it—I never forget that."

"JoBeth, dear, please." Her mother's gentle reproach went unheeded.

"And so is Wes fighting for what he believes. No one here, in this family, gives him credit for that. Except *me*. I love him! And he may be dying or being killed this minute, and nobody cares—" Her voice cracked hoarsely, and JoBeth ran sobbing from the room.

※

When JoBeth woke up, she knew it was late. The house was silent. There was not a sound of movement downstairs or in the hallway outside her bedroom door. Had they all gone to church without calling her? She knew that her mother thought she was ill last night and had made excuses for her to the others. Why else the outburst, the tears?

She remembered running upstairs the night before, throwing herself down on her bed, weeping uncontrollably.

She vaguely recalled falling into an exhausted sleep and her mother coming in later, placing a cloth, dampened with cologne, on her burning forehead, drawing her quilt gently over her shoulders, tiptoeing out again.

How long had she slept? Was the battle at Gettysburg over?

Who had won? Was Wes still alive? Or was he dead—had he made the ultimate sacrifice for his beliefs? A vivid picture of him lying, bloody, broken, in some forsaken place flashed before her. The image pierced her like a bayonet. *Oh, God, I hope it has all been worth it!* New tears rolled down her cheeks and into her mouth, and she tasted the hot saltiness on her lips.

She rolled over and buried her face in the pillow, wishing she could go to sleep again and not wake up until the war was over.

For three hot, humid, miserable days, people clustered around the telegraph office of the Hillsboro train station, awaiting the latest news of the battle being so fiercely waged.

Gettysburg—few had even heard the name, but afterward few would ever forget it.

Chapter Fifteen

❦

My Darling JoBeth,

Such wonderful news, I can hardly contain myself as I write. I have been reassigned. My captain discovered my educational background—that I could read, understand Latin, and had read law. He called me into his tent and said I was wasted as a foot soldier and would be of more value to the Union as an aide-de-camp or secretary to a commander. He gave me a field promotion to officer, and I am to go to Washington and await assignment.

This means that we can soon be reunited. As an officer assigned to a noncombatant status, posted in Washington (possibly at the war department), I will be able to send for you. I will arrange papers of passage as soon as I am settled. We can be married at last. I will, of course, keep you informed and send details. I love you, long for you, want to spend the rest of my life with you. God be praised that this has been brought about.

Ever your devoted,
Wes

After receiving this letter from Wes, JoBeth had to take her mother into full confidence. Both mother and daughter wept, knowing that this would mean an inevitable separation that both of them dreaded.

"Mama, you must help me get to Wes." JoBeth clutched Wes's letter to her breast.

Johanna gazed at her daughter and saw reflected in her eyes an intensity she recognized. She was no longer a little girl, someone to be told what she could or should do. She was a woman in love and determined to follow that love through, wherever it led.

"You will help us, won't you?" JoBeth pleaded.

"I'll do whatever I can," Johanna promised.

The next week, another letter from Wes brought a new urgency.

It would be too dangerous for him to come to Hillsboro, where he was so well-known, so a meeting place had to be decided upon. Richmond seemed the most logical place, being closer to Washington. It would be easier to slip across the guarded border there. Richmond was also the capital of the Confederacy. Careful arrangements must be made. No one must know of their plans. Secrecy insured Wes's safety.

Even though they were both convinced of the necessity, Johanna and JoBeth quailed at the duplicity this would involve. Especially the idea of keeping it secret from the Cadys, who had given them a loving home all these years.

Johanna wrote to Amelia Brooke, who had been her closest friend when they both attended Miss Pomoroy's Academy as girls and who now lived in Richmond. They had kept in touch all these years. Without going into details, Johanna asked if she would allow JoBeth to stay in their home until her fiancé could get the necessary travel pass to cross the line from Washington.

Many Southerners had been "stranded" away from home when the war broke out and travel became restricted. So it was not an unusual situation. Johanna did say they planned to be married and that JoBeth would remain up north until the war was over.

They waited anxiously for a reply. It was not too long coming. Amelia wrote she would be more than happy to have her friend's daughter as a house guest. In the same letter, Amelia gave them other information that was rather disquieting. Amelia's husband was now a high-ranking Confederate officer on President Jefferson Davis's staff. She went on, saying, "Needless to say, we are often hosts to a number of young officers far from home and on leave from their duties, so I believe JoBeth will find our household one that is lively and merry in spite of this dreadful war. Jacob and I are both looking forward to welcoming your daughter."

Reading the letter out loud to JoBeth, Johanna looked at her daughter with raised eyebrows.

"You realize we are taking unfair advantage of my long friendship with Amelia by not telling her the whole truth? What would she—or more important, her husband—say if they knew Wesley was a Union officer? I think they would have grave doubts about having you come." She paused, then said very solemnly, "You must be careful not to do anything that would risk them in any way."

"I wouldn't, Mama. I'm sure as soon as Wes knows where I am, he'll move heaven and earth to come, take me safely to Washington. We wouldn't put the Brookes in any kind of danger of exposure."

"This could be construed as giving aid and comfort to an enemy," Johanna said thoughtfully.

"But *I'm* not an enemy, Mama!"

"Yes, but you must understand that *Wes* is," her mother said sorrowfully.

"He only did what he thought was right. What he was *honor bound* to do."

"And that is in direct opposition to what Amelia's husband considers right." Johanna leaned forward and grasped JoBeth's hands. "Oh, my darling, I don't think you fully realize the risks both you and Wes are taking. If Wes should be, for any reason, stopped and questioned when he comes to Richmond to get you—he will be in *enemy territory.* He certainly won't travel in his army uniform, and if they detain him and check his identification and find out who he is— JoBeth, he would be arrested as a spy."

The full impact of what her mother was saying made JoBeth draw in her breath. She felt the blood drain from her head. She put both hands up to her suddenly throbbing temples. *What did they do with spies? They shot them.*

"Oh, Mama, we'll just have to pray."

"Of course we'll pray, JoBeth. But darling, maybe you and Wes should reconsider this plan. Wait until the war is over . . . be patient . . ."

There was a long moment as mother and daughter looked into each other's eyes, Johanna's bright with tears. "We can't wait, Mama. We've waited long enough already. Wes needs me, Mama. His family has abandoned him, and the Spencers act as if he never existed, even though at one time he was like a son to them. Of course, there is still his grandmother, but even she did not want him to join the army—*any* army! I am all he has," JoBeth said simply. "I must go to him."

"Yes, of course you must, my darling," Johanna said and held out her arms to embrace her. "I understand, JoBeth, even though I cannot give my approval. I have done the same as you in my day. Left mother, father, family, friends, all that was dear and familiar—for love. So how can I possibly tell you not to follow your heart?"

"And did you ever regret it, Mama?"

"I only regretted the hurt my going caused others. My father—*your* grandfather. I don't think he was ever reconciled to my marriage. Although he never spoke one word of recrimination to me. Of course, I'm afraid your uncle and aunt are going to feel that your action is a betrayal. But that cannot be helped. Perhaps in time they will understand. Anyone who has ever been young and in love cannot fail to." She sighed. "Much as I hate to part with you, I have no right to stop you."

When Johanna presented Amelia's letter as an invitation to her daughter from an old friend, Aunt Josie seemed delighted. It was not difficult to persuade the Cadys that JoBeth needed a change. It had been clear to them that over the past months, JoBeth had not been herself, so no further explanation was necessary. Even Uncle Madison agreed.

"Best thing in the world for the girl! Better than a tonic," he said gruffly when the matter was presented to him.

JoBeth's trip to Richmond would involve a train ride, and a traveling companion had to be found to accompany her. It would, even in wartime, be improper for a young single woman to journey alone. As it happened, Bernice Fulton, a middle-aged cousin of Uncle Madison, was going to Fredricksburg to visit a daughter-in-law and would be delighted to have JoBeth for company.

Aunt Josie entered enthusiastically into all the preparations for JoBeth's trip. She had been a popular belle in her day and thought a young woman's happiness was solely dependent upon having lots of beaux, lots of parties and gaiety to fill her life.

"With all the young men gone, Hillsboro is very dull for her. I hear Richmond is the hub of social life. And with Amelia being such a hostess, JoBeth will have many opportunities for some fun and frivolity in spite of the war," she nodded happily when Johanna told her what Amelia had written. "We must outfit her properly," she declared, and ordered an immediate evaluation of JoBeth's wardrobe, which had become sadly depleted for the last two years, having had no additions. Aunt Josie clucked her tongue. "Well, we must do something at once. We cannot have her outshone by some of those Richmond ladies. Luckily, I put away some material I purchased before the war and the terrible blockade. We'll have Mrs. Harversahll, my dressmaker, come and make JoBeth some lovely dresses."

Aunt Josie went to the trunk, where she had stored some yardage, among them a fine, soft, coffee-colored wool for a traveling suit, exquisite lace for trimming, and a length of shiny forest green taffeta. As she showed these to JoBeth, she never dreamed that one would become her niece's wedding gown.

Chapter Sixteen

~❧~

At last the train pulled into the Richmond station. It had been a long, arduous journey. There had been delays of all sorts—breakdowns of the worn-out engine, times when the passenger car had been shunted onto a sidetrack to let boxcars of military supplies and soldiers go through. Mrs. Fulton had been an irritating traveling companion, talkative and complaining. JoBeth had been glad to see her get off at Fredricksburg junction. She hoped the woman's daughter-in-law had more patience than she herself had been able to muster for the last hundred miles.

Alone and nearing her destination, JoBeth felt both excitement and exhaustion. The trip had seemed endless. A combination of nervous tension and discomfort had made it almost impossible to sleep. There were frequent unscheduled stops, and looking out the grimy window of the car, she had seen wounded Confederate soldiers helped onto the train. The sight was depressing—the haggard, hopeless faces, the stretchers being lifted, men missing arms or legs, others with heads bandaged, still others hopping on crutches or leaning heavily on canes. Obviously the South had suffered enormous casualties and heavy damage. JoBeth was confronted head-on with the terrible results of war.

It seemed almost selfish to close her eyes and send up a prayer of thanksgiving that Wes was out of the fire of battle, when her uncle and cousins were in the thick of it and probably on the losing side. But it was only natural, she knew, that whatever catastrophic events are happening in the world, it is only how they affect one personally that matters. Her prayer turned into an earnest plea that soon those in charge of such things on both sides would see the futility, the cost in human terms, of this conflict and, as Wes had once written, declare peace.

"Richmond! Richmond!" The conductor's shout brought both a relief and a tremor of nervousness. Here she was. For the first time completely alone. The enormity of what she had undertaken and what she planned to do made her almost dizzy. Life was scary and unpredictable, and for one awful moment, JoBeth wished she had never left Hillsboro. Thrusting back all those feelings, she gathered her belongings and made her way to the end of the aisle to the door.

Wearily, JoBeth descended from the train onto the platform and stood there looking around dazedly. She felt stiff and achy from the cramped coach, and she felt suddenly bereft. There was no one to meet her. Not that she had expected anyone. Amelia Brooke had no idea when she would arrive, just the approximate week. The station was filled with people, some saying good-bye, others greeting a variety of persons—women, soldiers, children. Voices raised all about her, sounds of children crying, women sobbing. People jostled by her, pushing their way toward the train, some elbowing their way out. She had to find a carriage to take her to the Brookes' house. Her heart was hammering. She had never had to do anything like this before, not on her own, not without someone to look after her.

Slowly she made her way through the crowd, the handle of her portmanteau in one hand, the wicker basket in the other cutting deeply into her palm. Breathing hard, she finally reached the curb of the street. This, too, was lined by a variety of people—civilians, soldiers, women with children—all looking for some sort of conveyance.

After seeing several possible vehicles taken by more aggressive types, JoBeth finally got the attention of the driver of a shabby rental carriage just as he was unloading his passengers. She was forced to share it carrying a woman with a baby in her arms and with a fussy toddler hanging onto her shirt. She had been standing helplessly alongside JoBeth, frantically waving at several passing hacks. The toddler was crying hysterically. So JoBeth, taking pity on the distraught mother, helped her get her luggage, valises, baskets, parcels, into the carriage.

Bunched uncomfortably inside, at least they were off the street and moving. Between sighs, the woman told her she was to be let off at the Spotswood Hotel, where she was to meet her soldier husband. Leaning her head out the coach window, JoBeth relayed this information to the driver. After getting rid of her fellow passenger, she would worry about getting to the Brookes' residence. There was nothing she could do about this delay. The woman looked drained and certainly had her hands full.

After they and all their paraphernalia were safely deposited at the hotel, which looked as war weary as everything else, JoBeth gave the driver the Brookes' address.

Richmond looked entirely different from the time JoBeth had accompanied her mother here on a visit before the war. Everywhere were the effects of war on the city. Everything looked shabby—the buildings, the streets, the people. They left the main part of town and soon were driving through a pleasant, tree-lined residential section of the city. When they came to a stop in front of an imposing red brick house, JoBeth peered curiously out the carriage window.

After checking the number on the black ornamental iron gate against the one on the small card in her hand, she alighted from the carriage. Almost as soon as she did, the front door opened and a lady in a bell-skirted lilac dress hurried down the steps.

"Well, well, darlin' girl, welcome!" she greeted JoBeth in a soft Virginia accent. JoBeth was immediately enveloped in a rose-scented embrace. "I'm Amelia, your mother's best friend, and I'm so happy to see you," she declared, then turned to direct the driver to set down JoBeth's luggage. In spite of JoBeth's murmured protests, Mrs. Brooke paid the driver and sent him on his way.

"You shouldn't have, Mrs. Brooke....," JoBeth began.

"Nonsense, honey. My pleasure. Now, come on along into the house. I declare, this has been one of the muggiest summers I can remember. We'll just get us some cool refreshment."

Used to the cooler climate of the Carolina foothills, JoBeth thought that Richmond was sweltering. It was a relief to step into the dim interior, where the closed window shutters kept the outside heat at bay. The house felt refreshingly cool, and the fragrance of potpourri faintly perfumed the air.

"Do take off that jacket and your bonnet, honey," Mrs. Brooke urged. "Then we'll go into the parlor and have some lemonade." She took JoBeth's biscuit beige bolero and hung it across the banister of the stairway, placed her bonnet on the hall table, then gave her a quick glance. "I do declare, you are so like your dear mother! I want to hear all about her and your dear little brother, Shelby. Although I reckon he's a big fellow now. Gone into the army, I've no doubt, like most all of our brave young men."

There was a sharp silence. Amelia put her fingers to her lips, smothering a tiny gasp. At first JoBeth wondered if she had forgotten what her mother had written about Wes. But a moment later Amelia apologized.

"Oh, my dear, I didn't mean anything by that! I am sure you know that I *do* understand." She moved hurriedly ahead of JoBeth into the parlor.

Whatever Amelia thought she understood, JoBeth realized that the woman had too much courtesy, too much tact, and too much affectionate consideration for her friend to ever express any disapproval. JoBeth whispered a tiny prayer that Wes would complete their arrangements speedily so she wouldn't have to impose longer than necessary on this gracious lady's hospitality.

"Sit down, honey." Amelia gestured to one of two wing chairs on either side of the fireplace. On the low table between was a tray holding a pitcher of lemonade, glasses, and a plate of thin cookies.

Amelia Brooke looked younger than her forty-plus years. She was slender as a girl, and her movements were graceful. She was sitting under a portrait of her that must have been painted when her doll-like prettiness was at its peak, and JoBeth saw that her once-golden hair had silvered, that there now were a few wrinkles around her eyes and mouth, but that she still was very attractive.

For the next twenty minutes, they chatted about inconsequential things, Amelia dwelling mostly on reminisces about her school days at Miss Pomoroy's with Johanna. At length, when JoBeth had refused a second glass of lemonade and another wafer-thin cookie, Amelia said, "Now, I know you must be simply *fatigued*, and I insist you take a little rest before we have supper. We eat late, because Jacob—Colonel Brooke, my husband—doesn't come home until after seven. He is on President Davis's staff, as your mama might have told you, and they work the most awful hours. I'm hoping he will be in good time tonight. He knew your mother, you see." Amelia gave a soft little laugh and said in a conspiratorial tone of voice, "In fact, I accused him of being smitten by Johanna Shelby first, when he met her at one of Miss Pomoroy's 'dansantes.'"

Despite the scarcities and ravages of wartime—the upholstery, draperies, and carpets being perhaps a little worn—the Brooke household had somehow retained its tasteful elegance. The guest room to which JoBeth was shown was equally charming, the bed's ruffled canopy and curtains crisply starched, a lovely bouquet of fresh flowers from the garden below daintily arranged on the bureau.

"There are fresh towels and an extra quilt if you should need it, which I doubt," Amelia said, darting around the room. "I hope you will find everything you need, and if not, you have only to ask," she assured JoBeth. At the door she paused to say, "Now, do have a little nap, honey. I'm sure you're worn out. I hear travelin' these days is deplorable. Of course, I have not moved an inch since this war began—and do not intend to, come the Yankees or high water." When Amelia left, JoBeth took a long breath. She was here at last. She walked over to the window and looked out, stretching her imagination farther than she could see. The Potomac River, which separated Richmond from Washington, was all that separated her from Wes! After all these months, they would soon be together.

Everything had worked out so much better than she could have hoped. Amelia couldn't have given her a more genuine welcome. Whatever she thought of JoBeth's reason for being here, it had not seemed to interfere with her spontaneous friendliness. How lucky it was that her mother had kept in touch with Amelia since their school days. How very convenient indeed. How fortunate *she* was to be in such congenial surroundings.

However, JoBeth had yet to meet Colonel Brooke.

After Amelia's warmth, Colonel Brooke was like a dash of cold water. He was a good-looking man in his late forties, with an erect, military bearing. He wore a mustard-colored mustache and sideburns, and his eyes, a steely gray, were keen, penetrating. He gave the impression of a man used to giving orders and having them obeyed. He was an exact contrast to his wife. JoBeth was at first quite put off by his aloofness. But although his manner was rather stiff, he was still a courteous host. JoBeth wondered how much he had been informed about her reason for being there. However, from the triviality of the dinner conversation, she felt reassured he knew nothing of the real circumstances.

Johanna had told JoBeth that Amelia was the type of person that "once your friend, was forever your friend." Amelia never gave the slightest hint that JoBeth's visit was cloaked in mystery and secrecy. She treated her as she would have any young house guest—with the kindest attention. Within the first week, JoBeth became very fond of her and understood why her mother had said she was such a delightful person.

The Brookes entertained a great deal. For the most part it seemed unplanned. Many nights, extra plates were put at the dinner table, because Colonel Brooke often brought home fellow officers. It did not seem to perturb either Amelia or her placid cook, Delilah. There always seemed to be another a batch of biscuits ready to pop in the oven, and no shortage of garden vegetables.

The talk was usually general. When it turned to the war or serious topics, JoBeth—who had learned to receive Amelia's discreet signal—rose with the other ladies and left the table.

These evenings were not out of the ordinary. They seemed, even if unexpected, not to upset the smooth running of the household. Weekends were different. Sunday nights, JoBeth discovered, the Brookes always held an open house. These evenings were attended by not only the colonel's contemporaries but younger officers as well. Mainly single, young men far from their homes, lonely for family. It was to these especially the Brookes opened their hearts and home.

The first Sunday JoBeth was with them, Amelia explained what had become the custom. "So many of these officers are just boys, like *your* own friends in Hillsboro. But they're homesick. Most are here in Richmond on furlough, some are stationed here temporarily, many are recovering from some injury or waiting to be sent back to their regiments. My heart goes out to all of them." Amelia shook her head sadly. "Even though I was never blessed with children of my own, I can just imagine how their mothers feel, and I try to give them a taste of home here." She went on, saying, "I also invite some of the young ladies I know, girls your age, to help make things light and let them have a little fun. Where they've been and where they're going to is dreadful— so I want them to have pleasant and happy memories to recall when they do." Amelia's wistful expression changed quickly into one of her radiant smiles. "Now, wear one of your prettiest dresses, honey." She wiggled a playful finger at JoBeth. "I know the sight of you will cheer some of these fellows enormously."

JoBeth felt a little reluctant to play the role Amelia expected. She felt awkward to be entertaining Confederate soldiers while *Wes* was arranging for her to join him in *enemy* territory! But there was nothing she could do but comply with her hostess' request.

She had brought a few summer dresses with her, having been warned by her mother that even in early September, Richmond might still be hot. From these, she chose a yellow organdy with a portrait collar embroidered with small yellow daisies. When she was dressed, she went downstairs and out into the garden.

Summer weather lingered, but in the late afternoon Amelia's brick-walled garden was shadowed by leafy fruit trees. Curlicued white iron benches and chairs were placed in small groups surrounding a lily pond in which goldfish could be seen under the lily pads. It was such a tranquil place, seemingly remote from the war and whatever was going on only a few miles away. For a few minutes JoBeth was alone there, relishing the serenity.

Soon Amelia, a lacy cloth over one arm, bustled out, followed by Deliah, who was carrying a large glass punchbowl. As she passed JoBeth, Amelia said over her shoulder, "It's so lovely and cool, I thought we could have our refreshment out here before we go in to supper." JoBeth helped them use the cloth to cover a table at the far end of the garden, then helped set out rows of small cups.

It wasn't long before the guests began to arrive. A half dozen young officers, smart in pressed gray uniforms, were soon followed by four extremely pretty young women. The young ladies immediately embarked on a lively repartee with the officers, as if this sort of party were something they did by rote. JoBeth had heard that wartime Richmond was a constant circus for belles. Now she believed it as she watched them ply their artful coquetry.

JoBeth felt suddenly shy. She had been so long out of the social swing of Hillsboro—having been not invited, overlooked, or simply left out—that she had almost forgotten her social skills. Feeling inadequate to the occasion, she retreated to a bench half hidden by a huge magnolia bush. Here she could stay until she got her bearings, felt a little more at ease, she told herself.

It was from this vantage point that she saw a tall, slim officer, his right arm in a black satin sling, escorted by Amelia to the trellised entrance of the garden. Then Amelia was evidently called back into the house on some domestic errand, leaving him standing alone. In a moment of startled recognition, JoBeth saw that it was Curtis Channing.

Chapter Seventeen

~❧~

Again JoBeth was struck by Curtis's extraordinary good looks. She noticed he had grown a mustache and that it suited him. He was perhaps leaner but still held himself with that combination of assurance and athletic grace shown to such advantage in his well-fitting gray uniform. There was something else about him, something not so familiar. His expression had a maturity and character that it might have lacked before.

As she stared, stunned by this unexpected arrival, his glance caught hers. For a full minute neither of them moved. Her heart gave a little leap. Before he had taken a step, she knew he was coming over to her. She half rose from the bench. A few seconds later he was standing there, towering over her. She saw he now had captain's bars on his collar. They looked at each other. Then Curtis said huskily, "JoBeth! What are you doing here? I never thought I'd see you again."

She swallowed, trying to find her voice. When it came out, it sounded high and rather shaky. "I'm staying with the Brookes. I've been here about a week."

His eyes swept over her, moving from her dark hair to her eyes, lingering on her mouth, where her lower lip was now trembling.

"I'm so—glad to see you," Curtis said slowly. "I could hardly believe my eyes. For a minute, I thought I might be dreaming—could it really be *you?*"

JoBeth found relief from her tension by laughing lightly. "Yes, it's me. No illusion." She was trying hard to regain her composure, to stop feeling so dizzy, so at a loss. She gestured toward the sling. "What happened? Were you wounded?"

He shrugged, dismissing her concern. "Nothing more than a flesh wound, actually. My shoulder took a slight hit." With a cynical smile, he said offhandedly, "Those Yankees are damn poor shots." Immediately realizing he had cursed in front of a lady, he quickly said, "Sorry. Now tell me about you. How do you happen to be in Richmond? I thought travel was difficult, nearly impossible, these days."

How much she should say without telling a lie? She sat down again on the bench, shifting her crinolines to make room for Curtis beside her, and said, "Actually, Mrs. Brooke is an old school friend of my mother's, and everyone agreed it might be a good idea for me to visit."

It seemed a plausible enough explanation, but JoBeth could see from the slight frown between Curtis's dark eyebrows that it didn't satisfy him. She might have been pushed into saying more, except at just that moment Amelia came upon them and greeted Curtis effusively.

"Ah, I see my hero has found my house guest! How lovely. He won't tell you, I'm sure, my dear, but Curtis is one of the bravest of our young men. With no thought to his own safety, he returned not only once but twice into the line of fire to rescue two of his badly wounded men." She smiled dotingly upon him, patting his shoulder fondly. "Now, you must give him special treatment this evening, JoBeth, since he is just out of the hospital and deserves our attention and care."

With that Amelia floated away in a swirl of ruffles to circulate among her other guests.

JoBeth looked at Curtis. "So you are distinguishing yourself in battle."

"Nothing more than any of us would do under the circumstances." His frown got deeper. "Enough of that. What interests me is, How long are you going to be here?"

"I'm not sure just how long," JoBeth answered. "What about you?"

"Until the doctors certify I can go back to my regiment. I have day passes from the hospital now. But the doctors want me to be out and exercising, getting back on my feet, starting to ride again, before they release me back to duty."

JoBeth glanced at the sling. "Can you do that? Ride, I mean, with one arm?"

Curtis shook his head slightly, indicating how unimportant he considered this. "It's almost completely healed. I have to get the strength back into it. Thank God that my horse survived. Both of my horses are stabled here in Richmond, and my man is looking after them."

The garden was filling up with new arrivals. The buzz of voices, laughter, the clink of punch glasses, began to flow around them. Curtis bent toward her. "The important thing is, When can I see you again? I mean, alone." Then he asked abruptly, "Do you ride?"

She looked startled. "Yes, of course, but—"

"What if I come tomorrow, then? You can ride my other horse. She's a lovely, sweet-tempered mare." He looked at her eagerly.

"I'm not sure, Curtis. I don't know if Mrs. Brooke might need me or have other plans . . ."

He dismissed her protest. "Never mind about that. I'll clear it with her. It would be a real favor. Zephyr needs exercising."

"Come along, you two," Amelia's voice reached them. "We're going in to supper now."

"Tomorrow, then? Say, two o'clock." It was more of a directive than a request.

JoBeth hesitated a split second. Perhaps it would be better to see Curtis alone and, without revealing to him the complete truth, tell him she had come to Richmond to meet her fiancé. He need not know who it was or that Wes was a Union officer. The bare facts were all that were necessary. This evening, among all this company, would be an inappropriate time.

"All right, tomorrow," she murmured. "Now I must go help Amelia serve," she said and hurried away.

At the supper table, she was seated between two of Colonel Brooke's junior officers and so did not have another chance to talk to Curtis. However, she was often conscious of his eyes upon her during the meal.

JoBeth was surprised that there was less war talk there in the immediate vicinity of the conflict than there had been in similar gatherings in Hillsboro. Perhaps here they purposely avoided speaking of the current Southern situation, being anxious for some respite from the constant pressure of campaigns, looking for a relaxing evening of enjoyable company.

The evening progressed pleasantly enough. However, even while she chatted with some of the other officers, JoBeth was aware of Curtis's eyes upon her. Anytime she happened to look his way, she met his gaze. There was both admiration and hope in it. Again she prayed she had not made a mistake by agreeing to go riding with him alone.

When all the party had left and JoBeth was helping Amelia gather up the empty glasses, the napkins, and the coffee cups, she told her about Curtis's invitation.

"I couldn't be more delighted, my dear!" Amelia glowed. "Jacob considers Curtis Channing one of the most outstanding young officers he's ever known. Not a shred of fear in him, not a timid bone. He's all man, all courage." She rushed on, saying, "I'm so glad you can make his leave a happy one. I'm afraid he's pushing his superiors to let him go back to his regiment. Maybe too soon." She clucked her tongue, and a sad, worried expression shadowed her face. "We've lost so many of our wonderful young men—" She halted, as if remembering JoBeth's particular circumstances. Then she gave a small shudder and, quickly picking up some more cups and saucers, bustled off in the direction of the kitchen.

JoBeth stood there for a minute, looking after her, holding two plates of crumbled cake in her hands, thinking about what an awkward situation she had put everyone in.

Chapter Eighteen

❧

The next afternoon, JoBeth, dressed in the dark-blue riding habit she had borrowed from Amelia, stood at the parlor window, waiting for Curtis. Since last night, she'd had all sorts of second thoughts about going riding with him. First of all, she worried that by accepting, she might have given him some kind of false hope, given him reason to think she might have changed her mind. After all, he *had* proposed to her. Secondly—and this was what bothered her most—she wondered if she was being disloyal to Wes. Perhaps it would have been more honest to have somehow found a private moment the night before and simply refused Curtis's invitation. Well, it was too late now. Whatever happened, she had to go through with it.

Just then she saw Curtis, on horseback, looking splendid in his gray tunic, sporting a black felt hat with a jaunty plume, coming around the corner. He had another horse, a sleek, cinnamon-colored mare wearing a sidesaddle, on a lead. In spite of herself, JoBeth's heart beat a little faster.

She heard the doorbell ring, footsteps along the hall, the door opening, then Amelia's lilting voice greeting Curtis. Next Delilah came to the parlor door.

"Miss Davison, yo' genemun is here to fetch you."

"Thank you, I'll be right there," she replied. Nervously she pulled on her leather riding gloves.

Taking a deep breath, JoBeth hooked her riding skirt to the loop on the side and went out into the hall, where Curtis was waiting. She couldn't miss his pleasure at seeing her. His eyes shone, his mouth lifted in a broad smile.

"Ready to ride?" he asked.

Amelia beamed at them both, like an approving mother. "I think it's just delightful you're taking JoBeth out into the countryside, Captain. It will do her a world of good—and you too, I've no doubt." As they went out the door together, she called after them, "Have a lovely time now, do."

JoBeth stepped up on the mounting block at the curb while Curtis held her horse's bridle. He assisted her into the sidesaddle, then handed her the reins. As he affectionately patted the horse's neck, he said, "Easy now, Zephyr has a sensitive mouth. You'll do just fine together."

Satisfying himself that she was comfortably settled, Curtis swung up onto his own horse, a feat he accomplished smoothly, even with his one arm still in the sling. They started off at a walk, then moved into a trot further along. There were other riders out, mostly men in uniform who saluted Curtis. He returned their salute smartly with his good arm while holding the reins loosely with the other. *What horsemanship*, JoBeth thought admiringly. Surely Curtis was as at home in a saddle as he would have been in a rocking chair on somebody's porch.

He had been right about Zephyr—an easy ride, a gentle mount. It took only the slightest touch of her rein or pressure of her knee to guide her.

Curtis looked at JoBeth, smiling, and pointed ahead. "We take a right turn down here at the crossroads."

Following Curtis, she soon found herself away from the main thoroughfare and on a beautiful stretch of road. All along the roadside, Queen Anne's lace and wild purple asters bloomed. The day was pleasantly warm but had lost the humidity of the last week. In fact, JoBeth sensed a hint of fall in the air.

She was riding alongside Curtis now, as there was no other traffic in the road. He glanced over at her with such open admiration that it sent a blush soaring into her cheeks and she had to turn away. Only a minute later Curtis reached for her bridle and brought both their horses to a stop.

"I can't help it, JoBeth. I could hardly sleep last night, thinking of what a happy chance seeing you again was. Remember, I believe in destiny. I told you that last Christmas."

JoBeth started to protest, but he shook his head and went on, saying, "I've never gotten over you. I've thought of you ever since—since I left you at the train station in Hillsboro. Thought about if we'd had more time, how things might have been different—"

"Please, Curtis, stop." JoBeth put up her hand as if to stem the flow of words. "Don't go on—"

"It's no use, JoBeth. Can't you admit that the two of us meeting again has some meaning?"

"I can't listen to this, Curtis. Please. Nothing's changed. The only reason I came out with you today was because I felt I had to try to make you understand."

"Understand what? I can't help loving you. What could you possibly say or do to change that?"

"I told you in Hillsboro and I'm telling you now, Curtis. There's someone else. I'm pledged to someone else." He *had* to know, she *had* to tell him, so she rushed on, explaining, "Last evening you asked me what I was doing in Richmond. Curtis, I'm here to meet him."

There. It was out, she'd said it. She watched for his reaction.

"He's a soldier, then." It was more a statement than a question.

"Yes," she nodded. Her breath was shallow, her heart pounding. He didn't need to know more. She prayed he wouldn't ask for details. Like information about his regiment, or what his commanding officer's name was.

Curtis frowned and stared over his horse's head at some distant point. Then slowly he turned back to her. A smile parted his lips under the mustache, showing a glimpse of his even, white teeth. He spoke softly, almost jokingly.

"Well, all's fair in love and war, isn't it? Even if I'm competing with a fellow soldier. *I'm* here and *he* isn't—at least not yet. Don't I have a chance to plead *my* case, try to win you?"

"There's no contest, Curtis," she said seriously. "This is someone I've known and loved most of my life."

"There's love, and there's *being* in love," he reminded her, still smiling. "Do you know the difference?"

She blushed. Had he read her mind? Had he somehow been aware that in spite of herself, she had felt excited, breathless, a little dizzy, at seeing him last evening? Had she inadvertently given him encouragement?

He leaned over, and she shrank back in her saddle, afraid he was going to touch her. The horses were getting fidgety at being held still.

"What are you frightened of, JoBeth? Your own feelings?"

"Of course not!" she said indignantly. Then she said firmly, "If you are going on like this, Curtis, we'd better turn around and go back."

He lifted his hand from her horse's bridle immediately.

"No, I apologize. I want us to go on. There's a spot up here I want you to see. It's by a stream, and the horses can get a drink and we can . . . talk." He flicked his reins, and his horse started off. Zephyr was glad to follow. The winding road, bordered with trees that were golden with the first touch of autumn, stretched before them. Enjoying her mount's easy gait and the beauty of the Indian summer afternoon, JoBeth relaxed a bit.

When Curtis left the road to go down a grassy path, she turned her horse in the direction he was heading. She soon found herself in a glade where willows bent over a rushing stream. Curtis dismounted and led his horse to drink. JoBeth did the same. Everything seemed stilled. The sounds of the busy city had been left far behind. A light breeze rustled the willow branches, and there was a scent of pine and of sun-warmed wildflowers. They sat down on a fallen log overlooking the stream, where sunshine glistened on the water as it rushed quietly over the rocks. For a few minutes the serenity of the place seemed to envelop them.

Feeling warm, JoBeth took off the riding hat and untied the attached velvet snood. She shook out her hair from where it had been clubbed under the net and lifted it to cool off the back of her neck.

"It's lovely here!" she sighed contentedly.

"I thought you'd like it," Curtis said. "I discovered it one of the first days they let me ride. A respite from the pandemonium of the hospital."

They sat there listening to the woodland sounds—an insect buzzing among the ferns, the sound of a woodpecker. At length Curtis broke the silence.

"Peaceful, isn't it? Hard to believe that a few miles from here, men are killing each other." The edge of bitterness in his voice startled JoBeth. She glanced at him. His expression was grave. He reached over and took her hand.

"That's why every moment counts, JoBeth. Time is so important now. None of us knows how much we've got, what the future holds, or even if we have a future."

JoBeth gazed at him, wide-eyed. In a flash of insight, she realized she had been wrong about Curtis Channing. He wasn't as shallow or unthinking as she had assumed. Or at least he'd changed since Christmas. Then he hadn't seen battle. It had all been an adventure he was embarking upon. Since then he'd fought and been wounded, seen it all firsthand. He knew what war was all about now, when he hadn't before.

His fingers tightened around her hand. "That's why telling you that I love you seemed important to me, JoBeth. I know that this man you say you love and are pledged to is a soldier, and maybe I should have some loyalty, some respect for that. But right now *I'm* here and he isn't and you're not sure, can't be sure, if he'll come—ever. He has just as much chance of getting killed as I do or anybody does." The pressure on her hand increased. "I'm sorry. I know I promised not to say any more, didn't I? It was a promise I shouldn't have made, one you shouldn't have asked for. Because I *do* love you, JoBeth. I don't think I ever really knew what love was until I met you."

"Oh, Curtis, love is so much more than what you're feeling now." JoBeth halted, then, daring to be truthful said, "Or even what *I'm* feeling. The reason I asked you to promise is because the person, the solider, I'm waiting for, who I'm here in Richmond to meet, deserves more than this—he deserves my loyalty to *our* pledge. So please understand." Her tone was pleading. "I know you're an honorable man. That you value honor. Honor my asking you not to say any more."

"That's the hardest thing anyone's ever asked me to do," he said, looking directly into her eyes for a long time. Then he raised her hand, turned it over, and kissed her wrist. His lips were warm on her skin, and in spite of the sun on her back, she shivered.

Curtis released her hand, then stood up. "I'll get the horses. You're right—we'd better go back."

He held her stirrup while she remounted. But when she leaned forward to give Zephyr a reassuring pat, Curtis placed his hand on hers. From her saddle, she looked down into his upturned face and saw such unabashed love there that it took her breath away. She withdrew her hand from under his, and he made the pretense of arranging the edge of her skirt over her boot.

"I shall try to keep my promise not to speak of it, JoBeth, but I cannot stop loving you." Curtis moved over to his own horse and mounted.

They rode back into town side by side, not speaking, but every so often JoBeth felt his eyes upon her and was irresistibly drawn to turn and meet his gaze.

Back at the Brookes' home, upstairs in her bedroom, she took off the riding outfit, thinking, *I should never have gone. What has come over me? What am I doing? Whatever it is, it's dangerous. Of course Curtis is attractive, of course his obvious, adoring attention is flattering. But it isn't right. It isn't right for me to enjoy it. I shouldn't allow it.* She closed her eyes and put her balled fists up to her temples, pounded them lightly.

It's only because I miss Wes so terribly. It's been so long! It's Wes I love, Wes I want. To substitute what Curtis is willing to give would be betrayal, nothing less.

Chapter Nineteen

~~~~

Curtis did keep his promise not to *speak* to her again of his love, but that did not prevent his sending notes, flowers, calling with candy and bouquets. Amelia thought him enormously charming—chivalrous, she declared—because she, too, was included in the gifts he never arrived without. He was always among the other young officers at the regular Sunday night suppers, but Amelia made him feel welcome anytime. She never tired of singing his praises to JoBeth. "Oh, honey, if I were a young lady, I would be swooning at having such a gallant young man courting me."

JoBeth hardly knew how to reply. Surely Amelia knew she was pledged and that all of Curtis's charm would not change anything. However, Amelia *did* try. During the next ten days, Curtis's visits became more frequent. Perhaps this was what prompted Amelia to tap at JoBeth's bedroom door one afternoon and ask if they could have a "wee chat."

"I hope you will take what I'm about to say in the same spirit as I shall say it. But I do declare, I'm worried sick about what you are planning to do, JoBeth." As JoBeth was about to protest, Amelia held up her hand. "Yes, I know—your Mama has written quite frankly about your situation. I know that this young man you love is a someone you've known all your life—but JoBeth, do you really agree with what he has done? Left home, family, his own people, to fight with the *Yankees*! If you knew what they've done—why, some of my friends in Winchester and Petersburg are *homeless* because of them!" She stopped. "Well, there's no use to go into all that! I know things because of Jacob's position that aren't common knowledge. Enough to say, I have some serious doubts about the wisdom of what you are planning to do." She paused, shaking her head. "Don't you understand? Once you go with him, *you* will be turning your back on your own family, too." Her eyes misted as she looked with real concern at JoBeth. "Oh, precious child, *think* of that!"

JoBeth's own throat was sore with distress at Amelia's putting into words what she had avoided thinking herself. All she could say was, "Wes is doing what he thinks is right. Surely when the war is over, people will forgive and forget and go on with their lives."

"Oh, child, you are so naive! The war has gone on longer than anyone imagined. This war has cost too many people too much to be over. The wounds dealt are deeper than one could have foreseen, will never heal, and the scars will last forever. At least for our lifetime."

JoBeth felt terribly depressed after Amelia left the room. Her argument, like Uncle Madison and Aunt Josie's, was so one-sided. They were all talking against Wes as if he were not every bit as committed to *his* cause as they were to theirs. They ignored everything but the fact that in their opinion, he had chosen the wrong side to fight for.

That night, JoBeth took out the picture of Wes she kept hidden in her handkerchief case. She studied his face, so intelligent, so kind, so candid. As she went to slip it back into its hiding place, her fingers struck something round and hard. Curious, she pulled it out and saw it was the shiny brass button Curtis had yanked off his tunic and given to her last Christmas. She held it in her palm for a minute, thinking that everyone would be so happy if it were Curtis she loved instead of Wes. Everything would be so simple then. But as Wes had said, nothing about this war was simple. And it was Wes she loved, Wes she was waiting for.

Oh, Wes, write soon. Come soon! Before anything more happens.

❦

Then one afternoon Delilah came to tell her that Captain Channing was waiting to see her in the parlor. The first thing she noticed was that he wasn't wearing his sling. He wasted no time telling her why he had come.

"I'm rejoining my regiment. I'm leaving tomorrow. I've come to say good-bye. I also came to say how much these last several days have meant to me. I cannot dare to think they have meant the same to you." He paused, holding up his hand to keep her from speaking. "But I can hope—pray— that when you remember them, you will think kindly of me and consider me to have been an honorable man. I kept my promise not to speak to you again of . . . love."

He frowned and walked over to the bow window and looked out for a few minutes before turning back into the room and saying, "I wish you loved me, JoBeth. I wish I could go back to whatever I'm facing and know that you did, know that I had something, someone—some reason to come back to."

"But you do, Curtis, you must. You have a family, parents, sisters who adore you, and you will have someone in your life—"

"The trouble is, it won't be you, JoBeth," he said flatly. "That is, unless—" He stopped, as if he wasn't sure whether he should voice his thought. "If anything should happen to change your plans—would you let me know?"

"Nothing's going to change, Curtis. I thought you understood that."

"Life is unpredictable. In wartime, more so. Just don't forget what I'm saying." He walked over to her. "I will never forget you as long as I live," he said solemnly. With that he put his hands on her waist and drew her closer. "Kiss me goodbye, JoBeth?"

Before she could demur, he caught her to him, pressed her against his jacket. His face buried in her hair, he whispered, "Please, JoBeth."

How could she not? She lifted her head and his warm, soft mouth was upon hers. The kiss was hard and there was something in it almost desperate. "Darling, JoBeth," she heard him say, felt his hands on her upper arms in a bruising grip, and then he released her and was gone. She stood there, shaken by the intensity of his kiss, listening to his booted footsteps on the hall floor, the click of the front door closing. Slowly JoBeth straightened herself. Fighting for control, she raised one hand to her lips and then to her cheek and found it wet with tears.

~✦~

After Curtis's departure, JoBeth's mood was melancholy. She was wracked with guilt and her own ambiguous feelings.

Even though she was preoccupied with her own troubled thoughts and impatiently awaiting word from Wes, JoBeth was not unaware of the tension her presence caused in the Brooke household. The longer she was their house guest, the more she could feel it. She had the distinct impression that Colonel Brooke was unhappy with her prolonged stay. She noticed it mostly in Amelia's nervousness when her husband was home. At the breakfast table or at dinner, there was an undercurrent in the careful conversation they conducted. While she understood the reason for that, it made her acutely uncomfortable. If only she would hear from Wes and she could leave.

Coming down to supper one evening, JoBeth inadvertently overheard a clash between her hostess and her husband.

"I know you don't want her here, Jacob, didn't want her to come—" Amelia's voice held anxiety.

"You knew that at the outset. I made my feelings quite plain at the time."

"But how could I refuse? Besides, I never expected it to be this long. Her young man is in a position where a privilege should be granted—"

Not allowing her to finish whatever she was about to say, Colonel Brooke cut her off. "I don't want to hear about her 'young man.' I don't want to know anything about him, their plans. . . . To me, *he* is the enemy."

JoBeth fled back upstairs feeling both humiliated and helpless. She had never not been wanted anywhere before in her life! She had tried so hard to be pleasant, amiable, to Amelia's taciturn husband. She had thought it was the pressure of his duties, his position, that made him seem so uncommunicative, almost surly sometimes. Now she knew he resented her presence in his house. More than that, he detested the whole situation his wife's accommodating nature had placed their household in.

It was all she could do to maintain a semblance of naturalness that evening at supper. Fortunately, the colonel was called away by an emergency at his headquarters office and left when the meal had just started. Sitting alone at the table with Amelia was also difficult. She did not want to embarrass her hostess by letting her know she had overhead the sharp exchange between her and Jacob.

What could she do but wait to hear from Wes? And pray that word would come soon and she would no longer have to strain Amelia's goodness and hospitality, as well as her marriage.

Chapter Twenty

The next morning, JoBeth came down for breakfast, murmured, "Good morning," then took her seat quietly. Amelia, looking as though she hadn't slept much, nodded and smiled absently. The colonel was drinking his coffee and reading the newspaper when Delilah brought in the mail. She laid it beside Amelia's plate, and distractedly Amelia sifted through it. Suddenly she came upon an envelope that caused her to jerk slightly. With a quick look down the table at her husband, then at JoBeth, she slid a letter over to her. At the same time, she signaled with her eyes and an imperceptible shake of her head. Immediately JoBeth was warned and slipped the envelope into her sleeve. In an agony of impatience, she had to wait until the colonel finished his breakfast and bid them both good-bye for the day and left the house. She then pulled out the letter and ripped it open with her knife.

It was the long-awaited letter from Wes. A direct answer to her prayers, and a much more prompt one than she had any reason to hope for. Hungry for details, she skimmed rapidly down the page. Although he could not give her the exact day and time, it *would* be within the week, sooner rather than later, so she must be packed and ready to leave at a moment's notice.

JoBeth looked up from the letter in her shaking hands. "Oh, Amelia, it's come! It's from Wes. He's coming to get me."

Amelia's reaction was a mixed one. She seemed both relieved and a little sad. "You have become very dear to me, JoBeth, even in this short time. And now you will be leaving." Her eyes brimmed with tears. "I worry about what you are going into and what may become of you."

JoBeth was too happy, too excited, to hear the note of sadness in the older woman's voice. Nothing could darken the elation she felt. "You mustn't worry, Amelia. I'll be fine. And I'll be so happy. You'll see. Wait until you meet Wes. You'll understand why I love him so. You'll see he's everything I told you."

⚓

Two days later another brief note came. He would be there within the next forty-eight hours. Almost two more days to live through! How could she bear it? The two days of waiting passed with agonizing slowness. Then in the late afternoon of the third day, Delilah knocked on the door of the bedroom, where JoBeth was packing. "Miss JoBeth, this jest come fo' you." JoBeth dropped the shawl she was putting into her valise and eagerly took the folded slip of paper the maid was holding out to her. "Oh, thank you. I think it's what I've been—," she said breathlessly and tore it open.

She read what she had so longed to know, in Wes's dear, familiar handwriting.

My Darling,

I'm in Richmond but of course in hiding. I cannot come in daytime, because of where you are staying. I'm sending this by a trusted servant in the house of a Union sympathizer. I'll be there this evening after dark. I have our passes and we can travel back to Washington as sister and brother going to see a sick relative. Not entirely true, I know, but of necessity. Be ready, be brave. Soon we will be together.

Hardly able to contain her joy, JoBeth ran down the hall to Amelia's room and knocked gently. To the answering "Come in," she entered.

Amelia was lying on the chaise, resting before dinner. She had a book on her lap but looked up as JoBeth approached her and said, "I hate to disturb you, but I have wonderful news."

"From the look on your face, I can only guess what it is," Amelia replied, unable to hide the tinge of regret in her voice.

Breathlessly JoBeth told her the contents of Wes's note. While they discussed just how his arrival and her departure should be handled, they heard footsteps on the stairway. Colonel Brooke had arrived home unexpectedly early. The two women exchanged wary glances. Amelia squeezed JoBeth's hand and mouthed the words "Leave this to me."

After greeting the colonel, JoBeth excused herself and went back to her bedroom and in breathless excitement continued happily packing.

However, down the hall the scene was anything but that of happy anticipation. In her anxiety, Amelia's voice was unconsciously raised. "But what else could I do, Jacob? She is the daughter of my dearest girlhood friend. We were at school together."

"Perhaps it is a case of choosing between loyalties," came the stern rejoinder.

"My dear husband, I beg you, don't put it that way."

"What other way can I put it? This is wartime, woman. We should have no choices like this to make. Our allegiance is to the Confederacy. I have taken an oath on it, and as my wife, you—" His tone was harsh. "You expect me to stay calm when you propose harboring an enemy in my household?"

"Surely you don't consider *JoBeth* an enemy."

"No, I consider her a foolish, uninformed young woman who does not realize the hazards—not only the risk she is taking but the danger she has put us in."

"Danger? What possible danger?"

"If it were known that there is to be a rendezvous of a Union sympathizer and her Yankee lover *here*, in the house of a high-ranking Confederate officer—why, I might even be court-martialed."

"But who is to know?"

"Richmond is full of spies. They are everywhere."

"But I can't refuse to help now, Jacob. Plans have already been made—"

"Plans? What plans?" he demanded. Then, as if understanding had suddenly burst upon him, he exclaimed angrily, "No! Don't!" He got up and stalked over to the window. With his back to her, he stared out into the street for a full minute before speaking again. "Whatever it is, I don't want to know about it, you understand? Whenever the time comes, give me some signal, and I will go back to my headquarters for a meeting—that evening."

❧

Ecstatic with anticipation, JoBeth was only vaguely aware of the high drama being enacted in the Brooke household as the hour of Wes's coming grew nearer. However, the undercurrent was high. Only someone totally insensitive to the electric atmosphere could have remained unaware of it. Late in the afternoon, Colonel Brooke came home briefly and left again after curtly telling Amelia to send word when it would be safe for him to return to his own home. Outside, the autumn dusk gathered quickly. In her bedroom, JoBeth ran back and forth from the window, where she watched anxiously for some sign of Wes's arrival, to her bedside, where she fell on her knees in frantic prayer that nothing would prevent Wes's coming.

Just after dark a tap came on the door, and Amelia stuck her head inside. In a whisper, which was no longer necessary, she said, "Your young man is here."

JoBeth's feet barely skimmed the steps as she flew down the stairway. In the hall stood a tall figure illuminated by the oil lamp on the table. Wes! Before she reached the last one, he was at the bottom holding out open arms, and she flung herself into them.

She pressed her cheek against the coarse greatcoat, smelling the damp wool smell, breathing in the fresh scent of rain and cold air. "Oh, Wes! Wes!" she cried, her voice smothered as he held her in a crushing embrace. "I can't believe you're really here!"

"Well, I am, my darling. Believe it!"

She hugged him tight, then drew back. "Let me look at you, see if you're real!" she exclaimed. "Oh, my goodness! You've grown whiskers!" she giggled.

"You don't mind, I hope!" he laughed. "I thought it gave me more dignity, made me look more like an officer and a gentleman." He grinned, then added quickly, "I'll shave it off if you don't like it."

"Let me see." She smiled and kissed him on the mouth. Their kiss was long, tender, infinitely sweet. Then JoBeth laughed softly. "It tickles. But I think I like it!" She hugged him.

Wes gave a low chuckle. "It's so wonderful to be with you again. To see you smile, hear you laugh. You don't know how I've missed that. Missed *you!*"

"*I* think I do know, as I've missed you," she said. "Oh, Wes, it's been so long. I didn't think it would ever happen!"

"Well, it *has*," he said almost solemnly.

For a long moment they simply looked at each other. Then she lifted her face and they kissed again. There was a difference in this kiss. It was the fulfillment of what had been only a hope, a longing. When it ended, Wes said, "Now, dearest, we will have to leave as soon as possible—you have your papers and I've brought your pass. It is best we leave when the sentries who have been on duty all night may not be as alert. There won't be too many questions when we show our passes. There is always a risk that if my true identity as a Union soldier should be discovered, I'd be considered a spy in enemy territory."

His words fell like heavy stones on JoBeth, briefly blotting her first happiness at their reunion. Stark reality of what they were facing hit. This was wartime. He was the enemy. They must flee under cover of darkness, like fugitives. Her heart thundered.

"How soon can you be ready?" he asked.

"Right away. I've most of my things packed."

Amelia, who had been standing at the top of the landing and had watched their meeting, overheard Wes's anxious question and came down a few steps, saying, "Come along, JoBeth. I'll help you get everything together. There's no time to waste."

Although Amelia had many doubts about this elopement—and was worldly enough to know that love did not conquer all, in spite of all the poems written, the ballads sung—she still felt exhilarated. These two star-crossed young lovers had excited her romantic imagination. JoBeth hurried back up the stairs and with Amelia's help put the last items into her valise. They both had to sit on her trunk to get it closed. Amelia held the gray melton cape for her to put on and hooked the corded frog fastenings under her chin. JoBeth pulled the hood over her hair. "Well, this is it!" she said breathlessly.

Suddenly tears sprang into Amelia's eyes as she looked at JoBeth. Then she placed both hands on the girl's cheeks, gazed at her for a moment, then kissed her fondly, saying, "Dear child, I wish you the best, all the best, and as much happiness as it is possible to find. God bless and keep you, my dear."

Impulsively, JoBeth put her arms around Amelia. "Thank you, thank you, for everything! I shall always remember your kindness and be grateful."

There was no more time to say anything. JoBeth went to the top of the stairs and called Wes. He took the steps two at a time and came into the bedroom to shoulder her small trunk. Quickly they went down the stairs and out into the night.

❦

Wes helped her into the carriage, then carefully arranged the rug over her knees. The sound of the carriage wheels against the wet pavement mixed with the hollow clip-clop of horse hooves. As she looked out the window of the cab, the whole world seemed wrapped in the mysterious yellow light from the street lamps. As the Brooke house faded into the rainy mist, JoBeth felt the same farewell she had the morning she left Hillsboro. Who knew when she would ever see it again?

Chapter Twenty-One

~~~

As they reached the city limits of Richmond, Wes took JoBeth's hand in his and said, "Now, don't be afraid and don't act frightened. This should go quickly. Our papers are in order, and there shouldn't be any problem. Just act naturally, answer any questions with yes or no. I'll do most of the talking." He squeezed her hand. "Don't worry, it will be fine."

The carriage came to a jolting halt. Even before it came to a full stop, Wes's hand was on the door handle. He opened the door and jumped out.

JoBeth could hear men's voices. Her stomach muscles knotted painfully. What if their passes—or at least Wes's— were found to be counterfeit? Would they be arrested, thrown into prison? All the horror stories she had ever heard about Yankee treatment of spies rushed into JoBeth's mind. She shrank back against the carriage cushions, holding her breath. She shivered, but not from cold. It was more the involuntary type of quiver that old Annie used to call "somebody walkin' 'pon ma grave." It was that same sort of childish fear of the unknown, fear of whatever might be going to happen.

Oh, *dear Father God, let us get through safely*, she prayed desperately. She leaned close to the carriage's open window. Wes was talking to the sentries, and she strained to hear what was being said. Wes's voice had taken on a distinctly Southern drawl—more pronounced than it was naturally. Most native North Carolinians' accents were never as noticeable as that of someone from Georgia or South Carolina. If she had not been so tense, she might have smiled. She realized Wes was intentionally trying to distract the sentries as their passes were being examined. And it worked. In a matter of minutes, their passage into Washington was approved and they were again on their way.

Back in the carriage beside her, Wes took off his hat, wiped his forehead, and said, "Whew!" Not until then did she realize what a strain the encounter must have been for him. She'd had no idea how worried he'd been about getting by the Virginia border. She shuddered, remembering Amelia and Jacob talking about danger. It was wartime. Danger was everywhere. But surely they would be in no danger as they passed through the Union lines, JoBeth thought to herself. She shuddered again.

"Are you cold?" Wes asked with immediate concern. He put his arm around her shoulders and drew her close. "It won't be long now, dearest. Washington's actually not far. Ironic, isn't it, that the seat of the government and that of the rebellion are located so close together." He sighed deeply. "Only a few miles apart in distance, yet a million in purpose." His arm tightened around her.

The combination of emotional excitement, the wakefulness of the night before, and the rocking motion of the carriage gradually lulled JoBeth to sleep. Her head cushioned on Wes's shoulder, his arm supporting her, she was hardly aware as they traveled through the night.

Grayish light was seeping through the slits in the carriage curtains when JoBeth stirred. She came slowly awake.

"We're almost there," Wes told her gently as she sat up, blinking sleepily. "We're safe now. We're coming over the bridge into Washington."

JoBeth rubbed the back of her neck, moved her shoulders to ease their stiffness, and peered out into the misty morning.

"We'll be stopped again, and our passes checked, but there'll be no problem here." Wes was getting out the leather folder containing their papers, so he'd be ready to get out at the checkpoint.

No problem? Why not? she thought drowsily, remembering how nervous Wes had been as they had approached the Virginia border. Then she realized why. They were no longer in the South, where Wes would have been in mortal danger, branded as a traitor, if caught. A Union officer traveling out of uniform with false credentials would have been considered a spy there. If they had been found out, Wes would have been dragged off, thrown into prison, shot without a trial! Of course there'd be no problem *here*, because now they were in what her relatives considered *enemy territory*.

Before Wes got out, he reassured her, "This shouldn't take long." He got out as soon as they stopped, shutting the carriage door behind him. Minutes passed. He did not come back. Concerned, JoBeth looked out into the murky morning to see what could be delaying him. She saw him conferring with two soldiers. He was gesturing back to the carriage with the hand that held their passes. What could be wrong?

She did not have to wait much longer to find out. Wes opened the carriage door and put his head inside, saying, "I'm sorry, darling, but they insist you get out of the carriage and present yourself." He lowered his voice. "I tried my best to convince them this was not necessary, that I could send to Major Meredith for confirmation of who I am and why I am escorting you into Washington. Of course, it's too early for the major to have arrived at his office. And I don't want to disturb him at home. If we don't comply, they tell me we will have to wait until such time as they can receive clearance and let us pass."

"I thought you said there would be no problem," she protested.

"I didn't think so. Evidently, security has been tightened. Lately there have been a number of occurrences of Confederate spies getting through, carrying secrets, vital military information. Unfortunately, these recent incidents have involved ladies. Hiding messages on their person." He hesitated, as if embarrassed. "I apologize, but it seems unavoidable. Unless we want to sit here for a couple of hours while they send for validation of our passes and wait for confirmation." He paused. "I promise, you will not be subjected to any indignity. They just want to make sure you are who our papers say you are, that you match the physical description. They'll ask you a few questions, that's all."

JoBeth had heard some of the stories relayed through the Richmond ladies' "grapevine." She had listened, appalled, to tales of female travelers being stopped and interrogated, the linings of their bonnets being ripped open, muffs torn apart, parasols cut to ribbons. Worse were other stories of some being required to remove their hoops as they were searched for possible contraband being carried to the enemy. Now she had to face such a possibility herself!

However, there was nothing to do but get out and do as they had been requested. The two young guards seemed a little uncomfortable, but they bluffed it out. They shuffled through her papers, asked her date of birth, her mother's maiden name, and a few more innocuous questions. Then the corporal, who seemed to be in charge, gruffly asked her to swear that all her answers were truthful, upon the possible charge of perjury. Never before having had her honesty challenged, JoBeth drew herself up and replied with cold indignation. "Of course."

She was then required to take the oath of allegiance, which with Wes's prompting she managed to do.

"You may proceed," mumbled the sentry to Wes, handing him back the sheaf of papers containing their passes.

Once they were back in the carriage and moving, Wes apologized. "I'm sorry, darling, but the fellow was only doing his duty."

JoBeth gave a little shudder. "Horrible," was all she could say.

"Soon all this will be over—a bad dream, a nightmare. We're safe. Nothing more to worry about," he said confidently. "Everything's going to be fine now."

JoBeth wished she could feel as sure.

All the happy excitement of their elopement had drained away, leaving her feeling shaken. What had she done? Come all this way, gone through so much, for this?

She looked out the carriage window. What she saw alarmed her and disgusted her. As they rolled along, she saw acres of makeshift shacks, dilapidated tents, lean-tos, set up on a stretch of swampy ground. It was too early for the poor dwellers of these pitiful shelters to be up and about—still, it struck her to the core that human beings could possibly be living in such squalor. She had never seen anything like it. Wordlessly she turned to Wes for some explanation.

Seeing her expression, Wes sensed her reaction. "It's one of the degrading facts of wartime life. People have poured into Washington since the war—doubling, tripling, the population. They are of all sorts: freed blacks hoping for work, the families of enlisted men who have followed them here and can't afford even the cheapest place to live. There are others, I'm afraid: rogues, thieves, camp followers, pickpockets—disreputable types you always find in any big city when normal life is overturned."

"But it's dreadful!" JoBeth exclaimed. "Can't something be done about all this? Can't better places be found for them to live?"

"The local officials and the metropolitan police try, but the problems are overwhelming—and of course, Congress and the army are occupied with the war." His arm went around her, drawing her closer as if to comfort her. "Try not to be too upset, JoBeth. This is all on the outskirts, terrible as it is. Farther along, it is different. I've found rooms for us in a quiet residential section of the city. In a lovely house. The home belongs to Mrs. Caroline Hobbs, a Southerner but loyal to the Union. She is a widow of only a few years and has been lonely living by herself. That's why she's renting us rooms. She is looking forward to meeting you, and I believe you will find her delightful company when I'm away on duty."

"But that won't be too often, will it? We will have time together? You won't be gone all the time, will you?"

"No, of course not. I should be home every evening unless Major Meredith has some special assignment for me." He smiled at her tenderly. "What is a few hours apart now? It will seem like nothing after all these months." He looked at her lovingly, almost as if he couldn't believe she was really there.

She rested her head momentarily against his shoulder. She knew Wes was happy, wanted her to be happy—and she wanted to be. But just now she felt unsure, frightened.

After a while, the carriage pulled up in front of a stone house. "Here we are," Wes said. He got out and turned to help her down. The morning was still rather dark, clouds overhead threatening rain. While Wes saw to her valise and hatbox, and the driver got down her small trunk, JoBeth looked up at the place that was to be her new home. There were lights on in the downstairs windows. As she stood there waiting, she saw the edge of a lace curtain lift in one of them, then drop. A minute later the front door opened and the portly figure of a woman was framed in the entrance.

"Come in, come in! Don't stand there in the chill," a genteel Southern voice urged.

"Good morning, Mrs. Hobbs," Wes called back, then said to JoBeth, "Come, meet our landlady." He took her arm, and together they went up the walk to the house.

Mrs. Hobbs was a handsome woman in her mid-forties, with salt-and-pepper hair under a lace-ruffled cap trembling with bows. She was wearing a black bombazine dress with a white collar. She shook JoBeth's hand warmly, studying her with quick, curious dark eyes. "Oh, my dear, I am so happy to meet you. I knew you must be a very special young lady, because your young man was very particular about everything being just so for you. Such devotion, such attention to every detail in your rooms. Come along, let me show you," Mrs. Hobbs invited, leading the way up the stairway. JoBeth murmured something she hoped was polite and followed.

The rooms were quite nicely appointed. In the small sitting room, a fire burned cheerily, lighting up the corners. There was a love seat and two comfortable armchairs. In the center was a round table with a ruby-glass-globed lamp. Flowered chintz tie-backs over unpleated lace curtains hung at the three-windowed bay. Watching for JoBeth's approval, Mrs. Hobbs pushed open the door to the adjoining bedroom. The high-backed, heavily carved mahogany bed was piled high with pillows and covered with an appliquéd quilt. In one corner stood a chaise, of the type that was popularly called a lady's "fainting couch."

"Everything is very nice, Mrs. Hobbs," JoBeth said appreciatively.

"I did so hope you'd like it!" beamed Mrs. Hobbs, seeming satisfied.

For a few more minutes Mrs. Hobbs fluttered about the rooms, touching antimacassars on the furniture, shifting the china dogs on the mantelpiece, stopping to rearrange a knickknack on one of the tables, before finally leaving.

JoBeth looked at Wes, not sure what to do next. At last, after all the conflict, all her stubborn resistance, her determination to come at all costs, she was here. And there was Wes, the reason for all of her rebellion, her refusal to listen to the pleas, the threats, the warnings, of her family and friends. A wave of doubt left her cold and shaking. Suddenly, what she had given up flashed before her. Should she have come?

Wes stood at the door, remaining there after having closed it behind the departing Mrs. Hobbs.

"Our appointment at the church is for four o'clock. I thought that would give you time to have a rest after our journey. It's been pretty intense, I know." There was concern in his eyes. He hesitated, as if waiting for her to say something. When she didn't, he went on, "I've made all the arrangements. My commanding officer, Major Meredith, will meet us at the church. He has agreed to stand up with me. I wanted him to meet you anyway. He is a fine person and very sympathetic to us. His sister is married to a Southerner, so they have experienced some of the same conflicts we have endured." He paused again, looking anxious. "Are you all right, darling? You look pale."

"Just a little tired and"—she smiled wanly—"a little hungry."

"Of course. I should have thought of that. I'm sorry." He turned, put his hand on the doorknob. "I'll go right down and ask Mrs. Hobbs if she could bring you something to eat."

"If it's no trouble?"

"I'm sure that would be no trouble at all. I think Mrs. Hobbs is the motherly type, don't you?" A smile brightened his face for a minute. "Would you like some tea, or would you rather have coffee?"

"Coffee, I think. I've not tasted real coffee for some time. The blockade, you know. . . ."

A rueful look passed over his face, but he did not discuss whatever he was thinking. "I'll be back in a few minutes," Wes promised and went out the door.

He was back before JoBeth had time to do more than remove her cape. As he came in, carrying a tray, he grinned. "Didn't I tell you Mrs. Hobbs was the motherly type? She had already prepared this. I met her coming up the stairs as I went down." He set down the tray on the table in front of the green velvet sofa. He poured two cups of coffee from the silver server and handed one to JoBeth.

"Mmmm." She held it, inhaling its fragrance, before taking a sip. "What a treat! It's delicious." The pungent taste immediately seemed to revive her. She took one of the small, triangular-cut chicken sandwiches and bit into it.

With the food and coffee, JoBeth's fuzziness began to disappear. She didn't feel quite so overwhelmed by all that had happened.

"I really must report to my office and let Major Meredith know we've safely arrived. I will come back here at three-thirty. Does that give you enough time?"

"Oh yes, that's fine." She made a funny little face and said, "Everything seems to be moving so fast."

"Yes, I know, but all these horrible long months of waiting are over. That's what I'm grateful for, what I thank God for," he said earnestly.

"Yes," she nodded, wishing she felt more certain. He finished his coffee, set down his cup, and got up. He took her hand, raised it to his lips, and kissed it. "Good-bye for a little while." He picked up his coat and hat and moved over to the door. There he turned back, as if he had just remembered something. He looked at her with a broad smile.

"I almost forgot. Our rings, JoBeth. We must exchange them so that we can use them in the ceremony." He drew his from the finger of his right hand and brought it over to her. He waited while she detached hers from the chain she had worn hidden around her neck for all these months. As she handed it to him, he leaned down and kissed her.

The kiss was sweet, reassuring. A warmth went over her. Wes was right: everything would be fine now. For a few minutes after he was gone, JoBeth remained motionless. She looked around uncertainly. She was really here in Washington, with Wes, and this was where she would be living. In just a matter of a few hours they would be married. At last all her dreams were coming true.

Chapter Twenty-Two

*After Wes's departure, JoBeth stretched out on the sofa and tried to rest. But she was too excited, too nervous, to sleep. She lay there looking around the unfamiliar room. Everything seemed unreal. Pictures of the last forty-eight hours flashed in her mind like images in a stereopticon. Everything that had happened since they fled through the night came back in vivid detail.

Too restless to lie still, she got up, inspecting the rest of the apartment. She went into the adjoining bedroom, pleased it was so nicely furnished and tastefully decorated as was the parlor.

She did not want to bother Mrs. Hobbs to ask for hot water for a bath. So she poured water from the pitcher into its matching pink china bowl and, using the lavender-scented cake of soap she was delighted to find in the dish on the washstand, bathed as best she could. Afterward she soaked a small linen hand towel with some precious cologne she had brought with her, patting it over her neck, shoulders, and arms.

Clean and refreshed, next she brushed out her hair until it crackled, then sat down at the dressing table to wind it into a figure-eight chignon. As she started placing the tortoiseshell pins into her hair to secure it, she saw herself in the mirror.

Her brush still in hand, she stared at the girl in the glass as if at a stranger. In the unfamiliar setting, she hardly recognized herself.

The chimes of the ormolu clock on the mantel began to ring. Two-thirty. In an hour Wes would return. *I must dress. Wes will be here soon, and then we will go to the church, and then*—her imagination took her no further. Everything seemed unreal. She was here by herself, with no loving relatives to get her ready for her wedding. She pushed away any regrets. This was what she had chosen to do. This was what she wanted.

She unpacked the jade taffeta dress, made from the beautiful material given to her by Aunt Josie, who had never dreamed it would be worn as a wedding gown—*to marry a man of whom they do not approve!* JoBeth thought guiltily.

She shook out the tiered skirt and stepped into it. Then she slipped on the bodice, which was embroidered with darker-green soutache braid. Starting to fasten the tiny hooks cleverly concealed under a narrow placket, she recalled instructing the seamstress to put the hooks down the front. She had known there would be no one to help her dress on her wedding day.

Lastly she slipped in her small pearl pendant earrings, then got out her hatbox and opened the lid. Unwrapping her bonnet from the tissue paper in which it was swathed, she took it out. She held it in front of her for a moment, admiring it. It was the prettiest one she had ever owned. Lined with fluted pink chiffon, it was trimmed with green velvet leaves in which nestled a single pink silk rose. Aunt Josie had selected the trimmings herself at her milliner's, declaring it perfect to wear with the green dress. Tying the wide green satin ribbons under her chin, JoBeth fervently hoped her aunt would eventually forgive her for eloping.

She was just buttoning on her gloves when a knock came at the door. It had a jubilant sound, as did Wes's voice announcing, "JoBeth, I'm here."

Her taffeta skirts swishing, she crossed the room to open it to her smiling husband-to-be.

⁓≈⁓

The interior of the church was dim and drafty. To JoBeth it had a strange, almost mysterious aura with its curved nave and shadowy arches. Entering, she felt the full impact of this solemn occasion. Wes covered her trembling hand with his, smiled down at her while they walked together down the long aisle. In the vestibule, JoBeth had been introduced to Major Meredith and to the regimental chaplain's wife, who were going to serve as their witnesses. Major Meredith was exactly as Wes had described him. His face, with its strong features and determined expression, revealed much of the qualities and character Wes had attributed to him. There was also an unexpected compassion in the deep-set eyes as he looked at them. Why? she wondered as they took their place and the chaplain opened his prayer book to begin the ceremony.

It was certainly not the wedding of her girlhood dreams. There was no organ music playing the traditional marches, nor was there a chosen soloist to sing her favorite hymns, nor did she know the clergyman who officiated. He read the ritual in what Wes told her later was a New England accent.

The ceremony was brief, but they both gave their responses in clear, sure tones, gazing happily at each other. JoBeth felt slightly delirious, as if her head were floating somewhere up over them and she were looking down on the scene. The words of the ceremony seemed natural to her. She had memorized them by repeating them each night after her bedtime prayers. She used to take out her pledge ring, hold it, and say the same promises she was making today. Ever since Wes had told her about betrothals in the olden days, she had cherished the idea. Speaking the words out loud "before God and this company"—although the church was empty except for them—was only a confirmation of the promise she had already made in her heart. Of course she would love, cherish, and obey Wes, in sickness and in health, for richer or for poorer, keeping only to him however long they both should live. There was no question, no doubts. All the uncertainty she had felt earlier had disappeared. This was a sacred moment. These were sacred promises, to be kept forever.

Exchanging their rings was only a repetition of what they had done in the Hillsboro churchyard, the fulfillment of all their hopes, prayers, dreams.

After they had all signed the register, Wes and JoBeth thanked the chaplain and his wife, then left the church with Major Meredith. As they came out onto the steps, they saw that a light drizzle was falling. The late afternoon sky was dark, heavy with clouds. Standing on the church steps, Major Meredith said, "You have a few more days of leave coming, don't you, Lieutenant? If I weren't required to report back to duty, I would insist on treating you two to a wedding supper at one of the city's finest restaurants. As it is, I have done the next best thing. I've taken the liberty of ordering a catered hamper from that same restaurant to be delivered to your address with my compliments. Perhaps it is even better this way. I know you both have waited a long, worried time to be together." He gave a brisk salute to Wes and bowed to JoBeth. "So I will not delay you. I admire your bravery and render my best wishes for a long and happy life together."

He saw them into their hired carriage waiting at the curb and bid them good-bye. By the time they arrived at Mrs. Hobbs's house, it was raining steadily. Wes held his military cape over JoBeth to protect her bonnet, and they ran up the steps. They had been given a key to the front door, and they let themselves in, then went quietly upstairs to their apartment.

JoBeth moved to the center of the room and stood for a minute, idly picking up a porcelain bird figurine, examining it. She could hear the rain pounding on the roof, giving the cozy little parlor a feeling of sheltered intimacy. Slowly she turned around and smiled.

Wes walked over to her, placing his hands gently on her shoulders, then very carefully untied her bonnet ribbons and removed her bonnet. He tossed it on the nearby table, then smoothed back her hair from her forehead, regarding her with infinite tenderness. Cupping her face in both his hands, he said softly, "Welcome to our home, darling wife."

"Oh, Wes, *wife*! That sounds so wonderful, so special."

"It is wonderful, and *you* are special. I thank God for you, JoBeth. I want always and only to make you happy, make you glad that you went through all you did and married me."

"Married. It hardly seems possible."

"But it is, my darling," he said, then kissed her. It was a long kiss but very gentle. "I love you, JoBeth, more than I can ever tell you." He took her hand and led her over to the sofa, eased her down to sit beside him, took her into his arms, and began to kiss her.

His kisses were slow and sweet, as if they had all the time in the world. He whispered her name over and over, kissing her again and again. An unspeakable joy surged all through JoBeth. The promise of their dream had been fulfilled. Their pledge had held, their wait had not been in vain, their faith had been rewarded.

Just then a discreet knock sounded at the door, and reluctantly they moved out of their embrace. They looked at each other questioningly. Then Mrs. Hobbs's voice came from the hall. "Lieutenant Rutherford!" Wesley gave JoBeth a helpless shrug, then got up, went to the door, and opened it to an apologetic Mrs. Hobbs.

"I wouldn't have disturbed you, but this was just delivered." She held out a wicker basket, its handle tied with a silver-edged white satin bow. There was a card on which was written, "Best Wishes to Lt. and Mrs. Wesley Rutherford."

"Thank you very much, Mrs. Hobbs. We were expecting it. A gift from my commanding officer." Wes took the basket from her.

Mrs. Hobbs peered around Wes at JoBeth. "Is there anything more I can do for you? I thought perhaps Mrs. Rutherford might not be used to our Northern weather—a hot water bottle, maybe?. . ." Her voice trailed away as if she suddenly realized the ridiculousness of her statement.

"That is most kind of you, Mrs. Hobbs. JoBeth—Mrs. Rutherford—*is* tired, of course, but we shall be just fine. Thank you." Wes stepped back, ready to close the door, but she stood there for a few seconds longer.

"Good evening, Mrs. Hobbs, and thank you again," he said firmly.

"Ah yes, Lieutenant. Well, if there should be anything—"

"That is indeed most kind—" Wesley again made an attempt to shut the door and this time succeeded. He turned around, made such an exaggeratedly bewildered face that JoBeth smothered her giggles with her hand. However, the ludicrous incident somehow broke through whatever stiffness either might have felt. As they unpacked the wonderful gift basket of delicacies—roasted squab, shrimp salad, dinner rolls, pears, grapes, chocolate eclairs, and a split of French champagne—they laughed and talked like old, carefree times.

Part Four

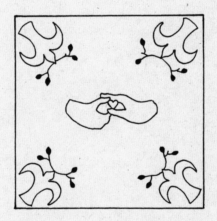

Chapter Twenty-Three

⚜

JoBeth awoke in the depth of the feather bed alone. Dazzling October sunlight spilled in through the bedroom window. Wes was already gone. She must have slept through his departure. She felt disappointed to have missed fixing him at least a cup of coffee before he left, as a proper wife should. She sat up, yawning. Then she saw the note he'd left on his pillow beside hers.

Dearest One,

As you're beginning to find out, soldiers reveille early. Did not want to disturb you. Love you and will miss you all day until I return this evening.

Ever your devoted husband,
John Wesley Rutherford.

She smiled fondly, kissed the signature, saying softly, "And *I* am Mrs. John Wesley Rutherford." Saying it still thrilled her. They had been married nearly six weeks, and Wes still treated her as a bride.

She stretched out her left arm, gazing proudly at her hand, on which the gold pledge ring circled her third finger. The ring she had worn on a chain next to her heart for so long. How lucky she was, how blessed! All the partings, all the sadness, all the heartache, for them was over.

She tossed the covers back, got up, and dressed. She boiled water on the little spirit burner and made herself a cup of tea. Sipping it, she went to the window and looked out. The day promised to be delightful. The leaves on the elm tree outside had turned golden and were dancing in a brisk wind. Perhaps she would go for a walk.

When she had first come to Washington, Wes had cautioned her about where she should go on her own. Washington was a dangerous place these days. All sorts of unsavory people had come to the Union capital for all kinds of reasons, many of them nefarious. Crime and vice were rampant, and certain streets no sane person would risk going into. The police tried to keep the most flagrant lawbreaking in check, and the newspapers were full of floridly written accounts of raids on gambling dens and houses of ill repute.

However, this neighborhood was filled with other homes like Mrs. Hobbs's and was pleasant and safe. Although in the beginning JoBeth had felt somewhat timid to venture out by herself, she no longer felt at all that way. Washington was a cosmopolitan city and a stimulating one, and she very much enjoyed exploring it. She liked to stroll on the tree-lined avenues, and she especially liked window-shopping along the streets of fine stores displaying all sorts of luxuries and commodities unavailable in the blockaded South. Here was no visible shortage of anything. Certain items that Southerners had long been deprived of having were displayed in abundance.

Sometimes it appeared as if there were no such thing as a war going on. People on the streets were smiling, fashionably dressed women promenaded, others drove by in barouches. Children, often accompanied by black nurses, rolled hoops along the sidewalks or wheeled velocipedes. There were also soldiers in many kinds of uniforms: whole regiments who had rallied to the Union cause, colorful Zouaves who looked as if they were on their way to a costume ball. Vendors of all sorts plied their trades: there were ice-cream dealers in small booths, chestnuts being roasted on small portable stoves, flower stalls, an Italian organ grinder playing melodies as his little pet monkey held out a tin cup to passersby.

All this was fun and entertaining diversion for JoBeth, who, in spite of her new happiness, had times of homesickness. She was often alone, because Wes's duties in Major Meredith's office required his putting in long hours, working late. If she had not followed her own inclinations of curiosity about her new surroundings, coupled with her sense of adventure, time might have often hung heavily on her hands.

The letter that JoBeth had both waited for and dreaded receiving came.

Dearest Child,

You may be sure there were mixed reactions here to the news of your marriage to Wes. Although Aunt and Uncle Cady, after their initial shock, were tactful enough to refrain from expressing what I am sure they must have discussed—and certainly how they feel—in private. You know Uncle Madison, and it is understandable when you realize how strongly he feels about the Cause, and of course, they have two sons fighting on the opposite side from Wes. I realize there are other families divided like ours, only none that we personally know of. I truly believe it was mostly dismay that by this you have cut yourself off from the rest of the family—at least for the duration of this horrible war. Aunt Josie came to me later and asked me point-blank if I knew about it before you left. I could honestly tell her only that I felt somehow your love would show you a way to be together. Truthfully, even when you left here to go to Richmond, I wasn't sure what would be the outcome. I did get a letter from Amelia, which I now enclose so you can read for yourself.

JoBeth unfolded the other letter and read it.

Dear Friend,

I sit down with hammering heart and trembling hand to write to you. I have just seen your precious daughter off into the night with the man she loves. I pray we can trust him to protect and love her as she deserves to be loved. I can only commend you, Johanna, on the job you have done in rearing this lovely young woman. She is a credit to your training, nurturing, and caring love. She is not only accomplished in all the ways our society demands but has an inner goodness that shines out through her outer self. A fine, sweet, true heart and soul. I feel sure by the time this reaches you, you will have received word from her. May God be kind to these two young people who love each other so dearly and face such hard times ahead.

She turned back to her mother's letter.

Of course, I agree with all that she says about you, my darling. I just hope Wes appreciates the jewel he has now in his possession. God keep you and bless you both. You have chosen a hard road to walk together, but I am sure our Lord will be an unfailing source of strength for you both.

Always your loving mother,
Johanna Shelby Davison

JoBeth finished the letter with mixed emotions. She was not surprised either at her aunt and uncle's reaction to her elopement or at Amelia Brooke's dire predictions. Both were to be expected, considering the circumstances. Especially Aunt Josie and Uncle Madison's response.

The feelings of her relatives could have only been deepened and hardened by the news her mother sent in a later letter.

> *It grieves me to have to add the news received here that Harvel was badly wounded in the terrible battle at Chickamauga in September. He is in a hospital in Chattanooga, and we hope for the best.*

This war was a scourge on the whole country, North and South. JoBeth had seen the trainloads of Union wounded, the lines of ambulances rumbling through the city on the way to the soldiers hospitals. Fatalities on both sides were heavy. Nobody escaped, no family was spared. She felt almost guilty that Wes was safe in his noncombatant duty. However, he had known the horror of the battlefield, although he refused to talk to her about it. When she allowed herself to dwell on it, JoBeth's heart was wrung with pain. When would it be over?

"Going out, dearie?" Mrs. Hobbs called to her from her parlor as JoBeth came down the stairway.

"It looks like a lovely day, and I need some fresh air," JoBeth replied, pausing at the door while she pulled on her gloves.

"What a good idea," Mrs. Hobbs nodded approvingly. "I'm a great believer in fresh air and exercise, even for females."

Her statement rather amused JoBeth, since the good lady rarely seemed to move farther than from her comfortable chair by her fire to the front gate for the evening paper.

"I've been meaning to speak to you, my dear," Mrs. Hobbs continued, setting aside her sewing, rising, and coming to the parlor door. "To see if you'd be interested in joining me for a project. I make quilts for the soldiers hospital. Of course, they're not intricate designs or unique in any way. But they are warm and seem to comfort the dear boys. Reminds them of home, I believe, and their own mothers tucking them in at night."

"I suppose I could, Mrs. Hobbs. My mother makes beautiful quilts. In fact, she's famous for hers. As are all my great-aunts. It's a kind of family skill. However—" She hesitated. "I've only made one of my own. I've helped finish quilts— that is, stitch the tops to the under padding, but—"

"Well, then, that's good enough. These quilts for the soldiers don't have to be works of art. I'm sure you'll do just fine. I've made so many of these, I'll be glad to show you. There's nothing to finishing. Just a matter of diligence," she chuckled. "And working with someone else makes it go fast. You know what they say, 'Many hands make light work.' We'll make a fine team, you and I," she said with a satisfied smile.

They began working one or two afternoons a week on the quilts for the hospital. JoBeth discovered that in spite of the difference in their ages, spending time with Mrs. Hobbs was enjoyable, and they became good friends. On one of the long rainy afternoons they were together, JoBeth told Mrs. Hobbs about the pledge patches she'd made during her separation from Wes.

"And did you complete the quilt then?" Mrs. Hobbs asked interestedly.

"No. I mean, I kept making the patches I'd designed, collecting them. But I didn't know when Wes would come home—to Hillsboro, I mean. I assumed it would be after the war. I'd made a kind of bargain with myself that I'd continue making them until the war was over and he was home safely." She paused, took a few stitches before going on. "I guess none of us dreamed it would last so long—*this* long."

Mrs. Hobbs nodded her head in sympathetic agreement.

"Anyway, then I went to Richmond, and then Wes came for me and—well, I just never have put it all together. I'm not sure I know how to do it myself."

"I'd be happy to help you, if you'd like?" Mrs. Hobbs offered.

"Would you? That would be wonderful. Wes has never seen the patches. It would be fun to have it all put together and then show him."

"A lovely surprise—your work of faith and devotion!" Mrs. Hobbs's bright eyes sparkled. "He'd be so pleased."

A few days later JoBeth got the patches out from the bottom of her trunk and laid them out over her bed to see if she had enough to make into a quilt.

When Mrs. Hobbs saw the squares with their unusual original design, she exclaimed, "Why, you're quite an artist, my dear. I'm sure your mother was happy to see you follow in her footsteps, wasn't she?"

JoBeth looked sad. "Well, not exactly—she never saw it. I had to keep it a secret, even from her. You see, ever since my father died when I was a little girl and we went to live in Hillsboro, it's been difficult. At least, since the war. All my relatives supported secession. Almost everyone I know is for the Confederacy." She paused. "So when Wes made *his* decision, everyone there turned against him, and I just didn't want to make it any harder for Mama, since she had to continue to live there."

"I think I understand, dear," Mrs. Hobbs nodded, then said briskly, "Well, I see we have work to do, but in no time you should have a beautiful quilt—one that you and the lieutenant will always cherish for its meaning."

Mrs. Hobbs was patient as she showed JoBeth how to complete her quilt. She was generous in her praise of JoBeth's design, her tiny stitches. Mrs. Hobbs's romantic soul relished that the theme had stemmed from their secretly exchanged pledge rings.

After that their friendship seemed to blossom. "Do call me Caroline," Mrs. Hobbs urged JoBeth. Together they pieced the pledge quilt together and attached it to a cotton under-pad filled with fluffy cotton batting. The finished quilt was indeed "a thing of beauty whose joy would last forever," as Mrs. Hobbs quoted admiringly.

As fall moved into a stormy early winter, there were many afternoons working on the soldiers' quilts together before a cheerful fire in Mrs. Hobbs's sewing room. Although Mrs. Hobbs dismissed these quilts as "necessity quilts," their joint endeavor brought back some of JoBeth's happiest childhood memories. As a little girl, JoBeth had loved sitting on a low stool by her mother's chair and going through the overflowing scrap bag, finding colorful material from which her mother would select appropriate pieces for the squares that would be put together for the top of a quilt. Next there would be the length of flannel for the lining, to be stretched onto the frame and held by small nails all along each side. Usually Johanna whipstitched the lining onto the frame, because these quilts were done quickly so that she could get on with the quilts for which she had orders and that people were waiting to have delivered.

The quilts that JoBeth made now with Mrs. Hobbs were like the ones her mother had made for their own personal use when they still lived in the mountains, before JoBeth's father died. Those were most often made from clothes that no longer could be mended, pieced, or turned or the many tidbits and pieces left over from the designs of patterns for the ones she made for sale.

JoBeth could shut her eyes and nostalgically feel the warmth of those quilts, remember their smell, recall the feeling of being caressed with love, security, warmth. No wonder

Mrs. Hobbs's quilts were so welcomed at the hospitals by wounded soldiers sick of heart and body, a long way from the comfort of their own home and mother.

Caroline Hobbs had fulfilled Wes's early prediction that JoBeth would find her delightful company. Their friendship provided JoBeth with the feminine companionship she had known at home and missed. Mrs. Hobbs kept JoBeth entertained with her recital of the daily events of Washington society. She was an avid reader of the society pages of the daily newspaper, and she recounted the social doings of the capital city as though she had attended every fete and levee.

She was a great expert on the president's wife, Mary Todd Lincoln, a controversial figure, the subject of much gossip ever since she arrived from Springfield, Illinois. "She is a woman of unpredictable temper, apt to explode at the tiniest thing." Mrs. Hobbs made a clucking sound with her tongue at this deplorable trait. "An implied snub or a gesture is enough to send her into a fury. Those who have been witness to such tirades say they are frightening to behold. It's said she is insanely jealous of her husband and has caused terrible scenes as a result."

Mrs. Hobbs's favorite personality on the social scene was Miss Kate Chase, a popular belle who was the daughter of the secretary of the treasury, and she read every scrap written about her. She served as her widowed father's official hostess and did a great deal of entertaining, as was required of a member of the president's cabinet, reaping inches of complimentary newsprint.

"She is a stunning creature," Mrs. Hobbs assured JoBeth. "Holds herself like a queen, has skin like snow, marvelous hazel eyes, and glorious bronze hair."

The fact that Mrs. Hobbs had never seen the lady in person did not diminish her knowledge of the details of the beautiful socialite's life. "She's being courted by the young senator from Rhode Island, William Sprague."

Eventually her wedding was the social highlight of the winter and became the topic of Mrs. Hobbs's monologues to JoBeth for several days. Having avidly read the accounts, she could give JoBeth a full report, as though she had attended the wedding along with the president (but *not* Mrs. Lincoln: "It's said she's extremely jealous of Kate and wouldn't want to be where *she* ain't the center *herself*—which of course she wouldn't be, with its being, after all, the bride's day").

Mrs. Hobbs relayed almost word for word the newspaper-article description of the elaborate reception following the ceremony, telling JoBeth that "the beautiful bride was a vision in white velvet, lace veil, and the matched set of diamond-and-pearl jewelry that was the gift of the bridegroom."

Listening, JoBeth could not help but compare this glittering affair with her own wedding—which no one attended or wrote about or deemed in any way special. A wedding far from girlish imagination. But JoBeth was sure the bride of Mrs. Hobbs's extravagant description could be no happier than she.

Sometimes JoBeth had to pinch herself to believe her own happiness. It seemed strange that she *could* be so happy, having been cut off so completely from family and friends. But then, she had felt even more isolated and lonely in Hillsboro without Wes. Any doubts that she might have had that she had been foolish to follow her heart vanished entirely. Wes lived up to her idealized image of him: his brilliant mind, his absolute integrity, the sweetness of their intimate relationship. All they had been through to be together had been worth it.

Chapter Twenty-Four

~∽⊱⊰∽~

*A*t long last, JoBeth's large trunk, battered, badly handled on its circuitous journey, finally arrived from Hillsboro. That it had come at all Caroline Hobbs declared a minor miracle, considering the "fortunes of war." It was scuffed, scratched, its leather straps worn, the brass locks rusted. Luckily, it had been well-made, and the contents were all safely intact.

JoBeth spent the day unpacking and putting away the embroidered petticoats, dainty camisoles, handkerchiefs, the peach dressing gown with its lace ruffles. She took a long time going over each dress before hanging it up in the armoire, contemplating where and on what occasion she might wear it. She lingered especially over the hyacinth blue velvet ballgown, fingering the folds. As she held it up to herself in front of the mirror, she remembered the last time she had worn it. It had been last Christmas, and she had danced with Curtis Channing.

Where would she ever wear it again? Perhaps a military ball here in Washington. For sure, if she ever *did* wear this gown again, she would most certainly dance with a soldier in a uniform of another color.

That possibility seemed dim. Wes worked long hours, came home weary. He often came home dejected from all the gloomy news he heard during the day, and it took all JoBeth's efforts to cheer him. The idea of any kind of social life for them seemed out of the question. Besides, just now a period of pessimism hung over the capital city. Things looked dark. The war was not going well. The North had lost its easy optimism about winning. Rumors were rife, morale was low. The draft for men was digging deep, dragging the bottom of the barrel for soldiers, taking all comers, including Irish and German immigrants straight off the boat who couldn't even speak English. The president was criticized at every turn, the generals were fighting among themselves, the Congress was in disarray.

The chance for any social occasion that would call for such a dress seemed remote. JoBeth sighed, putting the gown carefully away.

However, sooner than she could have imagined, an unexpected social opportunity came. To her complete surprise, Wes announced that they had been included in an invitation with Major Meredith's staff to attend one of Mrs. Lincoln's receptions. They were also invited to dinner at the Merediths' home before going to the White House.

JoBeth was beside herself with excitement. To think she would actually meet the president! Until she came to Washington, he had only been a shadowy figure to her, someone whose name she had heard denounced and vilified almost daily. Since then she had seen his name, headlines and articles about him, caricatures or cartoons of him, with regularity in the city's newspapers.

Mrs. Hobbs revered him greatly. When JoBeth told her of their invitation, she was as excited as JoBeth had ever seen the lady. Hearing his praises sung by Mrs. Hobbs when they worked together on the quilts had given JoBeth a different view of the president. She was curious to see him firsthand and form her own opinion.

JoBeth would have liked writing to her mother about all she was seeing, observing, doing. But since delivery of letters to the South was uncertain at best, she decided to start keeping a journal again. That way after the war, she would have a record of the places she went, the people she met, the things she could not tactfully or safely put in her letters. Certainly, going to the White House would be one such event she would have liked to share with her mother. JoBeth knew that Aunt Josie would faint if she knew to what "special occasion" her niece would wear one of the lovely outfits her own seamstress had made for her.

"Be careful not to outshine Madame President!" Mrs. Hobbs warned JoBeth when told of the invitation. "She don't like to be outdone in fashion—or anything else, for that matter. Especially by a pretty young woman like yourself."

Privately JoBeth doubted that the First Lady would give her a second look or a second thought. However, she did choose her dress carefully. A simple dusty rose silk, over which she wore a deeper-rose velvet jacket with a fan-shaped collar.

When Wes and JoBeth stepped into the entry hall at the Merediths' townhouse that evening, their wraps were taken by a rosy-cheeked Irish maid in a ruffled cap and apron over a black dress, just as Major and Mrs. Meredith came to greet them warmly. The major's wife, Frances, was equally as gracious as he. Taking JoBeth by the arm, she led her into the drawing room, where several well-coifed, elegantly dressed ladies and an impressive group of officers in dress uniforms shining with medals were already assembled.

She introduced her to a lady in purple taffeta lavishly trimmed with Belgian lace, who was seated on a satin-upholstered sofa. Then the major's wife called to welcome another group of arriving guests and left JoBeth there.

"What a lovely home," JoBeth remarked—a safe opening line she had been taught to use when starting a conversation with a fellow guest who was a total stranger.

The woman turned ice blue eyes upon her. "Do I detect a slight Southern accent?"

A little taken aback, JoBeth answered, "Yes, I am from North Carolina."

The woman moved her skirt an imperceptible inch. "How unfortunate! I've heard the city is filled with 'secesshes.'" With that the woman unfurled her fan and turned away, picking up the thread of the conversation she had been conducting with the woman on the other side of her.

JoBeth did not know whether to be insulted, amused, or grateful. Had the comment meant she was unfortunate to be from the South and far from home? Or unfortunate to be from the South when her husband was a Union officer? Or simply unfortunate on general terms? She certainly had not expected such blatant rudeness in such elegant company. She did not have a chance to either think of an appropriate retort or get up and move, because just then a splendid-looking officer bowed before her, saying, "I must be addressing Lieutenant Rutherford's charming bride?"

His flattering manner and the frank admiration in his eyes as he bent over her extended hand made JoBeth forget the enigmatic remark of the lady beside her. "May I introduce myself?" the officer said. "I'm one of your husband's fellow officers, Lieutenant Marsden Carlyle. May I have the honor of escorting you in to dinner?" He added with a smile, "I have your husband's permission."

At the table, JoBeth was seated between Lieutenant Carlyle and another officer. Wes was seated across from her, far down the other side of the table. Every so often he glanced approvingly over at her. It had been such a long time since she had been out socially, but JoBeth soon got the knack of it again. She recalled the advice Aunt Josie had given her before her very first dancing party: "If you can't think of anything to say, just tilt your head to one side, gaze intently at whomever happens to be speaking, look interested. It never fails. It is flattering to people to think you actually care about their opinions. Whatever they are."

As it turned out, JoBeth needn't have worried. Both men proved to be amusing conversationalists and flatteringly attentive.

After dinner, carriages rolled up to the front of the house, and the party divided into groups of four and left for the White House. Wes's approving look and smile as they left their hosts assured JoBeth that she had "passed muster" at her first Washington dinner party.

JoBeth felt as if she had swallowed a bunch of butterflies when they drove up to the imposing white mansion. Alighting from the carriage in front of the porticoed entrance, Wes held out his arm, and together they went up the steps, into the foyer, then on into the grand drawing room.

꧁ꕥ꧂

Late that night, JoBeth could not go to bed until she had written about her evening in her journal. She did not want to forget a single detail.

> *I feel like the cat who went to visit the queen in the old nursery rhyme. Although we are a republic and not supposed to be in awe of royalty, I suppose going to the White House is as close as I'll ever come to such magnificence.*

The White House has been newly refurbished, I was told, and there has been much malicious gossip about "Madame President's" extravagant expenditures for new velvet drapes and Italian carpeting. But the Green Room, where the reception was held tonight, is truly splendid.

Mrs. Lincoln, in comparison to her tall, rangy husband, appears very small indeed. Her gown was quite lavish—grenadine over silk, the bodice trimmed with point lace—and her hair was dressed with artificial roses. She may have been considered attractive as a young woman—her coloring is very vivid: bright blue eyes, rich mahogany-brown hair—but I found her animation forced, her manner of speech affected. What once might have been a "pleasing plumpness," at age forty-three has grown to fat. I thought her flushed face and rather petulant expression most unattractive.

Here JoBeth paused and reread what she had just written. She hadn't meant to be unkind, just truthful. There was something about Mrs. Lincoln that she couldn't quite define. An artificiality, a buried hostility she could not quite conceal, as though she viewed everyone—mainly young, attractive women—with slight suspicion. JoBeth had felt quite chilled as those blue diamond eyes fixed themselves upon her for a few seconds, and then the president's wife had given a prim little smile and held out her gloved fingers to JoBeth, who pressed them lightly, murmuring, "Good evening, Mrs. Lincoln," then moved down the line.

Although JoBeth knew that Mrs. Hobbs's unfavorable opinion was drawn largely from journalists who did not like the First Lady, she remembered Mrs. Hobbs's comment. After observing Mrs. Lincoln in person, JoBeth could not help but agree that there might be some truth in the rumor.

Her impression of the president was quite different. She looked into a face that was gaunt, deeply etched with lines, the eyes deep-set and dark, the expression of wisdom, sorrow, giving him the appearance of both determination and vulnerability. In the midst of all the music, the merriment, that flowed around him, he seemed to be troubled, brooding. She was too much in awe to do more than touch his hand briefly and move on. For some reason, she had felt drawn to turn and look back at him and was moved to instant sympathy. What burdens must be his to carry, what responsibility—the lives of so many to be lost or spared at his command.

JoBeth continued to write.

> It was the person of Kate Chase Sprague (our landlady's "ideal"), the daughter of the secretary of the treasury, who quite outshone Madame President, in my opinion. A truly beautiful young woman with a slender, graceful figure, magnolia white skin, hair glinting with bronze lights, she was dressed in a lovely apricot satin dress and seemed always to be surrounded by admiring gentlemen.

Chapter Twenty-Five

⚘

JoBeth did not keep a daily diary. Her journal entries were sporadic. Sometimes days passed, even weeks, without her writing in it. However, there were times when something unusual happened during the otherwise rather uneventful passing of her days, and then she would write at some length.

November 1863

> President Lincoln issued a proclamation declaring that the last Thursday in this month be set aside as a national day of Thanksgiving. Mrs. Hobbs invited Wes and me to have dinner with her and a group of her friends to celebrate the event. She told me it was a holiday long observed in her husband's native state of Massachusetts, and I guess it is celebrated in other New England states also. The Pilgrims' landing at Plymouth Rock is as great a cause for celebration as almost any other.

> We dined on roast turkey, mashed potatoes, several kinds of vegetables, salad, and both pumpkin and apple pie. I could not help but contrast all this abundance with the probable fare of my relatives in the South. Even before I left, they were experiencing shortages of all kinds, due to the successful blockade of ports along the Southern coast.

Oh, that all this would soon be over and we could be one country again! That was the fervent prayer in all hearts, I'm sure, as we bowed our heads for grace before that festive meal.

❧

December 8th

President Lincoln offered amnesty to any Confederate who would restate his allegiance.

Would that it were that simple. He doesn't understand or realize the strength, determination, resentment, of most Southerners, who are fighting for what they believe are their states' rights.

❧

December 1863

The early days of the month passed by pleasantly enough, even though JoBeth had to fight back nostalgic thoughts of bygone Christmases in Hillsboro. This third year of the war, she knew that Christmases back there must be much different now than those she recalled so pleasantly. She was sure the Northern blockade of Southern ports intensified all the hardships, shortages, that had already begun to affect the lives of her family and friends before she left. Naturally, she missed her mother and Shelby terribly. Nevertheless, she was determined to make her first Christmas with Wes especially happy.

JoBeth was giving him her pledge quilt as a Christmas gift. For the first time, Wes would see her labor of love, the record of her constancy all during their separation. She worked in Mrs. Hobbs's apartment so that it would be a surprise. JoBeth spent hours stitching the squares onto the undercover batting and binding the whole with yards of blue trim the color of Wes's army uniform. When that was done, she carefully embroidered her name, the date of his departure, and the date of their wedding in one corner patch.

She planned to have a small trimmed tree, a new holiday custom popularized by Queen Victoria's German husband, Prince Albert, who had introduced it to England. Americans quickly adopted the idea, integrating it into their own Christmas decorations.

Besides giving Wes the now finished pledge quilt, she could afford only a few small gifts for him. A lieutenant's salary was small, and everything was so expensive. Still, she enjoyed being out among the bustling shoppers, who evidently had money to spend. JoBeth was sure that Washington was in sharp contrast to most cities in the South at this time. Downtown stores were blazing with lights until evening, windows displaying all sorts of attractive merchandise. One afternoon while mostly window-shopping, JoBeth happened to catch a glimpse of the newly wed Kate Chase, now Mrs. William Sprague. The woman was getting into her shiny, gilt-trimmed carriage outside one of Washington's most expensive department stores. She was extravagantly elegant, wearing a moss green brocade jacket with a pale mink collar and cuffs, a graceful skirt, a bonnet laden with shiny black and green feathers. JoBeth found herself gawking like a pauper viewing a duchess. She couldn't wait to tell Mrs. Hobbs about it.

JoBeth's time with Mrs. Hobbs was always amusing and diverting, and their conversations were not as gloomy as the war news Wes reluctantly brought home. The war seemed a seesaw: First, one side seemed to have the advantage, achieving some strategic objective; the next time the other won a decisive battle, claiming victory. However, Wes expressed the general feeling in Washington about the final outcome of the war, that the North would eventually emerge victorious.

JoBeth had mixed feelings—a Union victory meant a Southern defeat. She sometimes did not want to hear the latest news of battles. Perhaps she was acting like an ostrich, she thought. But if there was nothing she could do about the situation, what harm was there in being entertained by the reports Mrs. Hobbs related about the chaotic private lives of those in the White House?

Mrs. Lincoln's extravagance was notorious. Her frequent shopping sprees to the New York emporiums were widely reported. But even more interesting to JoBeth was the strange "behind the scenes" melodrama. It seemed that since their little son Willie died, Mrs. Lincoln had been consulting spiritists and attending seances. Although fascinated by these bizarre stories, JoBeth could not help being sympathetic toward this woman.

Christmas Eve afternoon JoBeth felt restless and a little homesick. She didn't want Wes to come home and find her melancholy, so to offset her mood she decided to go out for a while and mingle in the holiday crowds to try to capture some spirit. It worked. After browsing through a succession of shops, she made a few impulsive last-minute purchases. Some scented candles, a book of Browning's poetry, a pair of house slippers for Wes to wear when he kicked off his boots at night. Feeling better, she came out into the street to find it had begun to snow. She hurried home through the wintry dusk, anticipating the evening ahead. The snow was still falling when she let herself into Mrs. Hobbs's house, grateful for its welcoming warmth.

Upstairs in their apartment, she drew the curtains against the growing dark, looked around the cozy, firelit parlor with satisfaction. She fitted the spruce-scented candles into the brass holder on the mantelpiece.

Mrs. Hobbs had insisted they have Christmas Day dinner with her and some friends. But tonight was to be just for the

211

two of them. Soon Wes would be here and they could have a candlelit dinner before the fireplace. From one of the small catering establishments that flourished in this city, she had bought a small roasted chicken, salad, a plum pudding she could heat on the spirit burner. They planned to attend the Christmas Eve service at a nearby church, then open their presents.

JoBeth wrapped the poetry book and the slippers and had just placed them under the tree when she heard the sound of Wes's voice speaking to Mrs. Hobbs on the landing.

She turned to greet him with a welcoming smile as he came in the door. But one look at his expression stopped her. Something was wrong. Something had happened. She opened her mouth to speak. Then, without knowing why, her heart chilled.

"What is it, Wes?"

"I'm sorry, darling. A telegram. Your Uncle Harvel died of his wounds in Tennessee."

JoBeth felt her knees buckle, and she had to hold on to the table to steady herself.

Poor Uncle Madison and Aunt Josie—and all those poor, adorable little children. She felt dizzy. She swayed and Wes was beside her in a minute, holding her, supporting her over to the sofa.

JoBeth's gaze moved to the tiny trimmed tree, with its paper chains and gilt candleholders. It looked so gaudy, so bizarre, taunting, in the face of this tragedy.

In her mind she was transported to Holly Grove. Remembering the gaiety of that last Christmas scene, the merry laughter of Harvel's children as they ran through the rooms festooned with evergreen boughs, holly, and mistletoe. Everyone had been so happy—

JoBeth closed her eyes against the pain.

In wartime everything is on the precipice. No one is guaranteed even a full day of happiness. . . .

Chapter Twenty-Six

~⊱≈⊰~

February 1864

Access to the president and to the White House still amazes me. People seem to wander freely in and out, with very few being stopped or questioned about their intent or errand. Does it not seem strange that the man most responsible for the great struggle to reunite our nation is so open to whosoever would come?

I suppose it particularly affects me because of the difference between Lincoln and the Confederate president, Jefferson Davis. He is almost a recluse. When I was in Richmond awaiting my pass to Washington, he remained a mysterious presence. Rarely did I hear of anyone, outside his immediate circle of trusted advisors or army officers, having an audience. Occasionally he could be seen riding out in the afternoons with General Lee or one of the other generals, ringed by a protective guard on horseback. But it was also said that because the threat of Unionist spies meant possible danger to his person, his route was often altered and his driver took him for airings on back roads and country lanes.

Here it seems to me that no such caution is taken for President Lincoln's safety, although secessionist sentiment runs high. He and Mrs. Lincoln are often easily viewed taking carriage rides with only a few mounted soldiers in escort.

I suppose this is much on my mind because of an encounter I had today. Wes had asked me to meet him at the White House, where Major Meredith's headquarters are located. We were to go to a late afternoon levee, held at the Merediths' home, for some new officers on his staff, and it would be easier and save time if I met Wes there.

As I was seated in the corridor, waiting for Wes, I observed the constant parade of people from the desk of the president's secretary to his office. How could he see so many people, hear so many petitions, answer so many questions, make so many decisions? One would have to be almost superhuman to handle such a load of demands.

Suddenly I became aware of a young girl, hardly taller than a twelve-year-old child, carrying a large artist's portfolio. She came down the hall toward me, juggling a sketch book that almost seemed too heavy for her slight build. There was an empty chair beside me, and she asked me timidly if it was taken. At my negative reply, she sat down.

At closer view, I reversed my estimate of her age and guessed her to be about sixteen, not more than seventeen at the most. She was quite pretty, her features regular, and her dark hair fell in ringlets to her waist. We acknowledged each other with a smile and a nod. I had no idea who she was and what on earth her business with the president might be. However, after a few minutes she introduced herself and enlightened me as to her purpose in being there.

Her name, she said, was Vinnie Ream, and she was an artist and sculptor. Shyly, not bragging or a bit arrogant, she then proceeded to tell me she had been given permission to station herself in the president's office and make sketches of him from life with the ultimate goal of sculpting a statue of him.

I was completely taken aback by this statement. She looked so young, looked to be barely out of the schoolroom. Quite unaffectedly she filled me in on her background. She had attended Christian College in Missouri, studying art and especially interested in sculpting. She told me her father had moved the family to Washington, where he was employed as a government mapmaker. She told me that on her very first day in the city, she had caught a glimpse of the president, and the nobility of his face had made a profound impression. Even then it became her ambition to sculpt him.

She went on to say it was a "miracle" how her deep desire came to be, how she was allowed to sit in the president's office and sketch him "from life." She may consider it a miracle—however, from listening to the account, it might well have also been her own persistence. What I've learned from being here in Washington, close to the political hub, is that it is also a matter of "whom you know" which most often is the way of accomplishing your goals. And so I believe it to be with Miss Ream. She went on to tell me that through the Missouri congressman James Rollin, she was apprenticed to a well-known Washington sculptor, Clark Mills. Eventually, through her connections, she was able to gain her long-held dream of actually drawing the president from life, with the object being a bust or statue of him.

She was very sincere in telling me what a privilege it was, how intimate the sittings became with Mr. Lincoln. That he shared with her the grief he felt for the loss of his little boy (his son Willie died tragically of typhoid fever), for whom he still mourned so deeply. She recounted to me how he would sometimes stand at the window looking out on the White House lawn, where he used to watch his children at play. Tears brightened her eyes as she told me how his head would bow, great tears would roll down his hollow cheeks, his shoulders would shake, even as he tried to control his sobs.

About this time she was motioned forward by the lift of the appointment secretary's hand. It was time for her to go, the girl whispered, and she quickly rose and, almost like a will-o'-the-wisp, slid quietly down the hallway and disappeared through the door of the president's office.

How much of all she told me is true, how much her dramatic rendition, I cannot say. However, I did feel that putting down this encounter might someday be of historic importance, should this young woman's dream of sculpting a statue of the president be fulfilled.

❧

April 1865

Appomattox! Lee surrendered. The war is over!

From the pictures I've seen of General Robert E. Lee, stately and silver-haired, and the glimpse I once had of General Grant, the commander of the army of the Potomac, when he was in Washington—short, stocky, his uniform unpressed and rumpled—it's hard to imagine two more different men. Victor and vanquished. One could imagine that if they were actors in a play, their roles would be reversed. I wonder how this news is being received at home? Certainly not with the church bells ringing, celebrations in the streets, as is here.

~~~

JoBeth heard that some of the still staunchly loyal Confederates were moving their families to South America, to Brazil, to escape living under what they feared would be harsh treatment from the dreaded Reconstruction government.

She knew the heavy price many persons dear to her had paid. They had lost all, then had been deprived of the victory that would have made their sacrifice worthwhile. She grieved for them. Again—it was as true now as it had been at the beginning of the war—she had a divided heart.

Dearest Mama,

Good news. Less than a week since the surrender was signed, and the travel bans between North and South have been lifted by presidential decree, so it should be possible soon for me to come home for a visit. Do you think Aunt Josie and Uncle Madison will welcome me? Or are they still angry and bitter about what I did? I would come alone and Wes would join me later. Perhaps I can lay the groundwork for reconciliation before he comes? After all, the president is advocating that the country come back together as one nation again. Surely our family can do no less? Let me know as soon as you can how you feel my plan will be received.

Give them all my dearest love, for it is still as true and strong as ever. Give Shelby especially a hug and kiss from his sister. I long to see you all.

Ever your loving daughter,
JoBeth

Chapter Twenty-Seven

❧

*O*ut on the streets, hawkers passed out the handbills that had been hastily printed to announce the special performance that would be held that evening.

FORD'S THEATER TONIGHT !! *APRIL 14, 1865*
*Special Performance ** Farewell Appearance*
of
Miss Laura Keene
In the Celebrated Comedy by Tom Taylor,
Our American Cousin
We will be honored by the attendance of
President Lincoln

Wes came home early that evening. Smiling broadly, he held up two theater tickets. "Guess what, Mrs. Rutherford? Tonight we are going out! Compliments of Major Meredith. He and Mrs. Meredith were unable to use them for some reason. So we are the lucky holders of dress circle seats to see *Our American Cousin* playing for one performance only at Ford's Theater tonight."

"How absolutely marvelous, Wes! How kind of the Merediths."

"And the president himself will be attending."

"Oh, good heavens!" JoBeth struck her forehead theatrically. "How can I stand it? I am most overcome with our good fortune!"

Wes laughed. He always enjoyed JoBeth's antics. Playing to her nonsense, he held up his hand, declaring, "Wait, you haven't heard all—General and Mrs. Grant will be accompanying them."

At this JoBeth staggered toward the sofa in a mock swoon. "Spare me, kind sir. I can stand no more!"

"What's more, afterwards"—Wes took a declaratory pose—"we'll go to supper at an elegant restaurant." He followed her over to where she sank back onto the cushions.

"And to whom do we owe *that* luxury?"

"To your husband!" he told her, laughing as he gathered her into his arms, cuddling her to him.

JoBeth struggled up from his embrace. "Good heavens, what shall I wear?"

Frowning fiercely, Wes relaxed his hold and, pretending to be outraged, demanded, "Here I am, kissing you—and *you're* thinking about clothes!"

"Well darling, after all, this is quite an occasion. I must dress appropriately. The dress circle certainly requires my most elegant gown. I know—my blue velvet!"

She dressed with much excitement. It had been so long since she could look forward to an evening like this, so long since she had felt free to enjoy herself. She had not had a chance to wear this beautiful gown yet in Washington. This was the *right* event. Anyone who was anyone in Washington would be there tonight. The city had been exuberant since victory. And tonight both the president and the victorious general would be in attendance.

Her elation enhanced the honey-rose glow of her skin, deepened the sapphire sparkle of her dark-lashed eyes. The

Shelby Italian cameo set—brooch and earrings of pale carnelian stone set in filigreed gold with their creamy carving of a Grecian lady's profile—were perfect accessories.

Wes was ready first and sat on a chair beside her dressing table while JoBeth fixed her hair.

"We'd better leave a little early, at least forty minutes before curtain time. They've got posters out announcing the fact that the president is going to attend this evening. So crowds will be forming for a glimpse of him as he comes into the theater," he told JoBeth as she twisted her hair into a chignon. "Poor fellow, he deserves some relaxation and entertainment after all he's been through. You know, he's aged even in the two years since I came here to Washington. The war has taken its toll on him as well as the country. But now, thank God, it's over and we can rejoice along with the president."

As Wes suggested, they left for the theater a little earlier than would ordinarily have been necessary. He was right about the publicity surrounding the president's attendance that evening. True to his prediction, the streets were jammed with carriages, buggies, hansom cabs. The crush of vehicles all vying with each other to dispatch their occupants as close to the theater entrance as possible clogged the thoroughfare. It was so crowded that after making futile attempts to get them nearer, their cab driver gave up and let them out a block from Ford's Theater. Already two lines on either side were pushing toward the ticket booth. The whole front of the theater was crowded with hopeful last-minute ticket-buyers and scalpers vending tickets to latecomers. Gawkers, waiting to see the president when he arrived, pushed against the queues of theatergoers.

Holding JoBeth's arm firmly, Wes managed to get past the shoving crowd and into the theater at last. He handed their tickets to one of the harried ushers in the foyer. The lobby was full, glowing with the flickering gas lights of the chandeliers, bright with the colors of women's hoop-skirted dresses, the flash of jewelry. In the snatches of conversation buzzing all around JoBeth, there was a mixture of exhilaration and relief. The victorious end of the war had brought a special excitement to this gala occasion.

JoBeth squeezed Wes's arm as they followed the usher down the plushly carpeted aisle, found their row, and settled into their seats. She was thrilled to discover that from where they were seated, she had a very good view of the presidential box.

Draped with red-white-and-blue bunting, it was one of two at the upper right-hand tier and was decorated with flags and flowers. The interior was wallpapered in dark red and hung with Nottingham lace curtains. An upholstered rocking chair with a carved frame had been provided for the president.

Suddenly a hush descended as the house lights mysteriously dimmed, and the rustle of the curtain being raised could be heard in the quieted theater. JoBeth's surreptitious glance up at the presidential box showed no occupants.

Act one began. The star, Laura Keene, a well-known comedienne, was well into the humorous dialogue when a definite stir rippled through the audience. For a moment everyone was distracted and turned to see Mr. Forbes, the theater owner, lead the presidential party down a side aisle. As they went up the stairs and into their box, a murmur circulated. Everyone immediately became aware of the arrival. There was a general shifting. People began to stand up and applaud. Miss Keene immediately halted in her lines and also began to clap her hands.

Then the whole audience got to its feet and the place rang with enthusiastic applause. The orchestra leader tapped his baton, and the first notes of "Hail to the Chief" rang out. The shadowy, tall figure of the president, half hidden by the draperies, could be seen standing as he acknowledged the recognition. Then he seated himself beside Mrs. Lincoln.

JoBeth had only one swift glimpse of the president himself, the unmistakable profile, the noble brow, the long nose, the dark beard. But she could see Mrs. Lincoln quite clearly as the lady fluttered her fan, turned to chat with the couple sitting behind them, who were definitely *not* the Grants. They were much too young, much too handsome. Who were they? JoBeth wondered. While the actors resumed the play, Mrs. Lincoln fidgeted. She patted her hair, adjusted her skirt, leaned forward with her small opera glasses to her eyes to look down at the orchestra seating, then touched her husband's arm as if to draw his attention to something or someone below.

JoBeth debated whether she dared draw her own tiny mother-of-pearl opera glasses from their velvet case and focus them on the presidential box. She had only seen Mr. Lincoln once: as she passed through the reception line at the White House. This was a chance to study him more closely. She couldn't let it go by.

Cautiously she took them out. Surely she could pretend to be viewing the stage. Discreetly she put the glasses up to her eyes, moved the tiny wheel to focus the lenses, slowly turned toward the pivotal box. A single second and she saw his face, and in that moment its expression etched itself indelibly on her memory.

She thought of all the times she'd heard him derided, spoken of with scorn, anger, hatred! And even worse, his physical appearance had been cartooned and described as "apish," "ugly." Yet what *she* saw was infinite compassion, conviction, and courage. She lingered on that face. Then, fearful to seem too obvious, she moved her glasses to view the two other occupants of the box. An extremely good-looking officer in dress uniform and a strikingly attractive young lady sat directly behind the president and Mrs. Lincoln. Whoever they were would probably be in tomorrow morning's society news. And surely Mrs. Hobbs would inform JoBeth.

Perhaps they were relatives of Mrs. Lincoln's, decided JoBeth, putting down her glasses. The First Lady had often had family members visiting and staying at the White House, even though it had caused vitriolic press attacks. Especially when her younger sister, the widow of a Confederate general, had been a guest there over a long period of time. That fact had even brought allegations that Mrs. Lincoln was a spy! *Poor lady,* JoBeth thought, turning her attention again to the stage. Mary Lincoln was probably more glad than anyone that the war was over and she would no longer be the target of such scurrilous rumors.

Those thoughts lingered in JoBeth's mind as she tried to get back to the gist of the play. For some reason it did not seem to hold her interest. It was a tired comedy of manners, and the acting was overdone. Still, it was amusing and brought a few chuckles and murmured laughter from the audience. It was, after all, a farce. Not to be taken seriously. She might have preferred a drama, a Shakespearean play for which the dramatic family of the Booths was famous. Perhaps another time.

An actor blared out his lines. "Don't know the manners of good society, eh? Well, I guess I know enough to turn you inside out, old gal—you sockdologizing old mantrap!"

As appreciative laughter ran through the audience, at almost the same time, there was a loud, cracking sound, like a storm door banging closed. Suddenly there was a scuffling noise and raised voices that seemed to be coming from the president's box. JoBeth turned her head just in time to see two figures wrestling, and she heard several piercing screams. The figure of a man scrambled to the ledge of the balcony, then leaped to the stage. There he sprawled for a minute before scrambling to his feet and running across the stage. A hoarse shout from the president's box rang out, "Stop that man!" Onstage, the actors seemed frozen in their places, their startled looks turning to horror as hysterical shrieking shrilled out from the presidential box. A young woman leaned over the railing and cried pleadingly, "Water!"

The audience rose to its feet. A protesting roar swelled into a crescendo. Exclamations, cries, gasps, screams, echoed throughout the building. There was a rush to the aisles. People pushing and shoving each other, clustering below the president's box. Then the horrible word circulated among the stunned theatergoers: "The president's been shot!" "Someone tried to kill Lincoln!"

JoBeth felt her knees weaken. She slumped against Wes, who was standing behind her. His hands tightened on her bare arms.

"Oh, dear God!" she heard him whisper. "This is what we've all been afraid of—he wouldn't listen to tighter security. And now, dear God, it's happened."

JoBeth felt a wave of nausea sweep over her.

The heart-wrenching screams and broken sobs could still be heard coming from the president's box. They watched in helpless shock as uniformed men clambered into the Lincolns' party box. Confusion reigned. People waited underneath the flag-draped balcony, with raised, questioning voices.

Wesley grabbed JoBeth's cloak, dropped it over her shoulders, leaned down, and spoke into her ear so as to be heard. "I should report to headquarters, in case—whatever. I should be there until—until anything happens. You must go home. I'll try to get you a cab. If there are any available. Otherwise, we'll make it back to Mrs. Hobbs some way. But then I must return, get to headquarters. God knows what this is all about. You understand?"

"Of course," she said, shuddering from shock and fear.

The cries and sobs rose all around them as the dreadful event took hold of the crowd. JoBeth bit her trembling lower lip.

"Poor, poor Mrs. Lincoln! Isn't there anything we can do?"

"Nothing, I'm afraid—*pray*. That's all that's left—but it may be too late." Wes's hands gripped her shoulders, firmly manipulating her through the dense crowd. "I have to get you out of here."

<hr />

JoBeth was only aware of the confusion, bordering on panic, that surrounded their exit from the theater. To get a cab, of course, was impossible. They walked all the way back to Mrs. Hobbs's. JoBeth's feet, in her thin satin slippers, became sore trying to keep up with Wes's longer stride. They were both breathing hard when they finally saw the night lantern on Mrs. Hobbs's porch. Wes handed JoBeth the key, then kissed her. "I have to leave now, get to headquarters. There's no telling what this means. Perhaps it's some kind of conspiracy, some plot to assassinate not only the president but others in the government. It may be a full-scale insurrection."

"Oh, Wes." She clung to him, trembling.

"Be brave, darling. I'll send word or come home as soon as I can." He took the key from her and opened the door. "Now go inside—and pray for the president and our country!" he said tensely. Then he was gone.

Almost staggering, JoBeth climbed the stairway up to their apartment. She paused briefly outside Mrs. Hobbs's door, then decided against waking her. Tomorrow would be soon enough for her to learn the news.

The night seemed endless. She moved restlessly from room to room, unable to settle down, praying for the president. The hours ticked away, spinning out into eternity.

Outside, dawn was breaking. Its cold, misty light crept in between the curtains that JoBeth had pulled together the night before—as if to shut out the terrible truth, the inevitable news she dreaded.

Stiffly, JoBeth roused herself from her cramped position on the couch. From sheer emotional exhaustion, she had finally drifted off into a troubled sleep. She sat bolt upright. Wide awake. Her heart throbbed as if she were awakening out of a nightmare. Then memory struck with new impact and she remembered. It wasn't a nightmare. It had really happened. She had been there. She shuddered violently.

Almost at the same moment, she heard footsteps on the stairs and stiffened. Wes? The tread was slow, dragging. Outside the door they stopped, as if hesitating reluctantly. She watched the doorknob as one mesmerized. Slowly it twisted. Then the door opened.

Wes stood there on the threshold, his shoulders drooped, his face haggard, drawn. JoBeth held her breath. Her eyes, riveted on him, begged the question her lips dared not ask.

"The president is dead." Wes's voice was like lead.

"Oh, no!" JoBeth gasped. "Dear God, no!"

Wes walked over to her, then half fell onto the sofa beside her. He put his arms around her waist as she laid her head against his chest. Neither spoke for a full minute. Finally he asked, "You've been up all night? Not slept?"

"I couldn't. At least not for hours. And you?"

He shook his head. She put both her hands on either side of his face, searched it. His eyes were bloodshot, circled with dark shadows. His expression bore the signs of the night's vigil.

"What was it like—waiting there?"

"We were all locked into a kind of desperate trance. Hoping against hope. Nobody spoke much. Everyone prayed."

"Mrs. Lincoln?"

"Prostrated. They took her home to the White House. Poor woman. Out of her mind with grief."

"Poor, poor woman. This will break her." Tears of sympathy rolled down JoBeth's cheeks.

Wes sighed deeply. "The poor *South*." He shook his head sadly. "There'll be no magnanimity now ... nothing but revenge. Everyone blames the secessionist sympathizers. When I was coming home, there was already talk in the streets that it was a Southern conspiracy. Vengeance—" Wes put his head in his hands. His words were muffled as he said, "It's tragic. All *he* desired was amnesty, binding up the wounds, reconciliation...."

JoBeth wondered briefly how the news would be received in Hillsboro. In the Cadys' home. Many had hated Lincoln. But she knew Wes was right—the South would bear the brunt of the nation's anger at the killing of the president.

"Come, you must get some rest." Wes took both her hands and drew her gently up. The fire in the hearth had long since gone out and she shivered. Wes's arm went around her, supporting her as he led her toward the bedroom. She leaned heavily against him, feeling that all the strength had gone out of her. He eased her down to sit on the side of the bed.

"Here, let me help you." He proceeded to unbutton her long kid gloves, now streaked and stained with tears. His fingers fumbled with the pearl buttons, but she seemed to have no energy to assist him. Finally he pulled them off, finger by finger, then took her hand, lifted it to his cheek, pressing it there for a few seconds. Slowly he turned it over and kissed her palm. He laid her gloves on her lap. She smoothed them out and placed them in the long, narrow box he held out for her.

Then he knelt and took off the satin slippers with the silk rosette on each toe. For a moment, he held her feet in his palms, tenderly rubbing each instep.

"You must get into bed, darling." He helped her to her feet. She held on to the carved bedpost while he unfastened the hooks on the back of her bodice, unbuttoned the waistband of her skirt. The beautiful velvet dress slid to the floor. He picked it up and hung it carefully on the front of the armoire. But JoBeth knew she would never wear it again.

Wes turned back the quilt and covers for her. She sat down on the edge of the bed.

"Aren't you coming?" she asked wearily. "You need rest, too."

"I've been ordered home to get a few hours' sleep. However, we have a full day's work ahead, arrangements to be made, and . . ."

The last of what he said faded as, sighing deeply, JoBeth fell back upon the pillows and closed her eyes.

JoBeth didn't know how long she'd slept when she was aroused by movement in the darkened room. Struggling out of her heavy sleep, she squinted her eyes and glanced around. Then she saw Wes's figure silhouetted against the light seeping in through the draperies.

"Wes!" she called to him. He turned, then came over and sat down on the bed beside her. "Why are you up? Didn't you sleep at all?"

"I couldn't. I can't believe the president is dead."

"Oh, Wes!" JoBeth held out her arms to him. He leaned toward her and she held him, his head on her shoulder.

"It all seems so pointless," he said hoarsely. "He tried to make a difference. To bring this country back to its beginnings, hold the Union together. And now . . . I thought it was all over—the hatred, the killing . . . but it's not. It will begin all over again, and there will be no end to it—" His voice broke.

She could feel his body shake with deep sobs.

"Darling, darling," she crooned as if soothing a weeping child, her hands stroking his neck. She felt his tears dampening her shoulder through her nightgown. Her embrace tightened and she drew him down to her and they wept together, embraced in their mutual sorrow.

<hr />

When JoBeth awakened again, Wes was gone. He'd left a note for her. He'd gone back to report to Major Meredith to see if he could be of any use.

Her head throbbed. She felt shaky and ill. Her eyes were burning, her eyelids swollen from all the tears of the night before. Her hair was tangled, for in all this time, she had not even removed her hairpins or the ornamental comb she'd worn to the theater.

The remembrance of the tragedy made her shiver, and she pulled on her quilted robe. She had been witness to murder. Had seen the alleged assassin jump onto the stage in front of her very eyes! She would see that scene over and over for the rest of her life, hear Mrs. Lincoln's piteous screams echoing down the years.

JoBeth moved stiffly over to the spirit burner, struck a match to light it, but her hand was shaking so badly that she had to do it twice. She'd feel better when she had some tea, she told herself hopefully. She waited impatiently for the water to boil, the tea to brew. Hot tea should bring some warmth into her unnaturally cold body. She got a fire started in the fireplace, then huddled in the chair in front of it, sipping the scalding hot tea.

Over and over she relived last night's horror. The scene played itself out on the stage of her mind, as if she were again viewing it in all its tragic drama.

She would never forget it. Never, never!

Chapter Twenty-Eight

*R*emembering Wes's dire prediction about what would happen to the South in the wake of the president's death, she tried to imagine the mood in her own home when word came of the assassination. Lincoln had publicly stated his policy of rebuilding the nation. Even against the advice of some of his cabinet, and despite the fact that members of his own political party did not agree with him, he had advocated "malice toward none, and charity toward all." *Now* what would be the South's fate at the hands of its vindictive conquerors?

It seemed ironic that Lincoln's death should come on Good Friday. The great humanitarian, the emancipator of slaves, the president who had preserved the Union—struck down on the same day as the Crucifixion. Both Savior of the world and savior of the nation killed by their enemies.

She must do something—something personal—to mark this terrible deed, create something to memorialize this historic event. . . .

JoBeth began to visualize the design for a quilt—perhaps the outline of three crosses rising across a field of lilies. It would be her personal reminder that she must hold on to the belief that as senseless and devastating as this death seemed, it had some purpose in God's mysterious plan. It would say, in a very individual way, that there was hope beyond the crosses of life. The design formed very clearly in her mind. Excitedly she took out a piece of paper, a pencil, and began to sketch it.

The very act of doing this seemed to bring her mother very close to her. It was the tragedy of her father's early and unforeseen death that had been the motivation for her mother's lifework of making quilts to sell. Johanna had painstakingly disciplined herself to learn a craft for which she had no particular talent. She had done it out of necessity at first. She had gone back to her hometown a penniless widow with two small children, to live with relatives. Even though they welcomed her with love and generosity, she hated being a "poor relation" in the household of her affluent aunt and uncle. Johanna prayed for some way to support herself and her fatherless children. The answer came with her creativity. She soon became known for her beautiful quilts. Her skill and the demand for her work provided the education she wanted for her daughter, and her son's college tuition and seminary fees. JoBeth felt a surge of energy, a rush of elation. As her mother had done before her, *she* would make something beautiful out of this tragedy.

Later in the morning, an ashen-faced Mrs. Hobbs tapped at JoBeth's door, holding the latest edition of the newspaper with its black-banner headlines. She told JoBeth that they had almost certainly identified the assassin as the actor John Wilkes Booth.

Of course, JoBeth had heard of John Wilkes Booth. He was a matinee idol, adored by young lady theatergoers. She had seen his pictures, and he had once been pointed out to her in front of the theater. Tall, handsomely built, an Adonis with curling dark hair, high color, white teeth, features as finely sculptured as those on some Greek statue. Mrs. Hobbs had read extravagant raves about him in theatrical reviews of plays in which he had appeared in Washington. He was known as quite a "ladies' man," and it was even rumored that Bessie Hale, the daughter of Senator John Hale, was infatuated with him.

As more was learned about the assassin, the profile of a vain, arrogant man seething with a murderous hatred of the president emerged. Imbalanced, his weakness of character led him to believe he could commit murder and get away with it.

Three days later, his death—he was ambushed and shot as he hid from his pursuers—seemed almost judgmental, and few mourned him.

～❧～

In the days that followed, the assassinated president drew the most mournful expressions of loss. A poem by the well-known author Herman Melville was published in the newspaper, and reprints were offered.

Spontaneous expressions of sorrow, grief, and respect began to appear in front of Ford's Theater. Garden bouquets, floral wreaths, formal funeral arrangements—sprays of lilies and other spring flowers—seemed poignant reminders of the one who would never see another spring.

Drawn by some irresistible impulse, JoBeth also trod the pilgrim's way there. Because she had been in the theater when it happened, she felt some inexplicable bond to the slain president and to his widow. She had heard her screams, felt her pain like a knife through her own heart. Although her own short life had known few losses, her sensitive nature suffered deeply with the mourning wife of the slain president. She could only imagine what she would have felt had it been Wes. Her sympathy was very real as she moved forward and, her bell-shaped skirt swaying, knelt and gently laid her small memorial bunch of flowers with the others.

JoBeth attended service alone that Sunday, because Wes had to be at Major Meredith's side in case he was needed to facilitate any of arrangements for the funeral. As she walked the few blocks over to the church, the bright sun and the sound of birdsong in the blossoming trees seemed a bitter counterpoint to the dejected churchgoers. How could it be, when the dark cloud of national tragedy hung so heavy?

A pall of foreboding gloom hovered over the city. On Tuesday, Wes escorted JoBeth to where the president lay in state, so she could pay her respects. Her heart ached remembering the last, festive occasion on which she had come to the White House. Long lines stood patiently to file past the catafalque, draped in black silk, that had been erected in the East Room. At the head and foot of the casket—braided, studded, and starred with silver—in which the body of the slain president lay, uniformed officers stood at attention. Sepulchral light filtered in from windows hung with black drapery, and the veiled mirrors added to the somber atmosphere. The heavy fragrance of lilies and roses permeated the room.

The funeral on Wednesday was limited to six hundred guests. Two days later the president was to be taken by railroad car back to Illinois.

Friday morning, tolling bells awakened JoBeth to another day of sorrow. There would be a final, brief service conducted for the president in the Rotunda of the Capitol before the last solemn march to the depot.

From Major Meredith's office window, JoBeth watched the sad, solemn procession from the White House to the train station, where the body of the president would be placed in a special car for the journey back to Springfield, Illinois, to his final resting place. Black plumes adorned the heads of the six gray horses pulling the hearse, which was festooned in black crepe, as they moved along the street in slow, measured steps. Behind was the president's horse, his boots placed in the stirrups. People lined four-deep along the way, many openly sobbing.

The newspapers had been filled with eulogies. Even the great Confederate general George Pickett, the nephew of Andrew Johnston, and years before a partner in Lincoln's Illinois law firm, was quoted as saying, upon hearing the news of the assassination, "My God! My God! The South has lost its best friend and protector, the surest, safest hand to guide and steer her through the breakers ahead. Again must we feel the smart of fanaticism."

～❦～

After the mournful scene, returning to their rooms, JoBeth removed the black satin ribbons from her bonnet, sadly folded them, and put them in a box. As she did, an idea for another way of marking this particular time in her life formed. These years she had lived in Washington made up a period separate from all the others in her life. In the space of less than two years, momentous things had occurred. Unforgettable things. Besides her journal, which she'd written in only intermittently, how could she keep some sort of record? No matter how sharp they are at first, memories often fade.

She remembered Mrs. Hobbs' telling her about a new kind of quilt that was becoming popular. An elaborate, fancy kind, a "memory" quilt made up of pieces from special gowns, such as a wedding dress, or clothing worn at other special occasions. The material was not cut into patches but in a variety of shapes fitted together in any sort of pattern—thus it was also called a "crazy quilt." Trimmed with lace or satin braid, it was more a quilt to be displayed than used.

JoBeth had already decided she could never again wear the blue velvet she had worn to Ford's Theater that night. It held too many horrible memories. Yet it had been worn on a historic—if tragic—occasion, and as such should be kept. A crazy quilt such as Mrs. Hobb had described would be a way to memorialize her time in Washington, all the things that had happened to her during this historic era. She recalled Mrs. Hobbs' saying, "As yet in my life, nothing very important or dramatic has happened that I could make a quilt about!" But JoBeth realized that her experience had been different. Hers would be worth remembering.

Chapter Twenty-Nine

❧

JoBeth flitted from armoire to trunk, from bureau to port-manteau, back and forth, happy and rather distracted at the thought that she was at last going home—well, to Hills-boro. In this last week of May, Washington was already sweltering. She looked forward to being once more in the cool foothills town, surrounded by the mountains, sheltered by the tall pines.

It would be such a relief also to be away from the ferment of the capital city. Ever since the president's assassination, the air literally breathed of fiery speeches, of excoriating vengeance, of speeches swearing retribution for the murder. Wes seemed to grow more weary and worn each day from handling the bulk of correspondence flowing into the major's office.

Wes had insisted JoBeth go to Hillsboro as soon as travel became possible, promising he would follow as soon as he received his discharge.

At first she had refused to leave him. But as both the weather heated and his persuasion increased, she gave in. She was anxious to see her mother and Shelby. It had been over two years. In the last, desperate months of the war, Shelby had left his classes at the seminary and joined a local unit to make the final, hopeless stands against Sherman's irrevocable advance through the South. He had, however, contracted typhoid and become dangerously ill—he'd been sent home to die, in fact. Thankfully, with good nursing and heartfelt prayer he had slowly recovered and was planning to go back to resume his studies in the fall.

However, the deciding factor in JoBeth's decision to go was her happy suspicion. One about which she was not yet sure enough to tell Wes. By the time he could join her in Hillsboro, she hoped to be able to share the exciting news that they were to become parents.

JoBeth hummed happily as she packed. Then, hearing a familiar footstep on the stairway, she halted for a minute, her face turned to the door to welcome her husband home. She was eager to share with him the letter she had received from her mother that morning saying that everyone was happily looking forward to her "homecoming."

All her own doubts about not being welcome faded with this reassurance. But one look at Wes's expression gave her pause. She knew that since the murder of the president, Wes had been depressed. He had idealized and admired Lincoln for his noble purpose. She had thought recently that he was coming out of his deep melancholy, but today he looked solemn, almost sad.

After greeting her, he slumped into one of the armchairs and surveyed the packed boxes, the valises, and the open trunk thoughtfully. In an attempt to cheer him, JoBeth declared gaily, "I'm afraid we are going to have to make you some new clothes, Wes. You must have grown an inch in height and several wide in the shoulders and chest since you were a civilian!"

He made no comment, nor did his tired face lift in a smile as it usually did to her lighthearted teasing. Immediately she sensed something was wrong.

"Do you have a headache, Wes?" she asked worriedly. "Could I fix you some tea or a tisane?"

He shook his head. "No, thank you, but I do need to talk to you, JoBeth."

"You sound serious. What is it?" she asked, alarmed.

She put aside the garment she was folding and went over and knelt down beside the chair in which he was sitting. She took his hands, which hung limply, and looked anxiously up into his eyes. They were haunted, miserable.

"I can't go to Hillsboro," he said heavily.

"I knew that, Wes. Not right away, of course, but you'll come later. Mama says—," she began, but he cut her off.

"No, I don't mean just *now*. I mean *ever*." A muscle in his cheek worked, as if he were trying to control his emotion. "What I mean is, we can't *live* there. I know that's what we've talked about, what we've planned, but—" He took an envelope from the inside pocket of his tunic. "I've done some testing of the waters, so to speak. I wrote to Cousin Will, asked him to tell me frankly what the climate would be in Hillsboro should we return to make our home there once more."

"And?"

"This is his answer." He tapped the envelope on the palm of his other hand. "He says resentment runs very high. North Carolina feels especially bitter, not being a large cotton-growing state nor a large slave-holding one and yet having lost more men per capita in the war than many of the states in the Deep South whose property they were defending. They've suffered a great deal. They're very much afraid of the new reconstructionist policies now being discussed in Congress. This is what he wrote: 'They're not satisfied in bringing us to our knees—they want to place their foot on our neck, grind our faces into the dirt.'" Wes looked up and into JoBeth's eyes. "So you see how impossible it would be for us to go back—to try to live among people who would despise us?"

JoBeth drew her breath in a little gasp.

"I know Will wouldn't lie. He's telling me the truth. Because he cares about us"—Wes's smile was ironic—"loves us even." He sighed deeply, his jaw set, and he told her, "If we go back to Hillsboro, hate will surround us like a thick, smothering cloak. We won't be able to breathe. We'll suffocate. We cannot—I *will* not stay in such killing atmosphere, in an environment where love cannot overcome, survive."

"Then what, Wes? What do we do?"

"I don't know. At least, I'm not sure. I don't think we have many alternatives. But I do have an idea I want you to think about—"

"Tell me."

"I say we go west—a new life, a clean slate."

"Where out west?" She tried to keep her voice from shaking.

"California, that's where."

"California?" she gasped, then asked, "Not the gold fields, Wes. You don't plan to mine—"

"No, no, darling. There are all sorts of opportunities. And land and all kinds of things we can do once we're there."

"Oh, darling, but it's such a risk!"

"Life is a risk, JoBeth. The person who risks nothing does nothing, has nothing, is nothing, becomes nothing. He may avoid suffering and sorrow, but he simply cannot learn, change and grow, and live. He has forfeited his freedom. Only the person who risks is really free."

"It seems like you've already thought about this a great deal."

"I have. I didn't want to say anything until I'd investigated it more on my own." He took both her hands in his, raised them to his mouth, and kissed her fingers, saying tenderly, "I know how hard it would be for you to leave your family—"

JoBeth's heart recoiled from another parting with her dear ones. It had been hard enough the first time. But her own experience confirmed the resentment Will described. Even the warmth and closeness and love of her family hadn't been able to protect her before. How much worse it would be now if Wes, a veteran of the hated conqueror's army, returned and tried to make a home, earn a living.

She had always hoped that when the war was over, she and Wes could settle down happily in the town they both loved, where they had grown up among their family and friends. But everything had changed now. Nothing would ever be the same for them. Old friends had become cold, doors once opened to them were now closed, warm greetings had become outright rejections. The homes where they had always been welcomed would not receive them. Hillsboro was no longer a place where they would feel comfortable, happy, or wanted. Peace may have come to the country, but the South only knew unforgiveness and vengeance.

The truth was bitter and hard to accept. But she couldn't deny it. Wes was right.

JoBeth remembered her mother's saying, "When we love, we place our happiness in the happiness of another." If this was what Wes wanted—*needed*—to do, if this was what he felt was the best thing for them and for their future life together, then there was no question she would agree and go. His happiness meant everything to her.

"Oh, Wes, it will be hard. But don't you know that we promised each other never to be separated again? Wherever you are, that's where my home is, my heart." She thought of the long separation, how she had yearned for him. No matter what happened, they belonged together. Wherever he went, she would gladly follow.

"California." She said the word tentatively, as if trying it out. "California!" she repeated. She felt a prickle of excitement. Looking up, she met his steady gaze and smiled.

The Crazy Quilt

※

Sewed points and squares form a pattern like life's cares—old garments, old memories—and what is life? A crazy quilt, sorrow, joy, grace and guilt, a scrap of silk, a piece of velvet, a length of ribbon, a square of scarlet, here and there an edge o' lace to enhance the commonplace, and so the hand of time will take fragments of our lives and make out of life's remnants in patterns fall, to make out of our life a thing of beauty after all.

Douglas Malloch

American Quilt Series Bonus Section:

❧

Dear Reader:

The editors at Zondervan Publishing House and author Jane Peart would like to thank you for reading *The Pledge*, the second book in the American Quilt Series. This Special Bonus Section, offered as a token of our appreciation, contains the "Prologue" to the next book, *The Promise*, which continues the story of the next generation.

Also included is a brief outline of how to make the "heart-in-hands" quilt that plays such a prominent role in *The Pledge*.

Again, if you are enjoying the American Quilt Series, be sure to look for the third volume, *The Promise*. You will probably also enjoy Jane Peart's other fine series: The Brides of Montclair Series and the Westward Dreams Series. The twelve volumes of the Brides of Montclair Series tell the epic story of a single Virginia family from before the American War for Independence to the twentieth century. (Volumes 13, 14, and 15 of that series will be appearing in 1997 and 1998, making one of the most extensive novel series on the market!) The Westward Dreams Series contains four volumes, each of which portrays a different independent-minded woman from the East who travels to the Old West to find a new life for herself and, of course, romance.

Thank you again. Happy reading,
The Editors of Zondervan Publishing House

Prologue to The Promise

From her bedroom window, Jana Rutherford, christened Johanna after her Grandmother Davison, looked out at the familiar scene she loved. Beyond the rim of beach stretched the distant blue line of ocean against an orange-pink sky. As she watched, a single boat, its sails billowing like winged gulls, moved slowly along the horizon.

She never tired of the Hawaiian landscape. She would never forget her first sight of the Big Island ten years before. She was standing at the railing of the steamer coming from Oahu with her father. "Look, Jana," he had said, "there it is, Hawaii, the biggest of all the islands."

There, in the direction he pointed, the Big Island seemed to emerge out of a sea of turquoise water rising steeply into lush green walls of dark tropical vegetation from the beach below on which foam-scalloped surf swirled.

"That's where we're going to live, Jana; that's our new home," he said. "We're going to be happy there."

And they had been. Especially Jana. From the beginning she had loved everything Hawaiian. Even her name sounded better in Hawaiian: Koana. It sounded softer, more musical.

A gentle wind now rustled the fronds of the palm trees outside the house and stirred the lattice blinds. Reluctantly

Jana turned back to her bedroom. There were still things to do before tomorrow. More packing. The steamer left early from Hilo for Honolulu. There she would board the ship sailing to the United States.

One task had been left to the last—going through the koa-wood chest. It contained things stored through the years. It held her childhood, as well as an assortment of memorabilia of the last ten years. It was a job she had procrastinated doing. It would be like opening a Pandora's box of memories, some good, some bad. But she couldn't put it off any longer.

Kneeling in front of it, she lifted the lid. The collection of a lifetime was piled haphazardly within: old dolls long since put away; worn books; a ragged Teddy bear missing one eye and too scuffed and limp to pass along to some other child—yet too beloved to give away. There was a cardboard portfolio she had made to hold some of her first drawings and watercolors. And in one corner, there was a battered shoe box. When she picked it up a fine drift of sand spilled over her hands. Inside were all sorts of seashells. A whole parade of happy days spent searching for them marched through her mind.

Then she saw what lay underneath, at the bottom. Her memory book, a little warped, mildewed at the edges, its original pink cover turned brown. The spray of pansies painted diagonally across its front had faded. After taking it out, Jana sat back on her heels and placed it on her lap. Slowly she turned the yellowed pages, one after the other, until she read:

September 1884—Kimo left today. He has gone to Germany to be apprenticed to a famous cabinet maker. I don't know how long he'll be gone. A year, maybe two. We walked down to the beach together, and he wrote in the sand, "Kua kua makamaka." In Hawaiian that means "forever friends."

That was the last entry in the book. The rest of the pages were blank. So much had happened since she had written that. Why had she stopped writing in this book? Was it because of her grandmother's wish in giving it to her that Jana should record "only sunny hours, joy-filled days, and happy memories" in it?

Jana closed the book thoughtfully. She replaced it inside the chest and slowly closed the lid. She couldn't throw it away. So much of the last ten years was recorded within its covers. And so much was unwritten as well.

Was it the Christmas of 1886 when everything had changed for her . . . ?

◆◆◆

To read more, ask you local bookseller for *The Promise* by Jane Peart.

How to Make the Heart-in-Hands Quilt

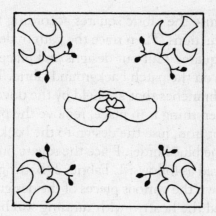

Unlike the "Carolina Lily" quilt pattern portrayed in *The Pattern*, Book 1 of the American Quilt Series, this "Heart-in-Hands" design is not traditional. It was designed specifically for this book by author Jane Peart, and she offers it as a way of thanking the many readers of her books. She would like to extend a special thanks to master quilters Connie Chapman and Liz Miller for their instructions and for the execution of the actual quilt.

Supplies needed for a 10-3/4-by-9-3/4-inch patch

Background Fabric: gray/blue, small print or plain
Doves: white fabric
Border Trim and heart: red fabric
Outer Border: blue fabric
Hands: peach or flesh colored fabric
You will also need: Fusable fabric or Wonder-Under

Copy the overall design onto paper to make the basic template. (You may trace the design by hand or enlarge the above design several times in a photocopier until it is the correct size).

Cut and fuse the fabric squares according to the manufacturer's instructions. Then trace the pattern design onto the fused fabric squares. Cut out designs and place them in the desired places on the patch background fabric. Then embroider the olive branches that are held by the doves.

When everything is in place, remove the paper backing, and with a hot iron, fuse the design to the background.

Sew on the blue border. Place the square on the backing, which is layered as follows: 1. Fabric. 2. Batting. 3. Muslin.

Stitch down the various pieces of the designs (the doves, the hands, and the heart—with running stitch, button-hole stitch, or pin stitch).

For the 1-1/2-inch border, cut 4-1/2 feet of red fabric two inches wide. Fold it in half lengthwise and press it to the width of 1 inch. Sew around front of patch, turn it over, and hand stitch it down.

Books by Jane Peart

The American Quilt Series
The Pattern
The Pledge
The Promise

The Westward Dreams Series
Runaway Heart
Promise of the Valley
Where Tomorrow Waits
A Distant Dawn

The Brides of Montclair Series
Valiant Bride
Ransomed Bride
Fortune's Bride
Folly's Bride
Yankee Bride/Rebel Bride
Gallant Bride
Shadow Bride
Destiny's Bride
Jubilee Bride
Mirror Bride
Hero's Bride
Senator's Bride